ROBERT B. PARKER'S GRUDGE MATCH

When Sunny's long-time gangster associate Tony Marcus asks for her help, Sunny is surprised—after she double-crossed him on a recent deal, their relationship is on shaky ground. But Tony figures that Sunny owes him, and she's willing to consider his case if it will clear the slate.

Tony's girlfriend and business partner has vanished, and he has no idea why. He just wants to talk to her, he says, but first he needs Sunny to track her down. While Sunny isn't willing to trust his good intentions, the missing woman intrigues her—against all odds, she's risen to a position of power in Tony's criminal enterprise.

Then a witness is murdered hours after speaking to Sunny, and it's clear there's more at stake than just Tony's love life. Someone doesn't want this woman on the loose . . . and will go to any lengths to make sure she stays silent.

PRAISE FOR THE SUNNY RANDALL NOVELS

ROBERT B. PARKER'S GRUDGE MATCH

"The superb plotting is enhanced by Lupica's well-written scenes set during Sunny's therapy sessions with Spenser's love, Susan Silverman, which deepen the reader's understanding of Sunny. Fans of tough, competent female PIs such as V.I. Warshawski will approve Lupica's continuation of the series."

—*Publishers Weekly*

ROBERT B. PARKER'S BLOOD FEUD

"Lupica hits the sweet spot by balancing Sunny's professional hypercompetence with first-person narration that exposes her fears and self-doubts. Parker fans will look forward to seeing what Lupica does with Sunny in her next outing." —*Publisher's Weekly* (starred review)

"The criminal honor codes are only understood by the criminals but are dismissed anyway when they interfere with personal enrichment. Even family loyalties come and go. Great stuff, Parker fans. Sunny's back!"

—*Booklist* (starred review)

"A fast-paced and entertaining read that is true to Parker's voice . . . Lupica hits all the right notes here. . . . I cannot imagine that anyone who was a fan of Sunny during the Parker years would be anything less than totally satisfied with Lupica's stellar handling of the character. . . . Terrific." —*BookPage*

ROBERT B. PARKER'S SPARE CHANGE

"Parker continues to add depth to his characterization of Randall as he explores her often contradictory feelings about love. . . . He never fails to entertain with humor and recurring characters whom we welcome back into our lives like old friends." —*Booklist*

"Engaging . . . Parker's signature bantering byplay and some borrowings of characters from other series . . . will delight fans. The outcome is never in doubt, but Parker hits . . . the right notes, and there's still ingenuity to his cat-and-mouse." —*Publishers Weekly*

ROBERT B. PARKER'S BLUE SCREEN

"It's all chemistry when Boston P.I. Sunny Randall meets Paradise Police Chief Jesse Stone. . . . Sunny and Jesse work well together." —*Orlando Sentinel*

"Let's thank Robert B. Parker for his new book."
—*Daily News*

"Sunny notches up a big one."
—*The New York Times Book Review*

ROBERT B. PARKER'S MELANCHOLY BABY

"Excellent . . . Sunny's own regulars hold their own in the tale. There's little here that Parker hasn't done before, but he does it so well here, with his impeccable prose and charismatic heroine, that fans will tremble with delight." —*Publishers Weekly*

"Parker can spin a tale with the best of them—most of the time, he is the best of them. . . . He riffs smoothly off Sunny's blue mood."
—*The New York Times Book Review*

"Parker's gift for plot construction quickly comes to the fore, delivering a tantalizing mix of standard mystery fare (threats, murders, suspense) and some intriguing shards from the characters' pasts. . . . Teasing . . . Riveting." —*Booklist*

ROBERT B. PARKER'S SHRINK RAP

"Parker turns in his strongest mystery in years with Boston PI Sunny Randall's third outing. . . . By focusing on an author's plight during her book tour, Parker writes about experiences close to his own, delivering sharp portraits of publishing types and fans. . . . With layers of psychological revelation, plenty of action, the welcome return of Sunny's supporting crew . . . and as usual, prose as tight as a drumhead, this is grade-A Parker." —*Publishers Weekly* (starred)

"Sunny Randall . . . private eye, [is] as brainy as she is beautiful. . . . Parker's trademark dialogue, always his strong suit, is as crisp and pungent as ever."
—*San Diego Union-Tribune*

"Parker knows how to settle an old score better than his characters do—he's tougher, smarter, and funnier than all of them." —*The Boston Globe*

ROBERT B. PARKER'S

GRUDGE MATCH

THE SPENSER NOVELS

Robert B. Parker's Someone to Watch Over Me
(by Ace Atkins)
Robert B. Parker's Angel Eyes
(by Ace Atkins)
Robert B. Parker's Old Black Magic
(by Ace Atkins)
Robert B. Parker's Little White Lies
(by Ace Atkins)
Robert B. Parker's Slow Burn
(by Ace Atkins)
Robert B. Parker's Kickback
(by Ace Atkins)
Robert B. Parker's Cheap Shot
(by Ace Atkins)
Silent Night
(with Helen Brann)
Robert B. Parker's Wonderland
(by Ace Atkins)
Robert B. Parker's Lullaby
(by Ace Atkins)
Sixkill
Painted Ladies
The Professional
Rough Weather
Now & Then
Hundred-Dollar Baby
School Days
Cold Service
Bad Business
Back Story
Widow's Walk
Potshot
Hugger Mugger
Hush Money
Sudden Mischief
Small Vices
Chance
Thin Air
Walking Shadow
Paper Doll
Double Deuce
Pastime
Stardust
Playmates
Crimson Joy
Pale Kings and Princes
Taming a Sea-Horse
A Catskill Eagle
Valediction
The Widening Gyre
Ceremony
A Savage Place
Early Autumn
Looking for Rachel Wallace
The Judas Goat
Promised Land
Mortal Stakes
God Save the Child
The Godwulf Manuscript

THE JESSE STONE NOVELS

Robert B. Parker's Fool's Paradise (by Mike Lupica)
Robert B. Parker's The Bitterest Pill (by Reed Farrel Coleman)
Robert B. Parker's Colorblind (by Reed Farrel Coleman)
Robert B. Parker's The Hangman's Sonnet (by Reed Farrel Coleman)
Robert B. Parker's Debt to Pay (by Reed Farrel Coleman)
Robert B. Parker's The Devil Wins (by Reed Farrel Coleman)
Robert B. Parker's Blind Spot (by Reed Farrel Coleman)
Robert B. Parker's Damned If You Do (by Michael Brandman)
Robert B. Parker's Fool Me Twice (by Michael Brandman)
Robert B. Parker's Killing the Blues (by Michael Brandman)
Split Image
Night and Day
Stranger in Paradise
High Profile
Sea Change
Stone Cold
Death in Paradise
Trouble in Paradise
Night Passage

THE SUNNY RANDALL NOVELS

Robert B. Parker's Grudge Match (by Mike Lupica)
Robert B. Parker's Blood Feud (by Mike Lupica)
Spare Change
Blue Screen
Melancholy Baby
Shrink Rap
Perish Twice
Family Honor

THE COLE/HITCH WESTERNS

Robert B. Parker's Buckskin (by Robert Knott)
Robert B. Parker's Revelation (by Robert Knott)
Robert B. Parker's Blackjack (by Robert Knott)
Robert B. Parker's The Bridge (by Robert Knott)
Robert B. Parker's Bull River (by Robert Knott)
Robert B. Parker's Ironhorse (by Robert Knott)
Blue-Eyed Devil
Brimstone
Resolution
Appaloosa

ALSO BY ROBERT B. PARKER

Double Play
Gunman's Rhapsody
All Our Yesterdays
A Year at the Races (with Joan H. Parker)
Perchance to Dream
Poodle Springs (with Raymond Chandler)
Love and Glory
Wilderness
Three Weeks in Spring (with Joan H. Parker)
Training with Weights (with John R. Marsh)

ROBERT B. PARKER'S

GRUDGE MATCH

A SUNNY RANDALL NOVEL

MIKE LUPICA

G. P. PUTNAM'S SONS
NEW YORK

PUTNAM
— EST. 1838 —
G. P. PUTNAM'S SONS
Publishers Since 1838
An imprint of Penguin Random House LLC
penguinrandomhouse.com

The Library of Congress has catalogued the
G. P. Putnam's Sons hardcover edition as follows:

Names: Lupica, Mike, author.
Title: Robert B. Parker's Grudge match / Mike Lupica.
Other titles: Grudge match
Description: New York: G. P. Putnam's Sons, [2020] | Series: A Sunny Randall novel | Identifiers: LCCN 2019052836 (print) |
LCCN 2019052837 (ebook) |
ISBN 9780525539322 (hardcover) | ISBN 9780525539346 (ebook)
Subjects: GSAFD: Mystery fiction.
Classification: LCC PS3562.U59 R65 2020 (print) |
LCC PS3562.U59 (ebook) | DDC 813/.54—dc23
LC record available at https://lccn.loc.gov/2019052836
LC ebook record available at https://lccn.loc.gov/2019052837

First G. P. Putnam's Sons hardcover edition / May 2020
First G. P. Putnam's Sons premium edition / March 2021
G. P. Putnam's Sons premium edition ISBN: 9780525539339

Printed in the United States of America
1 3 5 7 9 10 8 6 4 2

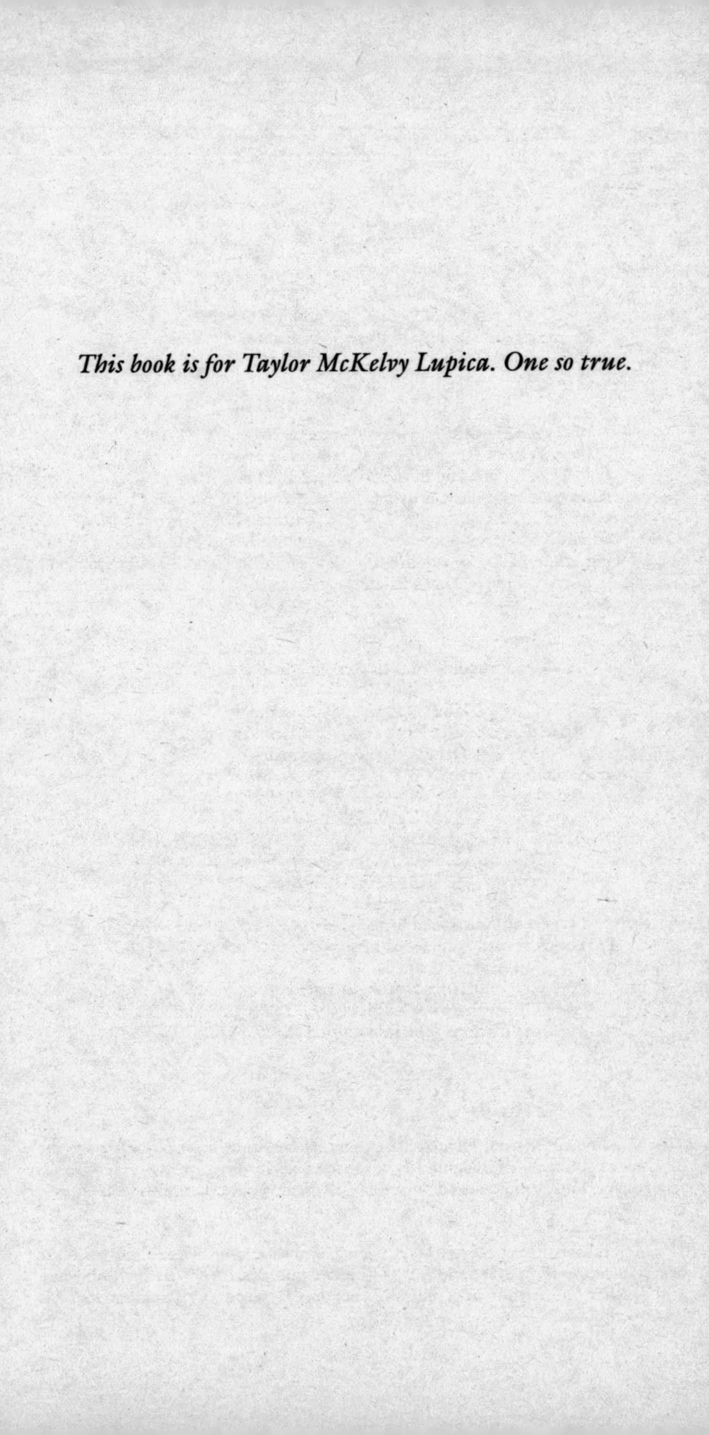

This book is for Taylor McKelvy Lupica. One so true.

ROBERT B. PARKER'S

GRUDGE MATCH

1

LISTEN UP WHILE I explain to you how you hold a damn grudge, Sunny Randall," Tony Marcus said.

We were in his office at Buddy's Fox. Tony's two most trusted troopers, Junior and Ty Bop, had driven me over here like they were Uber drivers, but only if Uber were hiring shooters and thugs this week.

"Tony wants to talk to you," Junior had said at my front door. "And before you say something smart, like you can't never help yourself, it really ain't a request."

"Fortunately, my schedule is wide open the rest of the afternoon," I said. "So you're in luck."

Junior had turned to Ty Bop then. "See that right there," he said. "She *can't* never help herself."

It occurred to me on the way to the South End that it was the most I'd ever heard Junior talk. He was as big as the Back Bay and usually just stood mute and scared the living shit out of you.

Now here we all were.

"Should I take notes?" I said to Tony.

He closed his eyes as he shook his head. I knew it wasn't because he thought I was funny, even though we both knew I was.

"What's the expression you'd use for a girl, you wanted to tell her she has balls?" he said.

"That she's got balls," I said.

"Well, you still got some balls on you," Tony said.

"Stop or you'll make me blush," I said.

Junior and Ty Bop were on either side of the door that led out to the bar area at Buddy's Fox. Ty Bop, who was Tony's shooter, still looked as skinny as a hairpin and so jittery I was always surprised I couldn't hear a faint hum coming off him, somewhat like a tuning fork. Junior, Tony's body man for as long as I'd known them both, seemed to be staring out the window and perhaps all the way to Portugal.

As always, Tony Marcus brought the word *bespoke* to mind. He was wearing a light gray suit, the gray so light you could barely see the pinstripes in it, a matching gray shirt, and a maroon tie and a maroon pocket square. His palms were flat on the desk in front of him. I couldn't help noticing his hands, and being more than somewhat jealous of his manicurist. In the constantly changing crime scene in Boston, Tony was somehow as powerful as he'd ever been, almost as if he were the beneficiary of crime-world gerrymandering. But he still played to and from his base, which had always been prostitution, in all its lousy and illegal forms.

"I believe you were talking about grudges," I said.

"Like the one we got going," he said, "since you jammed me up on that gun deal when I'd gone out of the way to help you save your former father-in-law's sorry old ass."

A few months ago I'd made a deal with Tony—he'd get a warehouse full of illegal guns in return for helping me save the life of Richie's father, Desmond Burke. But I'd never had any intention of letting Tony put that many guns on the street, and instead had tipped the warehouse location to the FBI.

"Most people," he said, "they think you got to act right away when somebody fucks you over the way you did me." He smiled. "Hell, that ain't how you hold a grudge."

I waited.

"What you do is, you *wait*," Tony said. "And then you wait a little more, until maybe the other person don't even remember how they did you in the first place. *Then* you find a way to settle accounts. And if they say, 'Why'd you fuck me up like that?' you say, 'See there, you forgot. We had a damn grudge.'"

He patted his hands lightly on the desk, as if to punctuate the thought. He smiled at me with about as much warmth as the small refrigerator next to Junior.

"You get my meaning?" he said.

"Tony," I said, "I'm as likely to forget that you're sideways with me as I would my email address."

He chuckled. "Balls on you," he said. "You forget all the other favors I did for you, back in the day. Remember that time I found out Jermaine Lister took a shot at you?"

Jermaine was a low-level pimp who'd once been Tony's brother-in-law. He *had* taken a shot at me, and ended up in jail because of that, if briefly.

"You remember what happened to Jermaine?" he said.

"You had him shanked in prison," I said. "And not because he took a shot at me. Because you were afraid he was going to tell the cops that you were the one who ordered him to take a shot at me."

"Did you a favor, that's the point of the story," he said.

"Yeah," I said. "Go with that."

He picked up an expensive cup and sipped whatever was inside it. He'd asked if I wanted something to drink, coffee or tea or water or stronger. I had declined. This was the first time we'd been together since the Feds had confiscated guns that Tony thought were going to belong to him.

"You know I could've taken you out anytime I wanted to," Tony said, "even if it would've gotten the Burkes all up in my shit."

"The thought has occurred to me."

"Somebody else did me like you did, I *would* have taken them out," he said. "But I like to think our relationship has evolved since then."

"Aren't I the lucky girl," I said.

"So," he said. "You wondering why you here today?"

"You missed me?"

"Want to hire you," he said.

I couldn't help myself. I laughed, loud enough that I was briefly afraid that I'd startled Ty Bop, who went through life like a grenade with the pin already pulled.

"Look to you like I'm joking?" Tony Marcus said.

I was at a point in my professional life where I had the luxury of picking and choosing my cases. After I'd saved Desmond Burke's life, he had insisted on paying me a vulgar amount of money.

But I had to admit I was curious.

"I'm listening," I said.

Tony smiled again.

"See there?" he said. "We all whores in the end."

"Not me," I said.

"You must be the exception proves the damn rule," Tony Marcus said.

2

THE PROBLEM, HE said, was that prostitution had gotten more complicated than the goddamn tax code.

"Boy," I said, "I wish I had a nickel for every time I've heard that."

He gave a quick shake of his head, like clearing the immediate air around him of a gnat.

"When I was coming up," he said, "you just put girls out over at the wharf, before they cleaned up that part a town, and in the Combat Zone, before they cleaned *that* up, and then you just sat back and counted your money. Was back when the girls was way more black than white."

Then he was telling me that he could still turn a better profit than I might think just putting girls on the street and with some of the high-end escort services he was running, but how more and more he was facing competition from gentlemen's clubs—he put air quotes around "gentlemen"—and online porn, and suburban madams who'd done everything with bored housewives except unionize them, and even what he called drive-through massage parlors. He said he was now dabbling in drugs, even though he said he didn't much like dealing in what he called that oxy-oid shit. And, he said, he kept a hand in the gun trade as well, even after the way I'd fucked him over.

"I'm still managing to get by, is my point," he said.

"I'll bet."

"But I've been forced to, ah, expand my management structure somewhat," he said. "Used to be just me and the pimps and the whores and hotel work and the high-end houses I run and whatnot. But now there's way more shit to keep track of."

Only Tony Marcus, I thought, could sound this nostalgic about this particular profession, as if he were talking about the covers Norman Rockwell used to do for *The Saturday Evening Post.*

"So," he said, "not only have I had to expand my operation to keep up with the goddamn times, I've had to do something else I never really done before." He sighed. "Delegate," he said.

I waited again. He always had to tell things at his own pace, there was no way to rush him.

"And now what's happened is I've got myself into an unfortunate situation with one of my delegatees," he said.

"Man or woman?"

"Woman," he said. "Moved up off the streets and even ended up running one of those high-end houses I mentioned, over near Symphony Hall. Calls herself Lisa Morneau. Like she French instead of Baltimore. That's what she calls herself now, anyways. No idea what it was when she first come to work for me."

"I don't mean to sound cynical," I said, "but often a move like that up through the ranks is facilitated by sleeping with the boss."

Tony smiled. "Hell, yeah."

"You care about this woman?" I said.

"I like this one more than most I've had, not gonna lie," he said. "Even got to where I was spending as much time at the place I put her up as in my primary damn place, leastways until she up and left."

"Left and went where?"

"Where you come in," Tony said.

I idly looked over to the door. Ty Bop's eyes looked closed, even though I knew they weren't. He had earbuds, and was moving his head up and down. He wore red-white-and-black high-top sneakers that I assumed had caught some sort of fashion wave, and a black hoodie with HOLLISTER written unevenly across the front, and black jeans. He looked, as always, as if he needed a hot meal.

Junior just leaned against the wall, arms crossed, as

if Buddy's Fox might come crashing down on all of us if he moved even a foot in either direction.

"Only woman ever left me before is Natalie, and that only on account of her switching leagues," he said.

His ex-wife.

"When you say Lisa left," I said, "does that mean she simply moved out?"

"Moved out, disappeared," he said.

"How long ago?"

"'Bout a week," he said. "Didn't empty the place. But the second bedroom she used as an office, she cleaned out the desk. Took her laptop, too."

"Clothes?" I said.

"Girl got so many, I can't tell how much she might've taken with her," he said. "Looking at her closet is like looking at the beach and deciding if there's less sand since the last time you looked. Only thing she likes more than shopping is running. Should see her. Runs like she the anchor leg in the Olympics."

"Luggage?"

"She took Louis *and* Vuitton with her, far as I can tell."

"So you don't think she was taken against her will?"

"By someone asked her to pack a bag?" Tony said.

"Why'd she leave?"

I thought I saw something pass across his face, as impassive as he tried to keep it. Something in the eyes, there and gone. Like Lisa Morneau.

"We never had that talk," he said. "But I can't lie. Thought we was happy. Happy in our relationship, happy with our business arrangement. Girl knows almost as much about my damn business as I do. She know who's doing what, where they doing it, how much they taking in, where I got strength, where I don't. She even had me using goddamn spreadsheets. People know me started to call her my other brain."

"If she's as smart as you say she is, she'd never use what she knows about you against you," I said. "That would make her an idiot."

"Doesn't mean the competition couldn't try to hire her," he said.

"I thought you had about as much serious competition these days as Amazon," I said.

"Might be a guy thinks he can change that up."

"Name, please?"

"Boy named Gabriel Jabari," Tony said. "Looks a little like that brother they was talking about playing James Bond."

"Idris Elba," I said.

Tony nodded. "Tries to act high-class," he said. "Talks like he some Ivy League motherfucker. But behind all the big words he's as street as me. Showed up in town 'bout six months ago, opened a high-class titty bar on Tremont, over there right 'fore it turns into Chinatown."

The place, Tony said, was called Suite. He spelled it for me.

"Cute," I said.

"Well, Gabriel Jabari ain't," Tony said. "'Fore long, I started to hear how the real reason he come here was to knock me off my perch. Like he was the one with a grudge, even though I don't even know where the fuck he was 'fore he got to Boston."

"Have you met him?" I said.

"I took Lisa with me over to Suite one time, just to check the place out," Tony said. "This boy Jabari finds out we there, he show us upstairs to the VIP area, comp us the best champagne, act like he wants to be my best friend. But while he blowing all that smoke up my ass, I see him looking at Lisa, and maybe her looking back at him. Then I find out she went back there on her own."

"Without telling you," I said.

He nodded. "Like I don't got people on the ground. What's it they say in Vegas? Somebody always watching? In Boston, the one watching is *me*."

"Did you ask her about it?"

"Never got the chance," he said. "I go over to her place later that night, and she's gone."

"And you're sure there was no precipitating event?" I said.

"There was a young girl got found OD'd a couple weeks ago," he said. "Looked like she got beat up before she did. Made Lisa real upset, had her asking me if I knew what'd happened. Turned out she was one of ours."

"How young?" I said.

"Younger than Lisa wanted me running," he said. "She told me I didn't need them that young. Said *we* didn't. Said that girl could have been her once."

"What did you tell her?"

"I told her that was fine with me, I didn't need those traffic cops up in my shit."

"You mean trafficking?" I said.

"Whatever," he said.

"You think what happened to that girl might have made Lisa run?"

"You the detective," he said.

"Aren't I though," I said.

He shrugged again.

"Anyway, Lisa's been off the grid since she did up and run," Tony said. "It's hard to do nowadays. But you *can* do it, long as you stop using your phone or spending money like the world about to come to an end."

"What about social media?" I said.

"I told her a long time ago to stay away from Twitter and Insta and Facebook and all the rest of it," he said. "Our business, you don't want to be sharing your business anywhere you don't have to. I mean, fuck Facebook and that Harvard boy runs it. He's no better than me when it comes to making as much as he can, however he can, wherever he can."

It was always fascinating listening to him talk, as he went back and forth between standard English and street, sometimes in the same thought.

"There must be other people you can hire to find her," I said.

"Normally I'd go to the dude does what you do, on account of him being the best," he said. "He and I got even more history than you and me."

I knew to whom he was referring. In my work, he was a bit of a local legend.

"But he's off in Los Angeles or some such," Tony said.

"So I was first runner-up," I said.

"Exactly," he said.

"I can't work for you, Tony," I said. "There's a lot of practical reasons. But there's a personal one, as well: I hate prostitution, no matter how much you try to make it sound like just another service industry."

"This ain't about that," he said. "This is a straight-up missing-person case."

"Thanks for clearing that up."

"You're not looking at the big picture," he said. "If you were, you'd know you almost can't *not* work for me."

"How do you figure?"

"Because what I am giving you here is a get-out-of-jail card with me," he said. "I clear your debt, and we start even. In fact, not only do we start even, I owe you one."

"One what?"

"A favor you can call in anytime you want to."

"I don't look at our previous business arrangement as a debt," I said.

"What you did was the same as stealing money from me," he said. "Like I said, you think I let shit like that go with anybody else?"

I uncrossed and then recrossed my legs. I knew he liked looking at my legs. It was one of my go-to moves with him when I was trying to buy time. Girl's gotta do.

"How do I know that if I find Lisa, harm won't come to her?" I said.

“You got my word,” he said. “And, let’s face it, now we got ourselves evidence that sometimes mine’s better than yours.”

I nodded. He had me there.

“What if I find her and she doesn’t want to come back?” I said.

He smiled. I smiled. My father used to quote some old baseball player, I forgot which one, who said that when you came to a fork in the road, take it.

“I just want to talk to her, ask her why she did me this way,” he said. “If she still wants to walk after that, she walks.”

“You love her, Tony?” I said. “Because it sounds to me like you just might.”

“Believe whatever the fuck you want to,” he said. “I’m trying to tell how it is.”

I shook my head slowly from side to side.

“Tony,” I said. “I’m still going to have to take a hard pass.”

“You didn’t ask how much I’d be willing to pay,” he said.

“If I owe you the way you say I do, why are you willing to pay me anything?” I said.

“Because then I’m officially your client,” he said. “You find her, you give me a bill, I pay you, we done.”

“If I don’t find her?”

“We still clear the books between us,” he said.

I couldn’t see myself ever taking any of Tony Marcus’s money, but I would worry about that later.

"You really want me up in your business from now till the end of time?" Tony said.

"Been there," I said. "Done that."

We were going in circles now, but Tony seemed to be enjoying himself. He'd always liked listening to himself talk. And for someone who had once again threatened to shoot me, he did seem to like me. Enough that he'd come to me to find Lisa Morneau, who seemed to mean even more to him than he was admitting.

I wasn't about to say it to him, but I was already more than somewhat curious about her, and how she'd managed to make it this far with Tony Marcus, in all ways, personal and professional, the whole damn thing. I found myself wanting to find this particular missing person just so I could meet the woman who had rocked this particular man's world. I wanted to know why she'd left. Wanted to know how much she might need my help if I ever did manage to find her.

"Let me think about this," I said.

"Nothing much to think *about*," he said. "We talking about a one-off here that's good for both of us. And you do take your hard pass? It comes off the table forever."

"I'll get back to you."

"Take as much time you need to make up your mind," he said. Then he paused and said, "Just make it up before the end of the day. The longer I wait to find her, the more gone she might get herself."

"I'll call you in the morning," I said. "And if I do say no, no hard feelings?"

Tony Marcus laughed. "Fuck no," he said.

Tony nodded at Junior as I stood up. Junior opened the door for me. I winked at him. Tony asked if I wanted Junior and Ty Bop to drive me home. I told him I'd call a car. When I was outside, I took my phone out of my purse and saw there were two missed calls from Richie, and one voicemail.

"Call me when you can," he said. "Or I'll call you back in a little while." There was a pause. "I, uh . . . Kathryn is back in town."

His ex-wife.

My day just kept getting better.

3

KATHRYN HAD BEEN living in London for years, along with their son. Hers and Richie's. Richard Felix Burke, I knew, was six now. She'd left for London before his first birthday. And once she had left, she'd done everything possible to keep Richie from the boy, especially after she'd moved in with a rich new boyfriend in Knightsbridge.

Now she was back. Developing story, as they said on the news shows.

I didn't call Richie back. I called Spike instead.

"The bitch is back," I said.

"Elton John's?" he said. "That bitch?"

"Richie's."

"The fair Kathryn?"

"Her."

"Fuck," he said.

"And, sometimes because there is bad news everywhere, I am considering doing some work for Tony Marcus," I said.

"I hope you're not driving," Spike said. "Because you're obviously drunk."

"Not yet," I said, "but perhaps soon," and I asked where he was.

He told me he was walking up Boylston, had just passed Trinity Church, and asked where I was. I told him. He said he'd meet me at the Bristol bar at the Four Seasons in half an hour. I told him not to start without me. He made no promises.

I fed Rosie, walked up Charles and across the Public Garden to the Four Seasons. I still didn't call Richie back. I wanted some time to think. And have a drink with Spike, which sometimes could be more therapeutic than a spa day.

We sat at a table near one of the windows. Outside, in what little was left of the afternoon light, snow had begun to fall. We were working on martinis. My plan was to stick with one, not just because of the hour, but because I didn't want to be half-drunk when I finally did speak with Richie.

When we sat down, Spike asked whether I wanted to talk about Tony first or Kathryn first. I said Tony. He said, "In the whole cockeyed grand scheme of things, wouldn't that be burying the lede?"

"Maybe it's simply avoidance," I said.

"Okay," he said. "But only until our second drink."

"I can't believe she's back," I said.

"That bitch," he said.

We drank to that.

"Okay, first things first," Spike said. "Why would you possibly think you can trust Tony?"

"He said it himself today," I said. "For a fancified thug, his word *has* mostly been good in the past. And the more he talked about Lisa Morneau, the more he made me curious about her."

"He's still a goddamn thug, and killer when he has to be," Spike said.

"Crazy world," I said.

"His or yours?" Spike said.

"Ours," I said. "But all things considered, I'd rather not be on his bad side until the end of days."

"When he wants something," Spike said, "that's his only side."

"I think that a lot of this might simply involve male ego," I said.

"That disgusting thing."

"He's getting older. Now he's been left by a younger woman, and a younger guy is making a move on him, in his own backyard."

Spike plucked an olive with his fingers, ate it, and finished his martini. As he waved at our waiter, he asked if I wanted another. I told him I was good.

"Our waiter's upper body looks rather well developed."

"Does it ever end?" I said.

"Rhetorical question?" he said.

He was wearing his new black cashmere jacket and a powder-blue shirt. There was, I noticed, and not for the first time, more gray in his beard than on top of his head. But then who was I to talk about coloring hair?

The waiter brought Spike his second martini. He said it was his last one, and then he was headed from here over to his place, Spike's, on Marshall Street, to get ready for the evening's festivities.

"A lot can go wrong between you and Tony," he said.

"I've spent my whole life trying to make my own way in a man's world," I said. "Well, guess what? The world in which this missing woman has somehow survived is a whole lot tougher than mine. Now she's knocked Tony back, at least a little bit. Come on. You'd want to meet her, too."

"But you're going to be taking his money."

"Not necessarily," I said, and explained the deal Tony had offered me.

"So it's pro bono work?"

"Might be," I said.

"I don't like that look," Spike said.

"What look?" I said, trying to sound innocent.

"The look that says you're already working on some kind of backup plan before you even tell him 'yes,'" Spike said.

"More like an exit ramp," I said, and sipped my drink. "And if something does go wrong, I have the same old backup plan as always."

Spike raised an eyebrow.

"You," I said.

"Shit!" he said. "I was afraid of that."

"You aren't afraid of anything," I said.

"Neither are you," Spike said. "So, if I might now change the subject, what has you so spooked about Kathryn?"

"Rhetorical question?" I said.

There was piped-in music now at the Bristol bar. I liked things better when they still had a piano player. It joined a long list of things, and places, I liked better the way they used to be. I sighed.

"What a day," I said.

"Not yet over," Spike said.

"Tony's woman left him," I said, "and the one Richie was married to after me comes back."

"Richie likes you better."

"She gave him a child."

"Not like it was family planning," Spike said.

"Still."

"She's also the woman in his life who moved to London with their son because Richie liked you better," Spike said.

That was exactly what she had done. Spike knew the story. Kathryn had gotten pregnant as a way of trying to save her marriage to Richie, certain that he would never leave her if she did present him with a child. I felt the same way when I found out she was pregnant, and when Richard Felix Burke was born. We both turned out to be wrong. It was about all Kathryn and I had in common, other than both of us loving Richie.

Richie told her that he always wanted to be a part of

the boy's life, that he knew he could be a good father to Richard even after the divorce.

"I thought you loved me," Kathryn said at the time.

"I did," Richie said. "And I always will. And I will love my son the best way I know how. But I can't stay with you while loving Sunny more."

Spike had always said it was amazing, Kathryn being a bad sport about something like that.

So she had moved back to London, where her mother still lived. Maybe she was still holding out hope that he would leave Boston and follow her there and the three of them could become one big, happy family. I could have told her there was as much chance of the Prudential Center moving over there.

More likely, or so I'd always thought, she just wanted to make it as difficult as possible for Richie to see his son, out of spite. Or all-around, world-class bitchiness.

At first Richie had tried, flying frequently over to London the first year after Kathryn had left. He always took a room at The Milestone, a boutique hotel where he and I had stayed once when I decided I needed to see Princess Diana's dresses. But the year after that, and after her mother had died, Kathryn had moved in with the richer, older boyfriend, one who was a big deal in the restaurant business.

Kathryn then informed Richie that the boyfriend would now become the primary father figure in the boy's life, at which point Richie asked her why, to learn how to make a proper kale salad?

Richie would still fly over occasionally. But Kathryn,

with the boyfriend's help, would sometimes make him wait days to even see his son.

When Richie complained about that, to both of them, the boyfriend had said, "Maybe you should take us to family court, dear boy."

"Or just go fuck myself?" Richie said.

"Or that."

Richie had flown back to Boston the next day. That was eight months ago.

Lately Richie had talked about being a father about as often as he spoke of the Kardashians. And we were back together, or as together as two people living apart could be. Still, I knew him well enough to know that the distance between him and his son was a lingering, constant, profound sadness in his life.

Except now his son was back. Along with his mother.

"We don't know why she decided to come back," Spike said.

"We do not."

"I'm assuming she has the boy with her," he said.

"Same," I said.

"But until you speak with Richie, we don't know how long they might be back for," Spike said. "Or if she might be back for good."

"Fuckety fuck," I said.

"You stole that from me."

"It seemed to fit the moment."

"You have clearly delayed speaking to Richie about all of this," Spike said.

"I wanted to organize my thoughts," I said.

"With old Dr. Spike."

"What does that say about me?"

"I'm afraid you and Dr. Silverman will have to sort that out," he said.

Susan Silverman was my therapist.

There was still a little bit left of my martini. I drank it. The vodka wasn't making me feel any better. But I had to admit, it hadn't made me feel any worse, either.

"I'll find out more when Richie and I do speak."

"No point in putting it off much longer."

"I know," I said. "You think it might help my thought organization to have a second martini?"

"If you have to ask that," Spike said, "I don't even know you anymore."

He reached over and picked up my right hand and kissed the back of it. He was my best friend in the world if you didn't count Rosie the dog. He was handsome in a rugged way, more ripped than he'd ever been, big and fearless and loyal and dangerous as hell when he needed to be. I'd always told him that if he weren't gay, I'd marry him.

He said he'd rather I adopted him.

"Maybe she got dumped," I said. "Kathryn."

"Ever hopeful," Spike said.

"You know what's crazy?" I said.

"Do tell."

"That I really might be more worried about Richie's ex-wife being back in my life, even temporarily, than I am about Tony Marcus," I said.

Spike paid the check. It was snowing harder when

we got outside. Spike said he'd walk me home. I said he didn't have to. He said he wanted to, and he liked walking across the park in the snow, it made him feel young and gay instead of old and gay.

When we got to my door he said, "This probably doesn't mean anything."

"Nope," I said.

"Probably just a visit," he said.

"Yup," I said.

"Talked out for now?" he said.

"Yup," I said.

He said I should call him in the morning, or later tonight, if I felt the urge. Then he put his arms around me. I told him he was almost the perfect man. He said, "Why almost?" I told him it might have something to do with his new scent.

"What kind of cologne is that?" I said.

"Not cologne," he said, trying to sound offended. "Tom Ford all-over body spray."

I told him that was way too much information.

"I might wait until tomorrow to call Richie," I said.

"That ought to show him," Spike said.

He kissed the top of my head and walked back toward Charles Street in the snow, and I went inside, where I was greeted exuberantly by Rosie. I had checked my phone before leaving the Bristol bar. There had been no further messages from Richie. I checked it again now. Still no messages. Were they having a family dinner? Where was she staying? Were Kathryn and Richard staying with him?

All I had to do was call. I always wanted to be the finder-out of things, smartest girl in the class. Just not at this moment. I took Rosie out, then fixed myself some pasta, melted some butter over it, added some Parmesan. I watched the *Nightly News* with Lester Holt, absorbed hardly any of it, except another story about legalized marijuana. Eventually they were going to be selling it at Stop & Shop. I went upstairs and took a long bath, came back down and built a fire, and put Ben Webster on Melanie Joan's world-class sound system. It wasn't yet eight o'clock. I fixed myself a small Jameson and took up one end of the couch. Rosie had the other. I had developed a taste for jazz long after a taste for Irish whiskey, but they seemed to fit together perfectly.

The way Richie and I had lately fit together, perhaps as well as we ever had, including when we were married and living together.

There was no reason for me to think things wouldn't continue to go well for us, perhaps to infinity and beyond, whether Kathryn was back in Boston or not. Richie and I had teamed up when he'd been shot and his family had come under threat. We were as close as we had ever been, even without any current discussion about ever moving back in together, or remarrying.

Where was he?

Where were *they*?

I picked up a book I'd been reading by Joni Mitchell that included song lyrics and poetry and sketches and oil paintings that I thought were quite good, wondering all over again how one woman could have that much art in her.

I read for a while and studied some of that art and then closed the book and said out loud, "How come he hasn't called again?"

Rosie instantly became alert, thinking a surprise treat might be in play. Even after establishing there wasn't, she continued to stare at me. There were a few similarities between her and the original Rosie, whom Richie and I had shared custody of after our divorce. The big one was this:

She seemed to have the ability to stare all the way into my soul.

"Okay, okay," I said to her. "I get it. I'm acting like a wife."

I knew I had no right to act like a wife wondering why hubby wasn't home from the office yet. I had no reason to be jealous. I told myself again that none of this was his doing. Since his divorce from Kathryn, their relationship had been about as amicable as the Israelis and Palestinians.

The snow was blowing sideways by now. The fire began to die out. I put on my coat, slipped into my new UGGs, took Rosie out one last time, cleaned up after her once she'd completed her nightly duties, locked the door when we were back inside, set the alarm, carried her up with me to the master bedroom, and set her down at her end of Melanie Joan's bed, which was big enough on which to land Air Force One.

I brushed my teeth, applied some moisturizer,

checked my bedside table to make sure that my Glock was where it was supposed to be. I checked my phone again. Still nothing more from Richie. It was only ten o'clock. But it had been a long day. I felt myself smiling, thinking that hanging with Tony Marcus might have been the highlight of it, and how crazy was *that*?

I had also decided that under the guise of working for him, I might actually be working for Lisa Morneau, if I could find her. Some kind of sisterhood thing. Just from different sides of the street, so to speak.

Still no calls or texts from Richie.

I shut off the light.

Then my phone.

That would show him.

4

WHEN I AWAKENED, after sleeping surprisingly well, I turned my phone back on and saw two missed calls from Richie that had come in after eleven o'clock, along with a text message from Tony Marcus:

So u in?

I knew he was a late sleeper. I texted back anyway, saying I was, and would call him later. I didn't know if Lisa Morneau wanted to be saved. Or was worth saving. Or wanted to stay lost. But I had made up my mind to find out.

Richie called about fifteen minutes after my first cup of coffee, right before I really was going to return his calls.

"Where were you last night?" he said. "I tried you a couple of times late."

"I went to bed early," I said. "Speaking of late, must have been a late dinner for you and Kathryn."

"I thought Kathryn and I needed to talk."

"What about?"

"Lot of things," he said.

"What's she doing here?" I said. "A short visit, I hope."

"She's come back here to live," Richie said. "She and Richard."

Shit.

"Didn't see that one coming," I said.

"I really need to talk to you about all this," he said.

"We're talking now," I said.

"I mean in person," he said. "I think the best way for us to get out ahead of this is if we *all* sit down and talk it through."

"How civilized," I said.

"We're on the same side, Sunny," Richie said. "You and me, I mean."

"Against the world," I said. "When would you like to do this?"

"How about right now?" he said.

"I haven't even showered yet," I said, "or made myself beautiful."

"You wake up beautiful," he said.

"Save it, soldier," I said.

"I explained a lot to her last night," he said. "I explained that I am committed to you and to us as much as I am to Richard."

"That must have gotten her motor running."

"She said she totally understood," he said. "The way she said she understood that whatever she and I had once ended a long time ago."

"Well, no shit," I said.

"So can we all come over?" he said. "I promise we won't stay long."

"Listen," I said, "there's something I needed to talk to you about, apart from our sudden family drama." I took in some air. "I've got kind of a situation going with Tony Marcus."

"Did he do something?"

"Yeah," I said. "He did."

"Did what?" Richie said.

"He sort of hired me."

"You took on Tony Marcus as a client?" Richie said.

"Well, in a manner of speaking."

"You're joking."

"Am not."

"Something else we need to talk about," he said. "Just not this morning."

"Agree," I said. "Let's deal with your situation first."

"Mine and ours," he said.

"Give me an hour," I said.

"See you then," I said.

"Sunny?" he said. "Thank you."

"Don't thank me yet," I said, and ended the call.

I had just enough time for what Spike liked to call "The Process": hair, makeup, clothes. Getting just the right look without looking as if I were trying too hard. I showered quickly, blew out my hair as best I could, did my face, put on a cornflower-blue cashmere pull-over that I knew was one of Richie's favorites and a pair of black Rag & Bone jeans that looked as if I'd had to apply them to my legs and butt with a Magic Marker. The whole time I was getting ready I tried not to dwell too much or too long on whether I was trying to make myself look this good for him or for her.

More likely it was both.

When I opened the door an hour later I had the same reaction I'd had the first time I'd ever laid eyes on Kathryn:

Holy Christ, she still looks like she could be my sister.

But I was more taken by the boy. I had seen plenty of pictures of Richard Burke. There had been times, across the years, when I'd been present when Richie FaceTimed with the boy, until Kathryn had even made that difficult for them. So I knew what he looked like and who he looked like, and who he looked like was Richie, just slightly more fair, because of his blond mother.

Mostly he looked like what I imagined a child of Richie's and mine would have looked like, if we'd ever had one. The gene pool would essentially have been the same. We had talked about having children when we'd first gotten married. We'd talked about it a lot. Decided to wait. Then we were divorced, and he had married

Kathryn, and then *she* was the one who had gotten pregnant. She was the one who had become a mom.

As I took their coats and hung them in the front hall closet, I noticed Rosie was standing in the doorway between the kitchen and living room. I had taken Kathryn's coat, so she was first into the living room. When Rosie saw her she began to quietly growl. It made me want to slobber over my own dog.

But as soon as Rosie saw Richard, she was running straight for him, her stubby tail wagging furiously. The boy immediately fell to his knees and let her lick his face, as if the two of them had already started a playdate.

"No point in asking if Richard likes dogs," I said.

"Seems as if yours likes Richard a lot better than she likes me," Kathryn said.

Makes two of us, I thought.

"He wasn't allowed to have dogs in London," Kathryn said. "My boyfriend didn't like them."

"Scum," I said.

"It's odd, isn't it?" Kathryn said. "Referring to a man William's age as a boyfriend."

"I've found there is no adequate way to describe the man in your life if he's not your husband," I said.

"How do you describe Richie?" Kathryn asked.

"The man in my life," I said.

I had a coffee setup on the mahogany coffee table. Richie and Kathryn sat next to each other on the couch. I sat in one of Melanie Joan's antique chairs across from them. Richard and Rosie behaved blissfully, and as if the rest of us weren't there.

The only thing the boy had asked was "What's his name?"

"Her name," I said. "Rosie. She's a girl."

"Sometimes girls are okay," he said, and then ran into the kitchen as Rosie chased him.

We all sipped coffee. *So far, so good,* I thought. Civilized, as promised.

"Daniel and I have ended our relationship," Kathryn said. "I explained that to Richie last night. Once we did end the relationship, there was no reason for me to stay on in London any longer."

"I'm sorry," I said, even though I really wasn't. My father said that no one faked sincerity better than his baby girl.

"I'm not," Kathryn said.

It was impossible not to notice that she was still able to elevate the concept of icy blonde practically to an art form.

"Who ended the relationship, if you don't mind me asking?" I said.

Richie chose to focus in that moment on the love fest between his son and my dog.

"I was the one who chose to leave," Kathryn said. "But he was the one who'd already chosen a younger woman. One unencumbered by a six-year-old child."

"I see," I said, just to say something.

"I only moved to London in the first place because of my mother," Kathryn said, answering a question no one had asked.

She sipped her coffee. I did the same. Richie continued to smile as he watched Rosie chase his son.

"In the long run, this will work out for the best," she said. "It will be a good thing that Richard will have his father back in his life."

"He should have been in his life all along," I said.

Civilized left the room, just like that.

"But we don't need to relitigate that today," Richie said.

"No, Richie," Kathryn said. "Sunny has a right. And *is* right. It was wrong of me to keep the two of you apart for as long as I did, a decision I will always regret."

Maybe she meant it. But it sounded to me like a line she had rehearsed, one that perhaps she thought might elicit my sympathy. Fat chance. For about the one thousandth time, I wondered how Richie had ended up with her.

He did his best to change the subject, at least somewhat, saying, "Kathryn will be looking for a place to live and finding the right school for Richard to attend second semester."

There was a lot more I wanted to say, mostly to her, things I had bottled up for a long time. But this wasn't the right moment. Richard and Rosie were chasing each other around the kitchen, loudly. He was laughing. If Rosie were capable of laughter, she would have been doing the same.

"Don't have much to offer on either real estate or schools," I said.

"And I wouldn't expect you to," Kathryn said. "But the real reason I asked Richie to bring me here today is because if Richard is going to be in Richie's life, he's going to be in yours, too."

I glanced at Richie. He hadn't changed expression, but I knew him. We had always been able to have entire conversations without a single word being exchanged. We did so now. I saw it in his eyes. He wanted me to let this go.

But he knew me. And perhaps knew I could not, or would not, just let this go.

"I have to ask you something, Kathryn, just because I can't not," I said. "Are we all just supposed to act now as if the last few years didn't happen? Seriously?"

She turned her face toward Richie as if she'd been slapped. Then looked back at me. Her face had reddened slightly. Or maybe I hadn't noticed before, and she'd simply overdone it with the blush.

"Maybe this was a mistake," Kathryn said. "Maybe things between us will never change."

"Maybe the mistake was keeping Richie from his son."

"I'm trying to make things right now," Kathryn said.

"For whom?" I said.

"For everyone," Richie said.

I had read something about a relaxation exercise where you took a few seconds to take in air, held it as long, exhaled just as slowly. I tried that now. It didn't help as much as I'd hoped.

"Kathryn, listen," I said. "I hope you find what

you're looking for here. I do. But you're not my concern. Richie is. And so now is that little boy in the other room. All I really care about is that they're together again."

"Fair enough," she said. She looked back at Richie. "I guess we're done here?" she said.

He nodded.

"We'll figure this out," he said. "All of us."

Kathryn went into the kitchen to collect Richard.

"He looks just like you," I said.

"Nothing is going to change between us," he said.

We were keeping our voices low.

"I want to believe that," I said.

I did want to believe it. But it was as if the ground underneath all of us had officially shifted the moment they had all walked through the front door. Or perhaps when Kathryn and Richard had landed at Logan Airport. Kathryn was right about one thing: If the little boy who did look just like his father was in his father's world now, he *was* in mine now, too. If Richie's world had changed, forever, so had my own. There was a longer conversation to be had about all of this, but this wasn't the right moment for that, either.

Richard was standing in the doorway to the kitchen. He had found an old tennis ball where I kept Rosie's toys, and had been throwing it to her. He threw it one last time. One last time Rosie brought it right back to him. I usually had to bribe her to get her to do that. Maybe she'd already figured out that he was Richie's.

When he had his coat on, the little boy thanked me

for letting him play with my dog. Then he looked up at me with Richie's eyes and asked if he could come back sometime and play with Rosie again.

"You bet," I said. "Rosie and I both want you to come back soon."

"Tomorrow?" he said.

"Maybe not tomorrow," I said. "We'll work it out with your mom and dad. But soon, I promise."

Kathryn took his hand and led him out the door. When the two of them were outside, and once again out of earshot, Richie said he would call me later. Then he kissed me quickly on the lips and told me he loved me. I told him I loved him, too. Then he walked to the car. I watched the three of them get in and heard the engine come to life, and then watched the car pull away toward Charles Street.

Rosie and I stood at the door and watched them go. Richard was behind his father in a forward-facing booster seat. He turned and waved. Probably at Rosie.

I stood there in the brittle, bright morning cold and told myself I was good at a lot of things, and had gotten better at other things as I'd grown up, and grown older, and lived a life. I knew more about myself than I ever had before. I did know how much I loved Richie Burke.

I just knew nothing at all about being a stepmom.

5

I HAD MY WEEKLY session with Dr. Susan Silverman a couple hours after Richie and Kathryn had left, and before I was to meet Tony Marcus.

At one minute after two o'clock, she and I sat across from each other in the downstairs office that was part of her residence on Linnaean Street in Cambridge. As usual she looked as if she had just come from a photo shoot for the world's best and best-looking therapists. She wore a black dress, her black hair was gleaming, her makeup looked as if it had been applied by a team of professionals, and her dark eyes were full of life and intelligence and curiosity. As always, she made me feel as if the best and most interesting hour of her entire day was about to begin.

"So," she said, "what's new and good with Sunny Randall?"

"Plenty," I said. "Hardly any of it good."

"Do tell."

I did. I described my meeting with Tony Marcus, and my conflicted feelings about him, then finding out as soon as I'd left Tony's office about Kathryn being back in Boston, and her subsequent visit to the house. By the time I finished, I was worried that my time was almost up.

When I finally did stop talking, she smiled.

"Well," she said, "it seems as if there is a fair amount of threat assessment going on, isn't there?"

I had changed out of my sweater and jeans before coming over here, into a new Elie Tahari shift dress. So first I had dressed for Richie today; now I'd done the same for Susan Silverman. No wonder I needed a therapist. Before long I'd need a second therapist to analyze my relationship with my first one.

"I honestly believe my arrangement with Tony, if you can call it that," I said, "is quite practical, if it really does remove *him* as a threat. Might as well pick it up there, okay?"

"We can pick it up wherever you feel most comfortable," she said.

"Even in an uncomfortable situation of my own making," I said.

"Mr. Marcus remains a violent and dangerous man," she said, "one who became even more dangerous to you because of the way your last business arrangement with him ended."

"I still think I made the right choice," I said. "Don't you?"

"I'm always more interested in how you feel about your choices, Sunny."

And . . . we're off, I thought.

"I'd much rather feel as if he owed me one, as opposed to the alternative," I said.

"And you believe that if you find this woman, that will reset your situation with him?" she said.

Somehow that word, *situation*, made me smile.

"Did I say something amusing?" she said.

"No," I said. "But I'm thinking that I have a situation with Tony, with his missing girlfriend, with Kathryn, with Richie's son. No wonder I'm here. I should have packed a lunch."

Her only jewelry today was a diamond stud in each ear, her look as understated and elegant as everything else about her. I continued to be curious about her life outside this office, upstairs in her residence. Even though she did make sly references about the man of her dreams from time to time, I knew nothing about him, the way I knew nothing of her life outside this room, and these sessions. But whomever the man was, he had to be a formidable presence, with a life force and intelligence—and perhaps even sense of humor—to match her own.

"Spike asked me why I seemed more concerned

about Kathryn being in my life than me being back in Tony's," I said.

She reached over and wrote something on the legal pad on the desk in front of her.

"I mean, there is no logical reason that I should view her as an actual threat," I said. "I know how much Richie loves me."

"But her appearance in Richie's life, and yours, has clearly unnerved you."

"Like I said, it hasn't been a dull twenty-four hours."

"Do you still view her as a rival for his affections?" she said.

"No," I said. "He made his choice. I don't see him unmaking it at this point. Or ever."

"So is it the child?" she said.

"You mean the child we never had together?" I said. "*That* child?"

She waited.

"Interesting way of putting it," she said.

"He's a sweet kid, he really is, you only have to be around him for five minutes to get a sense of that," I said. "I honestly can't look at him without seeing Richie. I don't want to see him as a complication. But how can I not?"

"Perhaps he's more an opportunity," she said.

"To do what?"

"Find out what kind of mother you might have been?" Susan Silverman said.

"There's a scary thought," I said.

"Is it?"

"Maybe it *is* the boy who scares me the most," I said.

She smiled again.

"Oh, boy," I said.

"So this is the kind of situation that you have always hated, one in which things are beyond your control," she said.

"Oh, boy," I said again.

"But the way you deal with all of it is entirely up to you," she said. "Worth remembering."

When I was with her, I always flipped my watch over so the band was on top and the face was on my wrist, so I could discreetly check the time when I thought we were coming to the end of a session. I glanced down at my wrist now. She probably noticed. But I assumed she noticed if I switched between soft pink blush and coral.

"I don't trust her," I said. "Never did."

"As you have never trusted Tony Marcus," she said.

I felt a smile come over me then. And saw her smiling back. "I think I spot a trend here," I said.

"Well, I should think," Susan Silverman said. "You *are* a trained investigator."

6

RICHIE CALLED WHEN I was on my way back to the Back Bay.

"I'm going to take Kathryn and Richard out for an early dinner, but thought we might have a drink later," he said. "Or something."

"Catch a movie?" I said. "Binge-watch *Mrs. Maisel.*"

"Or something," he said. There was a pause. "Just the two of us."

"Not just the two of us anymore," I said.

"We can handle this," he said.

"You're nicer to your ex than I could ever be," I said. "Or will ever be."

"What's the alternative?" he said. "I don't want to make this more awkward with her than it already is."

"You mean the way I do?"

"All things considered, I thought you were reasonably well behaved."

Somehow a laugh came out of me. "Relative to what?" I said. "Threatening to waterboard her?"

"I'm not asking you to be her friend."

"There's a better chance of me learning to skydive," I said. "Where's she staying, by the way?"

"Four Seasons, at least for the time being," he said. "Until she finds something more permanent."

"It's like she said, she didn't know where else to go," he said. "I don't think she has any idea how long she might stay, or whether she even wants to stay, to tell you the truth."

"She hasn't been this full of surprises since the pregnancy test came up positive," I said.

"And I'll always be grateful it did," Richie said. "He's in the world. In mine. Everything else is just noise."

"As it should be."

"Just remember that you're the one I always wanted," he said, "even when I couldn't have you."

"I know."

"I know you know," Richie said.

I told him to call me when he was done with dinner, parked the car behind the house, walked and fed Rosie, and booked an Uber instead.

TONY HAD SENT me the address of the small brownstone near Symphony Hall that he'd shared, at least occasionally, with Lisa Morneau. On the way over, I told myself that I had signed no contract with Tony Marcus, and was still allowed to change my mind if I wanted to. Just because he said he only wanted to talk to her didn't mean that was the whole truth and nothing but. He had his codes. But I had mine. I would never just turn her over to him. As my father liked to say, we'd burn that bridge when we came to it.

It got me to thinking on my way to Symphony Hall: Who *did* I trust more right now, Tony or Kathryn?

Or maybe the better question was which one of them did I trust less?

The two-story brownstone in which Tony had set up Lisa Morneau was actually around the corner from Symphony Plaza Towers, looking like a miniature version of the bigger brownstones on either side of it. It could not have come cheap. But I was sure that Tony, being Tony, preferred the privacy of the place, as opposed to a doorman building. I knew Tony didn't even want doormen knowing his business.

He said that the door would be unlocked when I got there. Good thing. Just the locks on the front door looked formidable enough to stop even the best pickers of locks in Boston, some of whom I knew. I took it on faith that the alarm system would have made Bank of America jealous.

As I was reaching for the handle, Ty Bop opened the front door for me.

"Yo," I said. "What's crackin', homeslice?"

He looked at me with the same indifference you got from snakes.

From behind him I heard Tony Marcus say, "Girl, you got about as much street cred as Sweden."

He was standing in the middle of the living room, which was open and sunny and, to my surprise, elegant. There were bookcases on both walls, to his left and right, an L-shaped couch, rustic coffee table, an expensive rug that I thought might be a Penfold, just because Melanie Joan had one quite similar to it.

"You said you'd bring a picture," I said.

Tony reached into the pocket of his overcoat and handed it to me. It was of Lisa Morneau sitting on the couch in this room. She was beautiful, with flawless skin, dark eyes, long hair. Killer smile.

"She looks young, Tony," I said. "Even for you."

"Yeah, but like they say, she got one of those old souls."

I put the picture into the pocket of my coat.

"What about credit cards, ATM, phone?" I said. "I assume you've been checking all of those."

"Easy to do," he said. "I pay for all of it."

"You told me she's been gone a week?"

"Six days, be exact," he said. "I left her here that morning, haven't seen her since."

"How long have the two of you been together? I didn't ask the other day."

"Coupla years," he said.

I grinned. "Personal best?"

"If we talking exclusive," he said, "pretty damn close."

He sat down on the couch, put his head back, then

moved it from side to side as if trying to relax the muscles in his neck. Or his brain.

"Tell me more about Lisa," I said.

"She smart, you can see for yourself she's nearly better looking than Beyoncé, a fast learner," he said. "Don't know how she learned what she learned about finance and shit, but she did. Like she was putting all her street smarts to good use. And the thing was? More I put on her, the more she showed she could handle. Businesswise, I'm talkin' about, not just the fucking. I told her where I was going, she could come along with me."

"And where *are* you going?" I said. "I thought you liked things the way they are."

"Town's wide open now," Tony said. "Maybe too wide open. Old guys like Richie's old man getting older. Felix Burke's dead. So's Gino Fish. Joe Broz is long gone. Don't know what the fuck Eddie Lee's family doing in Chinatown. DeMarcos are as fucked-up as ever. Casinos coming in, which means Vegas. Still plenty of drug business, even with them making weed legal. Somebody with vision, and muscle, and money, he could be bigger than anybody since poor old Whitey Bulger, he plays his cards right."

"You make it sound like Silicon Valley in the old days," I said.

"The way I see it," he said, "if you aren't looking forward you might as well have your head up your ass."

I smiled.

"What?" he said.

"Can't lie, Tony. I do like listening to you talk."

"Same old same old," he said. "Ain't nothing more than alabaster and sham."

"How much sham are you giving me now?"

"I just want to talk to the girl," he said. "Find out why she left when I thought things were going so good."

"Doesn't necessarily mean she thought they were going good," I said.

"No," he said, "it don't."

"I know we talked about this," I said. "But you can't believe she's with a direct competitor? It's as I said to you already. She'd have to know better. And know *you* better."

"I hear you," he said. "Still, I don't want to get cockolded here. Make me look weak as shit. And old."

"I believe it's *cuck*olded."

"Makes more sense my way," he said.

"It actually kind of does."

"Find the girl," he said. "As much as I know she knows about my business, might turn out she knows even more."

"I'm not handing her over if she doesn't want to be handed over," I said.

"Hear you on that."

"You don't think she might try to blackmail you with something she might know that you don't want her to?" I said.

"I just want her to keep all *my shit* to *her* own damn self, whether she's coming back here or not," Tony said.

I gave him a long look. "Is this more personal for you, or professional?"

"Ask her, you find her," he said.

"Deal," I said.

"Deal," he said.

He put out his hand. I shook it, resisting the urge to count my fingers after he released his grip.

"Lisa got any close friends?" I said.

"Only one I know of," he said. "Name's Callie. She come out of the life, too. Says she hasn't seen Lisa since I have. But that don't mean she hasn't." He pulled out his phone, tapped out something. I felt my own phone buzzing in my purse as he did. "I just sent you the number," he said. "You just got to be careful with her. She come up on the streets the way Lisa did."

"What's that mean?"

"We gone over this," he said. "Means whores lie, even after they stop whoring."

He stood up, telling me to take as much time as I wanted here, and to just let myself out. Told me the two locks on the front door would lock behind me.

"I'll bet," I said.

Tony said, "Upstairs is the master bedroom, where all that heavenly transport shit happened. And the little office she kept in the second bedroom."

"You know this is only a onetime thing between us, right?" I said, as Ty Bop opened the door for Tony.

Tony Marcus smiled brilliantly.

"What they all say," he said.

7

I HAD NO IDEA what I was searching for in the place that Lisa Morneau had called home until a week ago.

Tony had said that her clothes closets upstairs were always full, that he used to tell her that she better figure it out, he wasn't moving her to a bigger damn place because she couldn't stop shopping like the world was about to end. Now there were empty spaces and empty hangers in the big walk-in closet attached to the master bedroom, so some clothes must be missing. There was just no way of telling how many. And just because she had packed didn't necessarily mean she was safe. Or had left of her own volition. Or was still alive.

But the clothes that had been left behind told me she had outstanding taste, the closet featuring a lot of brands far more expensive than what I could ever afford. As much as Tony complained about what he had to spend on her, he had obviously kept spending. And the floor of the closet showed me that the woman sure did love her shoes, with a particular fondness for Jimmy Choo and Manolo Blahnik. And Prada. If I ever did find her, and before I called Tony—if I did call after hearing her story—I imagined that my first move might be asking her to go shoe shopping with me.

As Tony had said, the laptop was gone. I wondered just how much of Tony's business was on it. There was no landline, something hardly uncommon in the modern world.

There was no Alexa, the Amazon virtual assistant who'd managed to become one of the most famous women in the world, on either level of the place. I had once been aided in tracking down a missing college student by the memory on the Alexa she'd left behind in her dorm room.

I went back to the master bedroom, searching the closet methodically but finding nothing more exciting than some particularly bad-girl things from Victoria's Secret. In the second drawer of the bedside table I found some marijuana edibles that I recognized only because Spike had once tried in vain to get me to try them. I hadn't declined because I was a prude where weed was concerned, just remembering that in college all it had done was make me want to go stick up a Baskin-Robbins.

There was an unlabeled bottle containing some big

blue pills, with *Pfizer* written on them. If they weren't Viagra, I was going to turn in my license.

"Tony," I said. "You dog."

He'd told me he used the downstairs bathroom, and shower. I went to Lisa's much larger bathroom next, and conducted a brief inventory of makeup, facial wash, moisturizers, hair products. The basics. A lot of it was still visible on the large counter that included two sinks. But I felt as if there should have been more. I couldn't find a hair dryer anywhere. Or medication of any kind. There was no shampoo in her shower, or conditioner. More reason to believe she hadn't been taken, because clearly she'd taken at least some of her girl stuff with her.

I ended up back at the desk in the office, looking for something or anything. There were no false bottoms or compartments in the drawers, underneath the surface, or in the swivel chair. No old-school Filofax, no checkbook, none of the spreadsheets that Tony had described.

Nothing here to indicate that she had been taken, either.

But where had she gone? And for how long?

Maybe she had gotten a better offer, from Gabriel Jabari or someone else in Tony's orbit. Or she had simply found someone she liked or even loved more than Tony Marcus. Not hard to wrap my head around that one.

Somehow she had changed her life enough to make

it to the boardroom at Tony Marcus Inc., even if that involved being in the bedroom with him, too.

So what sort of change had she made this time?

Tony Marcus had said that somehow, in the years she'd spent on the street and the work she'd done for him since, she'd managed to stay out of the system, something he most certainly had not. But maybe Tony only *thought* she'd stayed out of the system. Or maybe she'd been in it before she went to work for him. I would call Lee Farrell, my best friend at the cops, and ask him to check.

Tony had said there was no safe, on either floor. It didn't mean there wasn't one that she had installed without telling him. But as hard as I searched, I was unable to find one.

I finally sat on the couch in the living room and tried to mimic the voice of Tony Marcus and said, "Where you at, girl?"

It sounded like a shout in all the emptiness and quiet around me, all the gone-girl-ness of the place.

Tomorrow I would regroup and reach out to her friend Callie. I felt there were things I could accomplish tonight, I just wasn't sure what. But one of Sunny Randall's boldfaced, tried-and-true rules of detecting went something like this:

When in doubt, find someone to annoy.

I called Spike at Spike's.

"Hi-ho!" he said in a singsong voice.

"I'd tell you that was too gay," I said. "But you know I think there's no such thing."

"How are things in your ridiculously complex life?" he said.

I could hear the sound of the restaurant behind him. It sounded busy. I asked if it was. He said never too busy for me.

"You up for going to a strip club?" I said.

"I told you I'm trying to quit," he said.

Then I told him I wasn't talking about HunkOMania.

8

SPIKE SAID I was usually much deeper into a case before I decided to go out of my way to annoy somebody like Gabriel Jabari. I told him that neither of us could be sure that I actually would annoy him, that maybe I'd just be making a new friend. In addition, I saw it as a constructive way to keep my mind off Kathryn.

He asked how the visit had gone. I told him that I was a sucker for the little boy, and how Rosie had practically thrown herself at him.

"How'd you take that?"

"Love me, love my dog," I said.

"And vice versa," he said.

"Rosie acted like she wanted to bite Kathryn on her skinny ass," I said.

"I assume this pleased you."

"To no end," I said. "The former Kathryn Burke acted like a total shit to Richie practically from the time the boy was born. Now it's like he's giving her a total pass."

"What choice does he have?" Spike said.

"That's what he said," I said.

"He and I are a lot more alike than you think," he said, "other than some fundamental differences."

"And you both love me."

"Madly."

We were in an Uber on our way to Suite, on a fixed-up block on Tremont right before Chinatown. I told Spike that Lisa and Tony had been here one time together, but that Tony said she had gone back without him.

"What I'd like to know is why," I said.

"Probably not the same reason I used to go to HunkOMania," he said.

"Oh, ick," I said.

My own firsthand knowledge of strip clubs, of any kind, was about as extensive as my knowledge of video games. I know there actually were Magic Mike places, both for men and for women. Having not done any research on the subject, I just felt there were more straight-guy places, fulfilling a need men had for easy and immediate and impersonal gratification short of outright paying for sex. And I had read enough about clubs like Suite to understand that the setting and ambience were supposed to make the patrons feel as if they were watching women undress at the Harvard Club.

But to me, whatever rationalizations young guys

with money in their pockets used on themselves, it still seemed to be like swimming with your clothes on.

"I still can't believe you actually went to places like this," I said to Spike.

"It was mostly for giggles," he said. "And with a former squeeze."

"But was there some kind of hinky turn-on?"

"Was for him," he said. He turned so I could see him grinning. "Want to hear more?"

"Sweet Jesus, no," I said.

We got out of the car and walked toward the front door of what looked like a pretty fancy Boston restaurant from the outside. I wondered how many couples showed up at Suite, if any. But Spike and I looked like one. He was wearing a blue suit and open-neck white shirt under his topcoat. I had decided to wear the same dress I had worn to Dr. Silverman's, trying not to dwell on the fact that I'd made the same fashion choice to come here that I'd made before seeing my shrink. Mostly I'd just wanted to find something that didn't make me look like a slutty job applicant.

When I mentioned that to Spike he said, "Liar."

The music was louder than I'd expected once we were inside. The cover charge was fifty dollars. Spike handed a hundred-dollar bill to the guy at the desk. If he thought it unusual that a man and woman had come here together, nothing on his face revealed it.

The guy said, "Been here before?"

"We have not," Spike said.

"Not many house rules," the guy said. "No drugs, no solicitation, no inappropriate touching."

Spike gently poked me with an elbow and said, "Sounds like our marriage, sweetheart."

No reaction from the guy on that, either. But then I hadn't expected the place to be a capital of lightheartedness.

He just said, "If you'd like to pay more, or even consider a membership on the spot, you'd both be entitled to the VIP area upstairs and the champagne lounge."

Spike said that he and the missus would like to just look around a little bit. As we moved away from the desk I told Spike, "If you call me 'missus' again, I will shoot you later."

"Little woman?" he said.

There were tables set around the dance floor, where a tall blond woman was just beginning a pole dance. She was nearly six feet tall, had short-cropped blond hair, was wearing only a G-string for the moment, and seemed to have some kind of sparkle thing going for her on her cheeks. Facial cheeks.

She was also more limber and flexible than some otters I had seen once on the Animal Channel.

We were able to find two seats at the bar. Spike ordered a Crown Royal, neat. I asked for a chardonnay.

When the bartender brought back the drinks, I said, "Boss around?"

"Got a lot of bosses," he said.

He was tall and wore a white T-shirt as tight as my

jeans, as a way of showing how ripped he was, upper arms and chest. Lot of brown hair on the top, not so much on the sides. What did the kids call it? High and tight.

"Gabriel," I said.

"Don't know anybody by that name," he said.

I reached into my purse and pulled out the photograph of Lisa Morneau that Tony had given me.

"You remember seeing this woman around here in the last week?" I said.

The guy looked at the picture and laughed, though his heart didn't seem to be in it. Then he handed the picture back to me.

"Don't know her," he said. "And me, so good with faces, usually."

I took a better look around, especially in the table area, where the waitresses were not only serving drinks in their short black dresses, but clearly presenting themselves to the customers like runway models. White, African American, Asian, Latina, they ran the gamut, but all were stunningly pretty. Even at a time in my life when young women had begun to look incredibly young to me, so many of these women seemed barely legal.

"They look like college kids," I said to Spike.

"A lot of them probably are," he said.

There was a tap on my shoulder. I turned around. A man taller than Spike, totally bald, broad-shouldered, and looking about as friendly as a prison guard said, "You come now, please."

If it wasn't a Russian accent, it was in the neighborhood.

Spike smiled brilliantly. "Least he said 'please,'" he said.

The guy said, "You are coming now, or we are wasting time fucking around, huh?"

We followed him past the stairway leading up to what we had been told was the VIP area, past the blonde now somehow working her way up the pole using only her long legs, to an elevator in the back of the place. The bald guy pushed the button for the third floor. On the way up, he checked my purse for a gun and quickly patted down Spike. But we'd both known better than to be carrying.

When the doors opened, we were in a spacious office that told me that the boss was indeed around.

The man behind the desk stood as we entered. I thought of Tony Marcus's description of Gabriel Jabari, but the man was even prettier than Idris Elba, if such a thing was even possible. He was wearing a skinny dark suit, shirt to match, silver tie.

"Ms. Randall," he said. "And should I call you Mr. Spike?"

"Spike will do," Spike said.

"I'm Gabriel," he said.

"So nice to meet you, Gabriel," I said.

He sat. We sat.

Gabriel Jabari said, "Gled, as I don't seem to be in much danger here, please go have a look around on the second floor."

The elevator doors opened and Gled was gone.

"Let's get to it, shall we?" Jabari said. "Why are you here showing around a picture of Lisa Morneau?"

"Your bartender said he didn't know her," I said. "But you obviously do."

"And you obviously know that already," Jabari said.

"Tony Marcus believes that the last time anybody saw her, she was here to see you," I said.

Jabari shook his head dismissively. "I offered her a job," he said.

"What kind of job?"

"A lucrative one," he said. "I am looking to expand my interests in Boston."

"At Tony's expense?"

He showed me so many white teeth I wanted to count them.

"From your lips," he said, "to God's ears."

"Soon after being here," I said, "Lisa disappeared."

"So I'm told," he said.

"Tony seems to think you might know where she has gone," I said.

"I think the French have a saying that covers that one," he said. "Fuck Tony Marcus and the horse he rode in on."

Spike said, "I knew that line had to start somewhere."

"You don't appear to have much use for Tony," I said.

"To me," Jabari said, "he is a sad old man refusing to accept that the world is in the process of passing him by."

Jabari said then that he'd forgotten his manners, and asked if we wanted a drink. "On the house," he said. I looked at Spike. Then we both shook our heads.

I said, "Why did you even invite us up here?"

"I've heard a lot about you, Ms. Randall," Jabari said. "Everybody in town knows about how you beat our friend Mr. Marcus out of all those guns. Which, to me, only validated my theory."

"About the world passing him by," I said.

"Precisely," he said.

"And you wanted to speed up the process by taking Lisa away from him."

"In a far more legitimate enterprise," he said.

I smiled.

"Well," I said. "Legitimate-ish."

"I will give you the same advice I would give Mr. Marcus, were he here," he said. "Stay *out* of my business."

"Eek," I said. "Is that a threat?"

He smiled again.

"As I said. Just friendly advice."

"Well," Spike said. "Friendly-ish."

"I am not looking to make trouble for you, or myself," I said to Jabari. "I'm just working a case."

"Work it somewhere else," he said. "I've told you everything you need to know about my interactions with Ms. Morneau."

"What if I need to speak with you again?" I said.

"Resist the urge," he said.

"Let me ask you something," I said. "If all you

wanted to do was offer her a job, why do you care whether I'm asking about her or not? *Is* she somehow in the middle of something between you and Tony in a way neither you nor Tony have articulated?"

"Say she is, just for the sake of conversation," he said. "It would not be a place anybody would want to be. Including, and maybe even especially, you, Ms. Randall."

"See, now," Spike said pleasantly, "that right there sounded like a threat."

The elevator opened. Gled reappeared. If Jabari has somehow pushed a button to summon him, I hadn't seen him do it.

"Gled, show our friends to the front door, please," Jabari said.

We got into the elevator, standing against the back wall. Gled hit the button for the first floor.

Spike whispered to me, "So I'm guessing the champagne lounge is out of the question?"

9

WELL," SPIKE SAID while we waited for our Uber, "if it was your stated mission to get under his skin, pretty sure we just checked that box."

"Before I'm through," I said, "I might have every big pimp in town mad at me."

I'd used my own address as the destination for our car. Spike asked if I wanted to go to Spike's for a nightcap instead. I told him I'd pretty much maxed out my fun card for one night. When we pulled up to the house on River Street Place, Spike walked me to the door.

"You want my opinion about your current circumstances?" he said.

"Always."

"You should drop this now," Spike said. "That guy was right. In the middle of something between him and Tony is not a place you want to be, at least not by choice."

"I said I'd find her," I said. "I'm going to find her. Kind of a thing with me. You'd know better than anyone."

"I used to have an expression when a bar fight would break out," Spike said. "Let's you and him fight. Let him and Tony fight, and you sit this one out. She'll probably come back on her own. Or not. But if she wanted to be with Tony right now, she'd be with Tony."

"We've gone over this plenty of times before," I said. "If I let somebody like Gabriel Jabari run me off, I need another line of work."

Spike said, "I have a bad feeling about this, Sonya."

It was always serious when he used my real first name. Same with Richie. And my dad.

"Lisa Morneau has been run by men her whole adult life," I said. "I want to find out what finally made *her* run."

"She's not your client."

I smiled at him. "You sure?"

"Be careful," he said, kissing me on top of my head.

I told him that I loved him then, and Spike said, yeah, yeah, yeah, tell him something he didn't know.

I unlocked the door. There was no beep from the alarm, which meant that I must not have set it before Spike and I went to Suite.

But when I stepped inside, Rosie did not come running.

Rosie always came running.

She did this even if she'd been asleep before she heard the door, from any room in the house. The original Rosie the dog did that. This Rosie was the same.

They both had mutantlike hearing.

I gave a quick whistle and called out "Rosie girl" as I instinctively reached into my purse for my gun, before remembering I didn't have one with me.

"Rosie girl," I said again as I reached into the drawer in the foyer for the short-nosed .38 I kept there.

I kept whistling as I searched the ground floor. She wasn't in any of the rooms, or underneath any of the furniture. I kept the gun out as I headed up the stairs to my bedroom.

The bedroom door was closed.

The only time I ever closed that door was when Richie and I were making love in Melanie Joan's old bed, which Richie said wasn't a bed at all, but more like a precinct. Other than that, I never closed it, even when I was alone. When I was out of the house it was a way of making sure that I didn't lock Rosie in there. I wanted her to be able to wander the house. I wanted her to be able to get to the water bowl next to the refrigerator in the kitchen.

Caution, I knew, was never a frivolous choice in the life *I* had chosen. So I gently opened the door with my left hand and quickly stepped through it with my gun still out, taking in the expanse of the room all at once.

The light was on. Sometimes I left it on before leaving, sometimes not.

"Rosie girl," I said, more softly than before.

I looked underneath the bed. She wasn't there.

It was then that I heard a soft mewing sound from the closet. That door was closed, too. I opened it. She was there, sitting on top of the shoes, staring up at me, clearly frightened, even knowing it was me. This from the small dog who thought she was big and who scared about as easily as I did.

I put the safety back on the gun, stuck it into the back pocket of my jeans, and gathered Rosie up into my arms, telling her that everything was all right. We went back downstairs, and I put a handful of food into her bowl, knowing that food generally made her feel better about everything.

While she ate, I took the gun back out and went up to the other levels of the old, narrow house, not thinking I would find anybody, but wanting to make sure.

No one here except Rosie and me.

But somebody had been.

I went back to the foyer and picked up my purse where I'd dropped it when I'd first come in and grabbed my cell phone and called Richie.

I had long since come to grips with the fact that as tough as I knew I was, and as good with a gun as I knew I was, there were still moments when I wanted to feel protected. Often by him. Man in my life. Susan Silverman called it duality.

“Somebody got into the house tonight while I was out of it,” I said.

That was all I got to say before he told me he was on his way and ended the call. I then poured myself a glass of Irish whiskey, which always made *me* feel better about everything.

10

RICHIE'S APARTMENT WAS on Salem Street in the North End, not far from the saloon that he owned and operated and loved. I had asked him once if he had to choose between the saloon and me, which way would he go.

"You," he'd said.

"Any particular reason?"

And Richie had said, "The benefits package."

He had never considered opening another one, no matter how much Spike, who now owned another restaurant up in Paradise, had told him he should. Richie would always tell Spike he wanted to own a bar, not a chain.

He had moved more than once since our divorce. When Richie and Kathryn had been married, she had somehow convinced him to buy a town house in Brookline, which Richie considered to be the suburbs, even though I told him that he couldn't be that close to Fenway Park and be in the suburbs. More recently he had briefly moved off Salem Street after being shot, into an apartment owned by his father, just because Desmond thought it would be easier to protect him there.

Now he was back on Salem Street. He made it to my house in twenty minutes. Rosie went running to him, as if order had returned to her world. I resisted the urge to do the same. But when he finished his love fest with Rosie he came over and put his arms around me.

"Hope I didn't interrupt anything important," I said.

"Nothing more important than you," he said. "Never has been, never will be."

We went into the living room. The bottle of Jameson was on the coffee table. I had a glass of it, neat, poured for him. Richie and I sat next to each other. He picked up Rosie and put her at the end of the couch. She wasn't happy about it, and tried to climb over Richie and get between us. Richie gently said, "Stay." She did.

"Tell me," he said.

I told him about my night.

"Was there any sign that the house had been searched?" he said.

"I didn't open every drawer," I said. "But if somebody did search the place, they're way neater than me putting things away."

"But somebody came here and didn't want to deal with Rosie, so they stuck her in the closet," he said.

"You know how noisy she gets with strangers," I said. "And Kathryn."

"Sunny," he said. "Focus."

"You sound like you're telling Rosie to stay," I said.

He shrugged.

"Someone came here after you left," Richie said, "and took a chance that you would be away for a while."

"Evidently," I said.

"Did you think they were looking for something specific," Richie said, "or just looking to scare you?"

"By scaring my dog?" I said.

"Does it have something to do with Tony Marcus?" Richie said.

He sipped some of his Jameson.

"Since I don't believe in coincidence and neither do you," I said, "I'd say yes. But I don't have anything worth finding yet because I haven't *found* anything yet."

"I'd ask if they took any jewelry," Richie said. He grinned. "But, well, you know."

It was a running joke with us. He knew that I'd never loved jewelry.

"I checked the box I keep the stuff in, top drawer of my dresser," I said. "I only lock it up when I'm going to be away for a while."

We both reached for our glasses now, as if on cue, and sipped whiskey.

"Tell me more about this Jabari guy," Richie said. "Could he factor into this somehow?"

"I don't see how," I said. "Somebody was in the house while Spike and I were at the club, but it's not as if we called and told him we were coming."

"If he's got nothing going with Lisa Morneau, why would he give a flying fuck if you were asking questions about her?" Richie said.

"Because he's lying and he *does* have something to do with her?" I said.

"He told you not to get between him and Tony, but maybe your friend Lisa has beaten you there," he said.

"Uh-huh."

Richie put his arm around me and pulled me closer to him and put his lips close my ear and said, "Get out of this now."

"Spike said the same thing," I said.

"I hate when that happens," he said.

"You agreeing with Spike?"

"Uh-huh," he said.

I somehow managed to move even closer to him, making me think of an old Marx Brothers line, the one where Groucho tells a woman that if they got any closer, he'd be behind her. As always, when we were this close, I felt as if some generator had started up inside me.

Richie, though, was still talking business.

"I don't know what the hell you're getting yourself in the middle of," Richie said. "But it really does sound like a shitty place to be, especially if you don't have to be there."

"Guys like Tony and Jabari have always controlled

Lisa," I said. "If she now has some power over one or both of them, I'd like to know why."

"You've got a client you can't trust," Richie said.

"Not the first time that's happened," I said.

"Not a client like this asshat."

"Maybe now I just want to find the asshat who scared Rosie," I said.

"That's not a good enough reason," Richie said.

I leaned up and kissed him under his ear. A place I'd always considered a power point. But, I knew from vast experience, there were many.

"You're not quitting," he said.

It wasn't even close to being a question.

"Not just yet," I said. "Lisa Morneau doesn't know it, but I'm on her side."

"A hooker you've never met," Richie said.

"But one who's in management now," I said.

He sighed and then turned and pulled me up and into a kiss that was always the same, which means like the first one we ever shared.

When I pulled back I said, "I need to walk Rosie at some point."

"This," he said, "is not that point."

As things developed, and rather quickly, it most certainly was not. We went upstairs.

I closed the bedroom door behind us.

11

I MET LIEUTENANT DARCY Gaines, who'd been a rookie on the cops when I was, at a Dunkin' in Brighton that was a few miles away from her office at the Family Justice Center on Commonwealth Ave.

She was taller than I was, just as blond, happily married with two children, now making a name for herself as the head of the BPD's Human Trafficking Unit. A few weeks ago there had been a feature about her in *The Boston Globe*, one in which she'd floated the idea of publicly shaming johns by sending them to what she called John School, where they could learn about the collateral damage associated with the world's oldest profession, especially when it involved underage girls.

She'd told me that when she first told the commissioner her idea about John School, he'd asked if it had a hockey team and what league it played in.

We were sitting at a corner table at midmorning. We both had hot coffee in front of us. Darcy had also ordered an old-fashioned plain donut, which I said reinforced negative stereotypes about the eating habits of cops.

"I still don't get the Dunkin' thing," she said, referring to the rebranding of Dunkin' Donuts.

"They do more than just sell donuts!" I said, like I was doing a television commercial.

"Next somebody will try to rebrand the Common," she said.

I had called her after Richie left, telling her I could use some of her wisdom on a case I'd just started working, about an ex-prostitute who'd gone missing. She was living in Watertown and said she'd meet me there on her way to her office, which was up near Boston University.

Now she sat across from me in uniform, *Boston Police* patch high on her right sleeve, name tag on the right front of her shirt, BPD pin on her collar. I studied the dark blue uniform, not a bad color for her, same as it once was for me, and wondered where I'd be in the department if I'd stayed on the job.

"So what's up?" she said.

I told her I was sort of working for Tony.

"You're shitting me," she said.

"It's complicated," I said. "But no, I am not shitting you."

"You are working for Tony Freaking Marcus?" she said, in a voice loud enough for the kids working the drive-thru window to hear, even wearing their headsets.

"Would it help if I told you that in my mind I'm working on behalf of the woman who's gone missing and not for *him*?" I said.

"No," she said. "Wait. Let me amend that. Fuck no. And quit calling her missing. Maybe she just finally came to her goddamn senses."

"Can I explain further?"

"About lying down with dogs?"

She wasn't my old friend Darcy in that moment. She was a career cop giving me the cop stare. I'd never been able to carry it off, but Darcy always could. And once you had it, you never lost it.

"Go ahead," she said. "This ought to be good."

I took her through it as quickly as I could, all the way back to why I'd needed Tony to find Desmond Burke when he'd been taken by the guy who'd shot Richie, and how I'd turned over the gun shipment to the Feds when Tony thought they were his.

"Blah, blah, blah," she said.

I couldn't resist any longer, and broke off a piece of her donut and ate it. She gave me a disappointed look. I shrugged.

"There's more," I said, and then told her about somebody breaking into my house while I was talking to Gabriel Jabari at Suite.

"Another beauty," she said.

"So that's where I am," I said.

"Working for somebody who represents everything I hate," she said. "And by the way? While you're going to work for this clown, we're seeing an uptick in the number of underage girls being turned out, on the street, in those cheesy massage parlors, even doing hotel work for some of these perverts. Another one died last week. OD'd after somebody beat her to an inch of what was left of her life."

"I heard," I said.

"It didn't even make the papers," she said. "That's how little these kids seem to matter. How'd you hear, by the way?"

"Tony."

"One of his girls?"

"Evidently."

Darcy spread her arms wide and put a fake smile on her face. "I wonder if he even knows her goddamn name," she said.

She wasn't done. We both knew it. It was like watching steam come out of her.

"Does your father know you're working for him?" she said.

"Richie knows," I said. "Spike knows. Jabari knows."

"Now you expect me to help you find her," she said.

I smiled now.

"Not expecting," I said. "Just asking."

She was staring at me again.

"For the good old days?" I said.

"You know what I remember best about the good

old days?" she said. "How many times you got me to do things that I knew I shouldn't be doing."

"Come on," I said. "We had fun. Remember that weekend at the Cape with the two surfers? You ever tell your husband about that one?"

"They weren't surfers," she said. "They were lifeguards. You want to blackmail somebody, at least do it with the right information."

I heard a phone buzz, realized it was hers. She pulled it out of the pocket of her pants, looked at it, nodded.

"I have to get to work," she said. "Just had a meeting with the boss moved up and I can't be late. He's been busting my chops since the story about me in *The Globe,* asking me when I get my own TV series."

"Help me find her," I said.

"So you can get the two lovebirds back together?" she said.

"I think there could be more going on here," I said.

"You know what a big ask this is," she said.

I said, "I'd do the same for you."

She nodded. "Yes," she said. "As a matter of fact, you would."

Then she said, "I am making no promises, but I will ask around about Lisa Morneau. I'll talk to my friends at this new task force they've got going."

"Vice?" I said.

"No such thing anymore at the BPD," she said. "This one throws an umbrella over sex and drugs."

"And rock 'n' roll?"

"Oh, and gangs," she said.

"Don't they get in your way?" I said.

She smiled. "Not for long," she said, and then wanted to know if I'd asked Lee Farrell to help me out with Lisa Morneau. Darcy knew that even though Lee worked Homicide, he really was my best friend in the department now that my father had retired, even though Phil Randall said you never retired, you were a cop until they closed the box on you.

"Nobody's died," I said. "At least not that I know of."

"Let's try to keep it that way," Darcy said. "You have any actual leads?"

"Tony gave me a name, a friend of Lisa's who used to be in the life and is out now," I said. "I'm going to try to see her today."

Darcy stood up and told me I didn't have to.

"We share information, right?" she said. "Just in case you come across something that would help me penetrate the force field around Marcus that somehow seems to keep getting stronger and lock his ass up once and for all."

"Well," I said, "I'll share up to a point."

"And what point might that be?"

"Like the old Supreme Court justice said that time about obscenity," I said. "I'll know it when I see it."

"You gotta be careful here, Sunny," Darcy said. "I know you think you're bad. These guys are worse."

"I'm always careful," I said.

"Not with the lifeguards," she said, and left.

12

I MET CALLIE HARDEN on her lunch break at the Copley Place Mall, on a bench in the open area across from the Tourneau watch store. The mall was attached to the Westin, and within walking distance of Trinity Church and the Boston Public Library. But if you set a mall exactly like this one in Omaha, or Scottsdale, or Eugene, Oregon, it would look almost exactly the same, with the same stores, the same music being played over the sound system.

I asked where she worked.

"Nearby," she said.

I asked where she lived, and she said in a section of the Old Colony neighborhood in South Boston, now being gentrified the way so much of Southie had been over the past two decades or so.

She had brought a tall coffee from Starbucks with her. I knew if I had more coffee I'd be running laps around the mall before long, from Tourneau to Tiffany and back.

If people walking past had taken notice of us, they might have thought us a couple of suburban moms looking for post-Christmas bargains.

"I told Tony I don't know where Lisa is," Callie said.

"What did he say to that?"

"He said that I should meet with you anyway," she said. "He said you're better at asking questions than he is, and don't have to threaten people when you want answers."

"Might be the nicest thing he's ever said about me," I said.

"But I want to ask you something," she said.

"Go ahead."

"I had no choice when it came to working for him," Callie said. "What's your reason?"

I told her what I'd just told Darcy Gaines, that it was complicated and, since I hadn't even taken as much as a retainer from him, I continued to view it as working on spec.

"Everybody always has reasons for taking Tony's money," she said.

Shots fired, I thought.

"It is highly unlikely that I will ever take a dime from him," I said.

"Got it," she said.

I hadn't known what to expect of her, looks-wise.

But she was quite lovely in an almost exotic way, perhaps with some Asian in the mix somewhere: dark hair, dark oval eyes. I understood that it was silly, even ridiculous, to think this way, but I did anyway: I couldn't imagine why someone so beautiful had ever needed to support herself by selling her body.

She might have been my age, or slightly older or slightly younger. Her makeup had been so artfully applied it was almost undetectable. The only sign of aging was around her eyes. Or perhaps behind them.

"Tony said that you and Lisa were friends," I said.

"*Are* friends," she said.

"I meant nothing by the past tense," I said. "If I honestly thought her dead, I wouldn't be here."

I asked where they had met. She said they had been working for one of Tony's escort services at the time, at a town house not far from where Lisa now lived, over between Westland Ave and Symphony Road.

"It looks like a normal brownstone," she said. "Tony's got a handful of places like it in a few fairly nice neighborhoods all over town, and some less nice neighborhoods, usually where there's enough foot traffic so that nobody sees anything out of the ordinary. And there's an entrance to this one from the public alley in the back."

"Real estate in that area isn't cheap," I said.

"Tony has always been willing to spend money to make money," she said. "Just not on us, of course."

Callie said she had been a runaway. I asked from where. "The Midwest," she said. She said she had just finished high school and bought herself a train ticket away from an abusive stepfather as a graduation present. I asked why Boston. She said she'd read online that there were a lot of art schools here, and she liked to paint.

"I paint," I said.

"I don't," she said. "At least not anymore."

One of Tony's men picked her out, and then picked her up, at South Station. Just like that, she was in that world. But she was pretty, and young. She wasn't on the street for long. They briefly had her doing hotel work after that, then put her in a house that catered to men with tastes for younger women, in Cambridge. She finally ended up working for Lisa, who was just becoming a fast-tracker in Tony's business. They became friends. Lisa was, she said, the first real woman friend she'd had since South Station.

"We both talked about putting together enough money to leave someday," she said. "Lisa used to talk about how she was giving herself an education on how to eventually get out of the life."

"You got out first," I said.

"I met a man," she said. "Not at the house. At yoga, of all places. A lawyer. This was about six months ago. He asked me out on a real date, and then another."

"What did you tell him you did for a living?" I said.

"I told him I'd saved enough as a personal trainer to go back to art school," she said. She shrugged. "One more lie. I even started taking some classes at Massachusetts College of Art and Design. And here's the thing: I still loved painting, I was falling in love with Dan, and I made the decision I had to get out. So I finally screwed up my courage and went to that awful place of Tony's in the South End and asked him if he'd let me go."

"Buddy's Fox," I said.

She'd probably sat in the same chair across from Tony that I had.

"He laughed and told me no, I was too good an earner for him," she said. "I told him that maybe I'd just disappear. He laughed again and told me good luck with that, that he'd own me until he was tired of owning me. I didn't know what else to do, so I went to Lisa. She had just stopped running the place over near Symphony Hall and had moved in with Tony. She said she'd talk to him. The next day, she called and told me I was out. I asked how. She said not to worry about it, maybe I could return the favor someday."

"You didn't press her?"

"Why? I was out, that was all that mattered."

"Just like that?"

"Just like that," she said. "Only I wasn't."

I waited. I watched her sad, dark eyes with a faraway look in them. It made me wonder if she were staring at her past, or future.

"The last thing for me to do was to tell Dan what I'd really been doing for a living," she said. "I had seen a therapist a few times, and she'd convinced me it was the only way for me to be truly free."

There was nothing for me to do except sit here and

wait for it. So I did, with an ending to the story I knew was as inevitable as shouting on cable news.

"You pay and pay and pay," she said.

I had to let her get us to wherever we were going at her own pace, in her own way. I did not want to rush her, or seem disinterested. Because I was not.

"I thought he cared enough about me to understand," she said. "Maybe it was some kind of insane *Pretty Woman* fantasy. But all he cared about was that somehow the friends he'd introduced me to would find out. Or someone at the law firm." I could see that she was starting to cry. "In front of my eyes he turned into every mean john I'd ever met."

I started to reach for a tissue. She simply wiped the tears away with the back of her sleeve.

"But you didn't go back to work for Tony," I said.

"I wasn't running this time," she said. "I have a good job now. I have friends."

"Do the friends know?"

"Not yet," she said.

"But you remained friends with Lisa?" I said.

"Yes," she said. "I felt I owed her that. I kept sensing that she was moving toward the door, just more slowly than I did."

"What kept her in?" I said.

"She was making real money for the first time in her life," Callie said. "She said that even though Tony controlled her bank account and credit cards, she had managed to put a fair amount away."

"Skimming from Tony, I imagine, would be more dangerous than your former life," I said.

"Lisa," she said, "has always had a good head for numbers. Even before it did her much good."

"When was the last time the two of you spoke?"

"We were supposed to have dinner about a week ago," she said. "She said she was closer than ever to getting to where she wanted to be. I said, 'Getting out?' She said, 'Everybody comes up on a line they can't cross. I can't cross the line with children anymore.' I asked her what that meant and she said she'd tell me all about it at dinner. But that afternoon she texted me and said that something had come up and she had to cancel, but she'd call in the morning. She never did."

I felt my phone buzzing inside my purse and ignored it.

"Did she ever mention a man named Gabriel Jabari to you?" I said.

"The man who owns that new club?" Callie said. "Just that she'd met him one time."

"Is there any chance that she could be involved with him in some way?"

"You mean sexually?"

"Or business," I said. "Or perhaps both. Jabari says no."

"If she was, she never mentioned it to me," she said. "And as far as a relationship, she'd only been with Tony for a long time."

"Did she have genuine feelings for him?" I said. "Because he seems to have had some for her."

"She told me Tony had said that he loved her," Callie said, "almost obsessively. I told her to remember that he was a pimp, and that pimps lie. About almost everything."

"Are we being honest here?" I said.

"No reason not to."

"Women of your former profession lie their asses off, too."

She smiled. "So we do," she said.

"You honestly don't know where she might be?"

There was the slightest hesitation. She tried to cover it by acting as if she were looking past me at someone in the mall, or something. I wondered how much she might have already lied to me today.

"I don't," she said. "Do you think Lisa might be in danger?"

"I don't know," I said.

I reached into my purse and took out one of my new business cards, which had my cell number on it, and the number for my landline at River Street Place.

"I have your number in my own phone," Callie said.

"Just in case," I said. "If Lisa calls you, please call me. Tell her I won't give her up. I just want to talk."

"If she still wanted to be with Tony, she'd be with Tony," Callie said.

She studied the card and then tossed it into her own purse and stood up.

"I do have a life now, Ms. Randall," she said. "It's not much of one. But it's mine. I owe Lisa because she helped me when no one else would. Whatever help she needs from me, I will freely give it to her."

"Maybe we can both help her," I said.

I shook her hand and said, "For what it's worth, I'm sorry about the yoga guy."

"So am I," she said. "All the lies I'd told to men in my life. And this time I screwed myself over by telling the truth."

13

TONY CALLED AS I was walking home from the mall. I thought about ignoring him, but knew that would only delay the inevitable. I knew from experience that he did not like being ignored.

He asked if Callie had told me anything he hadn't told her. I said she had not.

"She talk any shit on me?" he said.

"She did not," I said. "The only one doing that was me."

"You lying to me, Sunny Randall?" he said.

"I am not," I said.

"I want to know what you know as soon as you know it," he said.

I said, "It actually doesn't go that way, Tony."

"And how does it go?"

"I work this the way I work it and if you don't like it, you can call me off right now and go find her yourself."

I heard a low whistle on his end.

"Balls on you," he said.

"Ground already covered," I said, and ended the call.

The winter sun was high in the sky, but there was a big wind out of the east today, so even though the temperature was supposed to be in the thirties I felt colder than Admiral Byrd as I walked up Boylston and across Arlington and up Beacon. I passed the Bull and Finch, the pub whose exterior had been used for the old television show *Cheers*. The bar in that one, I remembered from my teenage years, was where everybody knew your name, and was always glad you came.

Where, I wondered, did Callie Harden go to feel that way, now that she was living a life that wasn't much, but was at least her own?

I had set the house alarm before walking over to meet her at the mall. I heard the reassuring beep when I came through the door, then punched in the code to deactivate as Rosie came running this time.

She was always glad when I came.

I put on some tea to take some of the chill out of me and called Sergeant Lee Farrell.

Even Lee admitted he wasn't yet the homicide cop that Frank Belson was. Lee hadn't worked the job as long or as well as Frank had. But he was damn good. He had told me last week that Belson and his wife were on a long-discussed vacation in Ireland, and while he wasn't rooting for someone to get clipped while Frank was away, there was a part of him hoping to give the higher-ups a chance to see what he could do when he was the one in the barrel.

He had been worried about being gay when joining the cops. But he was so clearly good at what he did, and obsessed with outworking everybody around him, that it had never really been an issue, except among a handful of idiots.

He was smart and funny and loyal and brave and handsome. More than once I had mentioned to him that maybe he and Spike would make kind of a cute couple.

"Of course," he said. "Because all single and attractive gay men are automatically attracted to every other single gay man they meet."

"You are two of my favorite people on the planet," I said. "You can't blame a girl for trying."

"You need to know something, Sunny," he said. "Only my mother tries to fix me up more than you do."

On the phone now I told him I needed help finding a missing employee of Tony Marcus's.

"You mean a hooker," Lee said.

"I believe they're now called sex workers," I said.

"Have it your way."

"Ex-hooker, not to make too fine a point of it," I said.

"No such thing," he said. "And why are you helping Tony Marcus, if you don't mind me asking?"

"He's sort of a client," I said.

"How is someone sort of a client?"

"It's complicated," I said. "And I promise to explain later. But for now I'm looking for a woman named Lisa Morneau who has essentially been acting as Tony's chief operating officer, in addition to being his main squeeze."

"I'm guessing it's not in Tony's best interest to file a Missing Persons report," he said.

"Nope," I said.

"You think she might be dead?"

"Please don't sound so hopeful," I said. "But hoping not."

"So why are you calling me?"

"Because you're the smartest cop I know, at least when Belson is on the other side of the Atlantic," I said.

"You know you're not as funny as you think you are, right?"

"Am too," I said.

"What's in it for me, if I do decide to help a girl out?"

"My undying gratitude," I said.

"Yeah, right," he said, and then asked me what I had on her, and I gave him the credit card numbers and cell phone numbers and bank cards and everything else Tony had given me. He said he'd get back to me.

I thought about calling my father, a trained detective himself. But for the time being, I didn't want to have the same conversation with him about Tony Marcus that I was having with everybody except Anderson

Cooper, who'd probably disapprove of my working for Tony, too. I thought about going back to Lisa Morneau's apartment, to see if I had possibly missed something. But I didn't think I had, and I could always circle back there later. For now I needed to get the address of the upscale house of ill repute nearby and talk to some of the women working there, if they'd been on the payroll when Lisa was in charge.

I was aware from my own police training that there was a protocol to be followed with missing persons on whom reports were actually filed. But there was nothing remotely normal about any of this.

I decided to bundle up as well as I could and still look like a sleek running machine, and make a couple laps around the Public Garden and the Common to clear my mind, not just about the case, but about my life.

Before Richie had left the house in the morning, he'd suggested a tentative plan, around my work schedule, for the four of us to spend some time together tomorrow.

"Four of us?" I'd said. "Kathryn, too?"

"You, me, Richard, Rosie," he said.

So I ran in Lululemon Toasty Tech Tights and a cold-weather mock turtleneck and a North Face vest and gloves and a Bruins knit cap that Richie had bought for me. Most days I loved running along the Charles. Just not today, and not in this wind.

Usually when I ran around the park, I was good for three laps. Today I ran two. When I got home I checked my phone for messages. There were none. Lee Farrell had not called, nor Darcy Gaines, nor Tony. Richie hadn't called, either. He had said something about apartment-hunting with Kathryn. Maybe they were doing that today. Or she was doing that with their son. Who was back in Richie's life, and thus very much in mine.

I showered and made more tea and fed Rosie an early dinner. Tired of waiting for someone to call me and without a plan for tonight, I went upstairs to paint. It was a piece on which I had recently resumed work after putting it aside for nearly a year, one of the buildings in which the original Rosie and I had once lived in Fort Point. A photograph I had taken of the building from behind and to the side, with just some of the ocean showing in the distance, served as the inspiration.

I had loved living at Fort Point. So had the original Rosie. I had loved being that close to the water, even though I was almost as close to the Charles now. But there had been far too many memories after I'd had to put the original Rosie down. Now the new Rosie and I were living on the perimeter of Beacon Hill for a ridiculously low rent that Melanie Joan Hall steadfastly refused to raise because I had saved her life once.

I painted until all of the late-afternoon winter light was gone and into the night, surprised when I finally stopped that it was past eight o'clock. I left my board on the table, cleaned my brushes, and put them away.

I was back downstairs, preparing to pour myself a well-earned glass of pinot grigio, when my phone did chirp.

It was Farrell.

"I caught a case after all," he said.

"Please tell me it's not Lisa Morneau," I said.

"It's not," he said.

But he was Homicide. He was calling me. Suddenly it was as if all the bitter cold of the day had found its way to where I stood in the kitchen.

"We found a woman," he said. "Near Joe Moakley Park in Southie. Looks like she got beaten up before somebody put two in her chest and dumped her there."

Joe Moakley Park wasn't far from Old Colony. Where she'd said she lived.

Farrell continued, "The vic's name—"

"Callie," I said. "Callie Harden. I was with her this morning. Talking to her about Lisa Morneau."

"She had your card in her purse," he said.

"I gave it to her," I said.

Then neither one of us said anything until Lee said, "You still there?"

"Yeah."

"You okay?"

"No," I said.

"Can you meet me at the station?" Lee said.

I told him I was on my way. Then I put my phone down on the island counter in the middle of the kitchen and closed my eyes and thought about Callie Harden, who now had no goddamn life at all.

14

LEE FARRELL AND I were in a small conference room at the new BPD headquarters at Schroeder Plaza. At least I thought of it as new, even though they'd moved here more than twenty years ago. But it still made the old place on Berkeley Street where my father used to take me when I was a little girl look older than the Old North Church.

I had given Lee my statement about my meeting with Callie at the mall. Now we were drinking coffee that he'd made from the Keurig machine in the corner. If I told my father they made coffee now at Homicide that didn't taste like embalming fluid he would surely see it as another sign of the apocalypse.

Lee was wearing a V-neck sweater, plaid shirt, tweed

jacket, and khaki pants. Frank Belson had always looked the part of Homicide cop in an old-movie way, right down to his raincoat and cheap cigars. Lee Farrell looked like a Brooks Brothers ad.

"Anybody see or hear anything?" I said.

"We're doing the normal canvassing," he said. "But it was a park in Southie on a cold winter's night. I think they just pulled up on William Day Boulevard, dumped her, left."

"She said she lived over near Old Colony," I said.

"I sent somebody to the address she had on her driver's license," Lee said. "Nobody saw anything unusual there, either. No one can remember the last time they saw her going in or out."

"You say she'd been beaten up," I said.

"Yeah."

"Like somebody was trying to get something out of her?" I said.

"Could be that," Lee said. "Or could be an, uh, assignation gone wrong."

"She didn't decide to go back to her old life a few hours after talking to me about it," I said.

"Just not ruling anything out at this point," he said. "Kind of a policy around here."

"She said she didn't know where Lisa might have gone," I said.

"Doesn't mean that was true." He sipped some coffee. "Who knew you were meeting with her?"

"Tony knew," I said.

"Would Tony have a tail on you?"

"Maybe," I said. "He still trusts me about as much as I trust him, which is as far as I could throw you."

"Easier with me now that I've slimmed down," he said.

"I talked to him after I talked to Callie," I said. "But I made it clear she hadn't told me anything useful."

"Maybe he thought she was being less than forthcoming," Lee said. "Or that you were."

"So he tries to beat the truth out of her and then shoots her in the chest and dumps her in that park?" I said. "How does *that* make any sense? He could have done that when he talked to her himself."

"Or she told somebody else she had talked to you," Lee said.

"But who?"

"Might your new friend Jabari come into play here?" Lee said.

"What could Lisa or Callie know that would be worth him killing Callie over?" I said. "I know Jabari's got skin in this game. But that makes no sense, either, unless there's a connection between Lisa and Jabari beyond what he's told me."

"If you find out, let me know," Lee said. "For now, I have no reason to talk to him."

"What about Tony?" I said. "You talking to him?"

He smiled. "Oh, yes," he said.

"If Lisa got herself jammed up between Tony and

Jabari, maybe Callie ended up in the same place," I said.

"Like they say in the movies," Lee said, "just when you're out, they pull you back in."

"*Godfather III*," I said.

"Godfather three hours of my life I can never get back," Lee said. He gestured at my foam cup. "You done with that?" he said. I nodded. He took my cup and his and tossed them in a wastebasket next to the door. My father was fastidious that way, too. Maybe it was a cop thing, liking things neat, even though it had never been that way with me when I was on the job.

Farrell disappeared around the corner. When he came back he was wearing his topcoat and had mine draped over his arm.

"Let me drive you home," he said.

"You don't have to do that," I said.

"I'll feel better if I see you all the way into your house," he said. "For now, you're the last person who saw my vic alive."

We got into his Land Cruiser and took two rights and a left onto Forsyth and then we were on Storrow. We talked more about Callie on the way, and the lawyer who'd dumped her when he found out the truth about her past.

"You gonna try to find the lawyer?" I said.

"Lawyer named Dan who took a yoga class somewhere in Back Bay," Lee said. He grinned. "Piece of cake."

When we got to River Street Place I asked if he'd like

to come in for one drink. As a matter of fact, he said, he would, and left the car directly in front of my front door. I told him he wasn't supposed to park there, that if there was nothing on the street you were supposed to park around back. He reminded me that he had police plates and was here on official police business, carrying a gun and everything.

I'd asked Lee to dog-sit Rosie plenty of times, so it was more like a reunion between them once he was inside. Lee said he'd take her out. I asked if he wanted whiskey or wine. He said he'd have what I was having. I said it was a whiskey time of night, and broke out the bottle of Midleton that Richie's dad had given me for saving his life.

We sat on the couch, Rosie on Lee's lap.

"You know you can't blame yourself for this," Lee said.

"Like hell I can't," I said.

"The choices she made, she made a long time ago."

"I brought her into this."

"Could have been random, what happened tonight."

"You said she didn't have her phone with her?" I said.

He shook his head. "My guys didn't find one at her place, either," he said.

"So whoever killed her took it," I said.

"She either told them what they wanted to know and they killed her anyway," Lee said, "or they decided to kill her after she couldn't, or wouldn't, give them what they wanted."

I drank some Midleton and put the glass down hard on the table, startling Rosie.

"Fuck," I said.

"She wasn't your friend, Sunny," Lee said.

"She only talked to me because Tony made her," I said. "In a way, it's like he was running her until the end."

He finished his whiskey and kissed me on the cheek, lifted Rosie off his lap, and got up off the couch.

"If you need any crime-fighting tips," I said. "Feel free to call."

"I got this," he said.

"Belson always welcomes my input," I said.

"Like hell he does," Lee Farrell said.

He left. I locked the door behind him and set the alarm. Then, despite my best intentions, I poured myself one more glass of whiskey and put Ben Webster and Oscar Peterson on the sound system and listened to the two of them chase each other around on "Bye Bye Blackbird."

I thought about Lisa and Callie and all the men they had known in their lives. I thought about the men with whom I had been romantically involved in my own life, before and after Richie, and all the men I'd gone up against in my work. I thought about all the ones at whom I had pointed my gun to resolve conflict, and wondered how many times women like Lisa and Callie had wished they had a gun in their own hands to resolve a conflict with some john.

I finished the last of the whiskey, took the empty glass into the kitchen, shut off the music and all the lights downstairs, and picked up Rosie, as glad as ever that my dog was a babe, just like me.

Even if I wasn't feeling like much of a babe tonight.

15

RICHIE SHOWED UP the next morning, having given me a courtesy call that he was on his way, and informed me that he was bringing biscotti from Bova's Bakery with him. The bakery, a North End landmark, wasn't far from his apartment on Salem Street and had various Italian pastries so delicious they could make you change your political beliefs, provided you still had any.

"Okay," I said, "you clearly want something, and it can't be sex."

"Too early in the day?"

I grinned. "Seems to me it's never been too early for us," I said. "But as much as I love Bova's, it would take more than biscotti."

"Cannoli?" he said.

"I don't know why that sounds dirty when you say it," I said. "But it does."

I took the bag from him, smelled inside, and said, "So what is it?"

"I was wondering, and you can say no if you want to, if you might possibly be able to watch Richard for a couple of hours," he said.

I walked over to the living room window, pushed the draperies aside, and saw his car out front, motor running.

"He's in the car, isn't he?" I said.

He smiled a smile like a kid who'd been caught doing something he shouldn't have been.

"Yeah."

"Kathryn, too?"

"Yeah."

"And what fun activities do you and Kathryn have planned that don't involve your son?"

"There are two apartments she needs to look at before she loses a chance at either one of them," Richie said. "One in Brookline, one in Needham. It will be easier without him."

"Speak for yourself."

"You're busy."

I said, "Little bit. Got one ex-hooker missing and another one that I talked to yesterday turned up dead a few hours later. Not that you asked what else is going on in my life."

"I should have asked before I came," he said. "Sounds like you're up to your eyeballs."

"Look who's talking."

"We can bring him," Richie said. "Richard, I mean."

"Kathryn can't put on her big-girl pants and go apartment-hunting on her own?" I said.

"She hasn't had to look at places to live for a long time," he said, "and hasn't done it in Boston since she and I moved to Brookline."

I knew there was nothing I had planned for the day that couldn't wait. The calls I needed to make I could make whether Richard was here or not.

And I already liked this boy, and not just because I trusted Rosie's judgment. There was a sweetness to him, and a vulnerability, that were both readily apparent, and quite appealing. And as much as I worried about how all of this was affecting me, Richard was the one who was going through the most.

"How long?" I said.

"Two hours, tops," Richie said. "So you'll do it?"

"I shall," I said.

"Cannolis next time for sure," he said.

Then he went to the car and came back with the boy, whose eyes got big and bright and happy as soon as he came through the door.

It wasn't about me.

It was about Rosie.

Already it was a love that seemed to passeth all understanding.

RICHARD FELIX BURKE immediately went looking for one of Rosie's tennis balls, before he even had his coat off. He threw it. She fetched it and brought it right back to him. Without bribes. Damn her.

They both seemed willing to play this game until Richie and Kathryn came back. Or, from the looks of them, until the end of time.

The boy was relatively oblivious to my presence but completely and joyfully and loudly engaged by my dog. At one point, I asked if he wanted something to eat or drink.

"No, ma'am," he said.

"You can call me Sunny," I said.

"Yes, ma'am," he said.

I reached into the Bova's bag and showed him the biscotti and asked him if he wanted some.

"No, thank you," he said, then smiled and added, "Sunny ma'am."

I smiled back.

He then resumed playing with Rosie. When he finally did get tired of the ball he would hold one end of one of her raggedy chew toys and she would hold the other, and the two of them would play tug-of-war until Richard would inevitably let her win. I watched them and tried to remember the last time I had babysat a child of this age. Maybe it was Mr. and Mrs. Cappabianca's boy Johnny, when his parents, neighbors of ours, were out to dinner with my parents. I was probably fifteen.

While they continued their playdate I went into the kitchen, away from the action, and made some calls. I spoke briefly with Lee Farrell about Callie. He said he was on his way to her apartment, wanting to look through it himself. I called Tony Marcus. When he answered his voice was thick with sleep, and impatience.

"You told that queer detective Callie'd been one of my girls," he said.

"I'm a good citizen," I said.

"Well, I ain't," he said. "So don't be telling your fucking cop friends my fucking business."

"Did you go see her or talk to her after I saw her?" I said. "She'd been beaten pretty badly."

"Wasn't me," Tony said. "There's ones in my world think that's part of the game, roughing up the help. But that ain't ever been me."

"You sure?"

"Yeah, I'm sure," he said. "But why you so worried about some girl who didn't work for me no more when you supposed to be worried about one who still does, least last time I checked?"

I watched Richie's son play with Rosie as Tony Marcus said, "You focus on the live whores and not the dead ones," and then ended the call, the silly old romantic.

About half an hour later Richie texted me to say that he and Kathryn were on their way back. It was close to lunchtime by then. I asked Richard if he was hungry now. He asked if it would be all right if he had a peanut-butter-and-jelly sandwich.

"With the crust cut off?" he said.

"Around here we don't make them any other way," I said.

I made one for him and one for me. Aunt Sunny. He asked if he could have a glass of milk, too. I told him I only had skim. He asked if that was real milk.

"Yes," I said, "but for weenies."

He looked at me and smiled his father's smile.

"Are you a weenie?" he said.

"Totally," I said.

As we ate I said to him, "How are you doing with all this moving around?"

He looked at me with his father's eyes.

"Not so good," he said. "But . . ."

He stopped there, and ate more of his sandwich.

"But what?" I said.

"But I try not to show it," he said. "I don't want my mom to worry about me."

I looked at him and wondered how much she was worrying about him right now, and how much she was worrying about herself. What the percentage might be.

"So you're trying to be tough," I said.

He looked at me again with the big eyes.

"Sometimes I don't feel so tough," he said. "I miss my friends in London."

"I'll bet," I said. "But you'll make new friends here."

"I don't want my dad to think I'm not happy to be with him," Richard said.

"Your mom and dad will figure this all out," I said.

"That's what my dad says," Richard said.

"He's a pretty smart guy."

Richard grinned at me. "Smart as you?"

"Heck no," I said.

"Why not?"

"He's a guy," I said.

"And guys aren't as smart as girls?" Richard said.

I put my thumb and my index finger close together.

"It's very close," I said. "But we get a little bit ahead at about the age you are now, and you guys spend the rest of your lives trying to catch up."

He giggled.

"You're just making stuff up now," he said.

"You got me," I said.

Suddenly he laughed. I didn't know why what I'd said was so funny. And didn't care. His father didn't laugh much, either. But I loved it when he did.

When he finished eating he said, "Thanks."

"For making such an outstanding sandwich?" I said.

"For talking to me," he said.

"I like talking to you," I said.

"Same," he said.

16

TONY HAD GIVEN me all the passwords for Lisa's credit and bank cards, at least the ones he had been paying for; I checked again after Richie and Kathryn and Richard left. There had been no activity on any of them.

If she'd run, she had put enough money away to keep her going. Maybe it meant she had been planning this for a while. There were still no clues in the bank or credit card statements that Tony had emailed to me indicating where she might be, nothing from New York or Los Angeles or London or Paris or Pawtucket, Rhode Island, or Portland, Maine. All of her recent purchases, from before she disappeared, had been from either Boston stores or online. Nothing from out of town.

I opened my laptop and looked for any references anywhere on the Internet to Lisa Morneau and found none. In all likelihood it wasn't her real last name, but it was the only one I had. Tony said she'd come from Baltimore. Maybe she'd been using her current name there, and there was some kind of sheet on her. I called Darcy Gaines and asked if she'd mind calling the Baltimore cops and asking if Lisa Morneau was in their system.

"After I'm done, do you want me to wash your car?" she said.

It took her only fifteen minutes. She said Baltimore had nothing on anybody using that name. I thanked her, then said, "You come up with anything here?"

She said, "Not yet," and told me she'd love to chat longer, but she had actual police work to do.

I looked down at Lisa's picture, which I had set next to my laptop, almost as if hoping that she would say something to me.

Maybe if we had Callie Harden's phone we could have checked her recent calls, but we didn't. Maybe Lee would find something at Callie's apartment that might point us in the right direction, even though Callie had sworn she didn't know where Lisa was. He said he would call me when he was free. Maybe Callie had lied to me. Why not? Lisa was the one who had gotten her out of the life. Lisa was her friend.

But maybe not her only friend.

There could be someone else with whom Lisa had worked, and in whom she had confided. I called Tony and asked who was now running the house between Westland and Symphony Road. He gave me the name Olivia Hewitt.

I asked him how the place worked in the middle of the day.

"You're asking me how a whorehouse works?" he said. "For real?"

"I'm just wondering how many of your employees and how many customers might be around right now," I said.

"We operate on that early-arrival-and-late-checkout deal," he said, and told me he'd tell them I was on my way.

"You could maybe pick up some spare change, you got a couple of hours free," Tony said. "Work a couple of shifts. Might turn out you like it."

"Too old," I said.

"Some of the johns, they like a woman of a certain age," he said.

Before I could reply he said, "Yeah, yeah, I know. Why don't I just go fuck myself?"

I HAD TO buzz to get in. One of Tony's guys opened the door for me, motioning me into a small foyer, which then opened to a larger area where a young black woman sat at a desk. Once, when this brownstone was likely a residence, this was probably the living room on the ground floor. Now it could have served as the reception area for a doctor's office.

Best little whorehouse near Symphony Hall.

I was about to give my name to the young woman at the desk when a much older woman, not much more than five feet tall, came out of the office behind her. She was blond and pretty and even whiter than I was.

"Ms. Randall," she said, putting out a hand that was much older than the face, which had had some work done to it. You could do something about faces. Never hands. "I'm Olivia Hewitt. So nice to meet you."

I shook her hand and smiled as she waved me into her office.

"You're not what I expected," I said.

"And what did you expect?" she said. "Someone younger, or sluttier?"

"Withdraw the statement," I said.

"Everyone in this profession is not the same," Olivia Hewitt said. "Some of us evolve. I am not the girl I was on the streets of Boston, or the refined woman I like to think I became in New York."

I told her that I would try not to be intrusive, or take up too much of her time. She said Tony had told her to give me all the time I needed, within reason. I asked how many women were on the premises at the present time. She said six, including Tonya, gesturing at the woman at the desk. She said that they ran both outcall and in-house services out of what she called "this facility." She made it sound like a power plant.

"I've heard about, um, facilities like this," I said. "Wasn't there a suicide involving one of the madams several years ago?"

"Her name was April Kyle," she said. "I'd actually worked with her in New York City, poor thing. She got herself in over her head."

"Perhaps as Lisa Morneau has?"

Olivia Hewitt said, "You'd know that better than I."

"From the outside," I said, "this could be any residence on the street."

She smiled. Her skin was so tight I wondered if she knew she *was* smiling.

"We do even better for some of our best and most generous customers," she said. "It was actually Lisa's idea. There are a few standalone apartments scattered here and there around the Back Bay, as well. One in The Fens. Another on Stanhope Street."

Olivia Hewitt said she'd met Lisa when taking over for her. She said before that she'd done similar work for a woman named Patricia Utley in New York, with whom Tony had done business in the past, and that Patricia Utley had recommended her to Tony as someone who was ready to move up and into a management role.

"How many women working here now worked for Lisa?" I said.

"Off the top of my head," she said, "I believe only Laura and Kourtney. With a *K*. But then ours is a profession where tenure is rarely a desired or stated goal. Perhaps I am one of the exceptions to that rule."

I was starting to think her smile, once deployed, was then frozen in place. Or maybe just her whole face was. Hard to tell, even sitting this close to her.

"You do seem to have lasted," I said.

"You find something you're good at," she said, "you stay with it." She shrugged. "And it helps that I have a good woman in my life."

"Behind every good woman," I said.

"Exactly," she said.

"Did you know a former employee here named Callie Harden?" I said. "Her stay here would have overlapped with Lisa's."

"No," she said. "Should I have?"

"Somebody shot and killed her and dumped her body in a park in South Boston last evening," I said.

"Good Lord," Olivia Hewitt said. "Was her death work-related?"

"She'd retired," I said. "Or so she told me."

There was an iPhone in a pink case on the desk in front of her. I heard it buzz. She did not look down. Finally she said, "Is there something else I can help you with today, Ms. Randall?"

I asked if either Laura or Kourtney with a *K* were around and she said I was in luck. She called out to the receptionist and asked her to go upstairs and get Laura and Kourtney. Olivia Hewitt showed me into a small living room off the foyer. A couple minutes later two women walked into the room. One was blond with long, straight hair that immediately made me jealous. The other was taller, but with shorter black hair. What we'd once called a bob. Did they still call it that? Both were young. I had long since come to grips with the fact that meant they looked younger than me, I now being, as Tony Marcus had said, a woman of a certain age. Olivia Hewitt informed them I was a private detective working for Mr. Marcus and looking into the disappearance of Lisa Morneau.

The blonde was Laura. Without being asked, she volunteered that this wasn't her full-time job. When I asked what was, she said, "Flight attendant." The other woman was Kourtney. I asked if this was a moonlighting gig with her as well. She said yes, her own full-time job was as a Pilates instructor.

I asked what had brought them both here. Laura said, "The money's good, my schedule is flexible, and I like sex."

"Same!" Kourtney said, as if encouraging me on my core blasting.

Before Olivia Hewitt had left the room, she had informed me that both Laura and Kourtney had appointments scheduled within the next half-hour.

"Mani or pedi?" I'd said.

No one in the room, including Olivia Hewitt, showed any reaction. It was apparently a mirth-free zone.

Both of the women sitting across from me on a small sofa were wearing short dresses. Both had crossed their legs, as if on cue. They had very good legs. I was almost certain both were wearing Louboutins. Once a shoe girl, always a shoe girl. I wanted theirs.

Work clothes, I thought, *for working girls.* I idly wondered just how many of these places Tony Marcus really did have in Boston, and how many young women like these were waiting for appointments at this time of the day. Darcy Gaines had told me once that it was like Whac-A-Mole. Close one down, another opened up. It was why her focus these days was on minors. She knew she could never cut off the supply. But, she had told me once, she could sure as hell try to slow it down.

"I'm here to ask about Lisa Morneau," I said. "But I was wondering if either one of you knew Callie Harden? She worked for Lisa here."

Kourtney looked at Laura, then shook her head. Laura said, "I started here just as Callie started talking about leaving. I think it was about some guy. Do you know her?"

"Somebody shot her to death," I said.

I knew they both had to be expert in faking just about every possible emotion. But their reaction to the news seemed authentic.

"Jesus," Kourtney with a *K* said.

"Does it have something to do with Lisa?" Laura said.

"Unclear," I said. "I just know that they were friends, and that Callie died not long after I had spoken to her about Lisa."

Kourtney said, "Do you think Lisa might be dead, too?"

"Hoping that's a hard no," I said.

Laura looked down at the Apple watch on her wrist. All the modern accessories for a modern career woman. "We don't have a *lot* of time," she said. "But how can we help?"

"Did Lisa ever indicate that she might be ready to move on?" I said.

"Once in a while," Laura said. "But every time she did, I thought she was joking. She was already sleeping with the boss. When we all heard that, we thought she had it made."

"In the shade," I said.

"Huh?" Kourtney said.

"An expression women of a certain age still use," I said.

They looked at each other and shook their heads. "Why get out," Laura said, "when you already had Tony in you?"

She giggled. So did Kourtney. *Oh, sure,* I thought. *They thought* that *was funny.*

Olivia Hewitt popped her head back into the room and said, "Tonya just received a couple of texts. Laura, your client will be here in a few minutes. Kourtney, yours is running a few minutes late but says he's on his way."

"Showtime," Laura said.

I stood and gave each of them one of my cards, just as I had with Callie twenty-four hours ago. I told them to call if they remembered anything about Lisa or Callie that they thought might be useful.

I thanked Olivia Hewitt for her time. Tony's guy wordlessly showed me out. On my way down the front walk, I passed a broad-shouldered guy in what looked to be an expensive topcoat heading for the same door from which I'd just left.

He nodded at me and smiled. I smiled back, then kept going. From behind me I heard him say, "Hey."

I stopped and turned.

"You new?" he said.

"The opposite, actually," I said, and kept walking.

Maybe I should have given him one of my cards, too.

When I got back home a black Navigator was parked where Lee Farrell had parked the night before. Gled, Gabriel Jabari's man, got out on the driver's side, came around, and opened the back door.

Jabari leaned out.

"Take a ride with me," he said.

17

THERE WAS NO point in refusing, any more than I would have refused Junior and Ty Bop when they showed up at my house and started this whole thing.

There was a faint scent in the backseat of what I thought might be cinnamon. But I was about as conversant in men's colognes, even Spike's, as I was tractor pulls.

"You could have called."

"Where's the fun in that?" he said.

"Where are we going?" I said.

He smiled. "Like I said. For a ride."

Sometimes it was just easier to go along. It occurred to me that that attitude wasn't vastly different from the one held by the women I had just visited. Another thing for me to discuss with Dr. Silverman.

"Have you been following me?" I said.

"Why would I?" he said.

"Maybe you think I could lead you to Lisa," I said.

"You're the one looking for her, not me."

"Ask you another question?"

"Ask away."

"Did you break into my house?"

"Why would I break into your house? I barely know you."

"Maybe you want to find Lisa even though you say you don't," I said.

"Didn't break into your house," he said. "But I might be more interested in talking to Lisa Morneau than I previously indicated."

"To make her another offer?" I said.

"An even better one," he said. "You hear all over town that she is Tony's other brain. I believe that's the expression? I would like to know what she knows. Hurt his business, help mine, win-win."

We had made our way past the Colonnade Hotel on Huntington.

"As a matter of fact," he said, "been thinking about hiring you as well."

I angled myself in the backseat to get a better look at him.

"You're serious," I said.

"I am."

"I sort of have a client," I said.

"I want to be a real client," he said. "By making you a better offer than Tony has made."

"At our first meeting," I said, "I'm almost certain you were the one telling me to stay *out* of your business."

Now he faced me more directly. Today he was wearing a zippered cashmere sweater and jeans and suede boots.

"I believe it was John Maynard Keynes who said that when the facts changed, so did his mind," Jabari said.

"Love the reference," I said. "But the answer is no."

"You didn't even hear my offer."

"Don't need to," I said.

"I am trying to get you to change your mind in a civilized manner," he said. "Normally ain't my style."

His transitions in tone and language were as effortless as Tony's.

"Am I supposed to thank you?" I said.

"In the very near future, I am going to make a big move on Tony Marcus," he said.

"Should I alert him? Or the media?"

"He knows," Jabari said. "And when I do, you are either with me or against me."

"The answer to your offer is still a polite no," I said.

"No such thing, least not with me."

"Well, I could have said 'fuck no.'"

He hadn't moved, or changed expression. But something had changed with his eyes. In that moment I imagined him looking at me the way he had looked at all the people he had gone through, from wherever it was he had been, to get to where he was now. He said nothing back, and did not have to.

"Ask you something else?" I said.

He waited.

"Do you know a woman named Callie Harden?" I said.

"Who that?" he said.

"A friend of Lisa's to whom I spoke yesterday," I said. "A former prostitute who was found shot to death in South Boston last night."

"Might be Tony's style," he said. "Not mine."

"Gonna have to take your word on that," I said.

He leaned forward now.

"I am offering you the opportunity to get on the right side of this," he said. "With someone who has a much more enlightened attitude about women than Tony Marcus."

"There is no right side of this that I can see," I said.

He reached over and tapped the window between him and Gled. I looked out the window. We had made our way back to Arlington and come to a stop in front of Smith & Wollensky about a block or so from the Mass Pike.

"You know what they say about people who don't learn from history," Jabari said.

Gled was already opening the door for me.

"They're doomed to repeat it?" I said.

I was starting to get out of the car. Jabari moved across the seat and put a grip that was far too firm on my arm. I looked down at his hand and then back up at him.

"Or just fucking doomed," he said.

His hand was still on my arm. I looked down on it again. My eyes told him to remove it. He did.

"I believe we're done here," I said.

"We are," Gabriel Jabari said. "Now get the fuck out of my car."

I did.

18

I TOOK A SHOWER when I got home, trying to wash away the stink of the day. Then I poured myself a glass of chardonnay and ate some leftover chicken and thought more about the sad life and death of Callie Harden.

I did not know for sure that someone had followed me to my meeting with her. If Tony knew that Lisa and Callie had been friends, it wasn't much of a leap to think that others did, too. Jabari said he wasn't having me followed. He could have lied. Pimps lied. Callie had said it herself.

But if I had led him to her, did that mean he'd killed her, or had her killed? Why, because she might have information that might make it easier for Jabari to hire

Lisa away from Tony Marcus? Kill someone who was best friends with the woman you say you want to hire?

And what possible gain would there be for Tony to have me followed to a meeting with Callie Harden? Clearly, he had her phone number. If he didn't know where she lived now, it would be no great challenge for him to find out.

Was I being followed?

If somebody had followed me on foot back to River Street Place after Gabriel Jabari had dropped me off, the person was very good, because I hadn't spotted him, or her. I looked out the front window now. As always, there were cars parked on both sides of the street. It was dark at this hour. If there was somebody in the front seat of one of those cars, I was unable to spot them.

One of the reasons I had taken this case was so I wouldn't have to look over my shoulder, but that's exactly what I was doing now. I didn't like the feeling that someone might be following me. I didn't like that I had made no progress finding Lisa Morneau.

And I hated what had happened to Callie. In a surprising and visceral way, and not for the first time, I hated feeling like a victim of life's circumstances.

If someone was following me, I was going to find out.

I went upstairs and put on a BU sweatshirt and a pair of jeans and some waterproof Merrells I wore for walking around in wet weather. I took the Glock out of my bedside table and brought it back downstairs and put it in my purse, replacing the .38 I'd been carrying. I put on a parka and a baseball cap with *Spike's* on the front, locked the door, set the alarm, and walked around to the back of the house where residents of River Street Place were allowed to park their cars. I drove around to Berkeley and got on Storrow Drive heading west. It had begun to snow again. After about a mile I picked up the black Nissan, no plates in front, about five cars behind me, keeping that distance no matter how much I slowed down or sped up, occasionally changing lanes. But always staying with me.

I took the ramp for Soldiers Field Road, finally made a left on North Harvard Street, and pulled into the lot at Harvard Stadium. The previous November I had attended the Harvard–Yale game here with Spike, "The Game," as it was called, with typical Ivy League understatement. Spike wasn't much of a football guy, but happened to be dating one of the Harvard assistant coaches at the time.

We'd had good seats, at midfield. I remember saying "Boola Boola" as we'd made our way to them, before he shushed me and told me that was a Yale song.

Before I got out of the car I removed the Glock from my purse and put it into the side pocket of my parka. I knew I was being emotional, borderline irrational, and didn't care. If you couldn't get emotional and irrational once in a while, what was the point of being female? There. I'd said it.

I knew that the root of my anger was that men, once again, seemed to feel as if they could set the rules of engagement in my life. But it was more than that roiling me, and I knew that, too. I should never have taken this case. I shouldn't be working for Tony Marcus, in any capacity. Spike was right. Richie was right. I should quit.

Only I hated quitting.

So now here I was, pretending to talk on my phone as I got out of the car, looking around as if confused, wanting whoever had been tailing me in the Nissan to think I was here to meet someone. The snow came harder.

I walked through Gate 1, out of the snow and into the bowels of the stadium, and immediately began sprinting toward Gate 2, hoping its gates weren't closed, wanting to see if the Nissan was in the lot and how close it might be to where I'd parked.

Just like that I was the one doing the following, as snow suddenly came blowing at Harvard Stadium from the west.

I poked my head out and saw the car, motor running, perhaps fifty yards from my car, closer to North Harvard than where I'd parked.

I couldn't see how many people were inside. Maybe it was only the driver. If so, I didn't know if he had yet followed me inside the stadium. The snow came harder, starting to blow sideways.

I inched along the outside of the stadium and saw the driver get out of the car. The headlights hadn't yet gone off, so I saw that he was black and skinny, and wearing some kind of sleeveless parka and a baseball cap. At first I thought it was Ty Bop, except that this guy was heavier. But then, almost everybody was heavier than Ty Bop.

He lowered his head and leaned into the snow and walked toward Gate 1. I moved more quickly along the outside walls, Glock in my hand, not really having played this all the way out in my head, not having known I was coming here until I started driving.

I just knew this: Whoever *they* were, they thought they were the ones in control. They didn't realize I'd flipped the script. What was the rallying cry for we modern women, and all the men who had ever tried to push us around, or worse?

Time's up?

The guy was standing a few feet inside Gate 1, shifting his weight from one leg to the other, trying to make himself warmer, perhaps wondering if I had even made my way to the field, when I came up behind him and put my gun into the small of his back.

I heard him grunt and then say, "Shit."

"Hands up," I said. "And if you try anything, I *will* shoot you."

"For what? Following you?"

"I've had a bad day," I said. "There's no telling how agitated I might get."

Then I said, "You got a name, tough guy?"

"Don't matter," he said.

I poked him harder with my gun.

"What, you gonna shoot me in the back?" he said.

"Who said it would be in the back?" I said. "Maybe in the ass, just for sport."

"Go ahead," he said. "Been shot before."

"Who told you to follow me?" he said.

"I tell you that," he said, "might as well let you shoot me."

We were at a standoff, and both knew it. I stepped away from him, in case he tried to wheel suddenly on me, with an elbow or backhand slap at my gun, or even one of the kickboxing moves I'd once learned from a trainer myself. I asked if he was carrying. He said he'd left his piece, he didn't get out of the car expecting no damn shootout at Harvard Stadium.

"You could pat me down, you want," he said. "Might like it."

I noticed an almost imperceptible drop of his hands.

"Don't even think about it," I said.

He shook his head.

"This shit is fucked up," he said. "Letting some little girl get the drop on me."

I racked the slide of my gun for effect. But he had to already know the magazine was loaded.

"I hate being called that," I said.

"What?"

"Little girl."

"Fuck you," he said.

"Who hired you?"

"Fuck you," he said.

"You got any ID on you?" I said.

He snorted. “Oh, hell yeah. I got my driver’s license in my pocket along with my Starbucks card.”

He made a snorting noise.

“You think you so bad.”

“I read in a book one time,” I said, “that the badass is generally the one holding the gun.”

He shrugged and turned and spit.

“Give me a name,” I said. “I have a couple of hundred dollars in my car. Tell me who hired you and it’s yours.”

“Then what? I spend it when I’m dead?”

I moved around in front of him now, keeping the gun pointed at him, still careful to stay out of his reach. If he’d been lying to me about his own gun, and did have it on him, it was going to take some time and effort to clear it. And I didn’t believe he wanted a shootout at Harvard Stadium any more than I did.

“What we do now?” he said. “You know you ain’t gon’ shoot me.”

“What *you* do is go tell the guy who hired you to tell whoever hired him to stop following me. Because if he doesn’t, I’m pretty sure somebody who does like to shoot people will be coming up behind him.”

“Like who?”

“Like somebody working for Desmond Burke.”

“Who the fuck is Desmond Burke?”

“Trust me,” I said. “Someone in your crew will know. Or your boss will. Or his boss.”

He shrugged.

“That car outside yours?” I said.

"No," he said.

"Stolen?"

"What the fuck difference it make, anyway? Ain't no plates on it."

"Start walking," I said. "And don't turn around until you're back inside the car. And if you decide to come back to my house tonight as a way of rolling things up, you'll see a cop car in front of it."

He hesitated, as if briefly considering his options, then said "Fuck it" as he headed in the direction of Gate 2. I watched him go, slowly began backing toward Gate 1. By the time I got outside, my car was the only one in the lot. Then I was inside my car and heading back toward North Harvard, and Soldiers Field Road, and Storrow Drive, without ever looking back myself.

I knew what I'd done fell into the category of what I called dumb-guy stuff. I had solved nothing and learned nothing and come no closer to finding Lisa Morneau. I had likely made more trouble for myself, even though I did not know with whom.

I still didn't know who'd had me followed.

But, damn, it had felt good.

"Boola Boola," I said, not caring whether it was the other school's song or not.

19

IT WAS PAST eleven o'clock when I got back. I was still too keyed up for sleep, so I sat at the kitchen table with a glass of whiskey and my trusty yellow legal pad, writing down what Tony had told me about Lisa Morneau and writing down things that Gabriel Jabari had told me and wondering which one of them was having me followed, because they were the only two players in the game that I knew about.

Each said they wanted to find her for a different reason. Perhaps each thought I might actually lead one of them to her.

But which one?

And why *had* she run in the first place?

Did she really know everything about Tony's operation, or just everything he allowed her to know? Did she know things that Tony would kill to keep secret?

And if she'd told Callie Harden these things, was that why Callie Harden had died?

I sipped whiskey. Rosie slept at my feet. I was working for the most powerful pimp in the city, whatever I told myself about our current arrangement. I had been threatened by someone who sounded like he wanted to be the most powerful pimp in the city. I was looking for an ex-hooker and had likely gotten another ex-hooker killed. But this was the life I had chosen, trying to answer questions like these about people like this, no matter how righteous my motives were.

I sipped more whiskey, picked up my pen, and wrote in big, cursive letters:

Is she gone for good?

A possibility that could not be ignored.

I looked down at Rosie, snoring at my feet, and said, "Where's Lisa?"

Rosie looked up, but clearly had nothing.

Made two of us.

I kept replaying my conversation with Callie, as best I could, wondering if I had missed something, if she might have dropped her guard enough to indicate she knew more about Lisa, or where Lisa might be, than she had told me.

But what?

I thought about calling Richie. I sometimes called him late at night after he'd closed up the saloon, the phone calls making me feel the way I did when we had first started dating and would talk on the phone into the night, neither wanting to be the first to hang up. Now it was all this time later and he was about to become a dad, really, for the first time in his life. In his life and our life together.

But if I talked to him tonight I would have to tell him about what had happened at Harvard Stadium, and I knew what his reaction to that would be. He would be less happy about that than he was that I was working for Tony Marcus. So I did not call him, nor Spike, knowing his reaction would be roughly the same as Richie's. I felt myself smiling. One thing I had learned with Dr. Silverman. I could project with the best of them.

Having gotten nowhere and decided nothing, it was time for me to go to bed. I got my parka out of the closet, got the .38 from the desk in the foyer, grabbed Rosie's leash, took her out for her final ablutions of the evening, congratulated her so profusely when she completed both of her tasks as if she'd won Best in Show. I looked out at River Street Place and in the direction of the Charles Street Meeting House and wondered if I was still being watched, and by whom, and from where.

I locked the door, set the dead bolt, set the alarm, gathered Rosie into my arms, was about to go up the stairs until I remembered I'd left my phone in the living room before taking Rosie outside.

There was one missed call, from an unknown caller, one new voice message.

I played it.

"This is Lisa," the voice said. "I need to talk to you."

A pause.

I could hear voices in the background. It sounded as if she had dropped the phone and picked it up.

"Nobody had to die over this!" she said.

That was all. I kept replaying the message. No matter how many times I did, it ended the same way every time.

20

DARCY GAINES AND I sat across from each other at the Dudley Café, about a twenty-minute walk from police headquarters at 1 Schroeder. She said she was here and not in Brighton because it was one of those magical days when she got to give a progress report to the commissioner.

"They're pretty proud of their micro-roasted coffee here," she said.

"What does that even mean?" I said.

"They roast it in smaller batches," she said. "Trust me on this. I'm a cop. We know things that civilians like you don't."

I had called her cell when I knew she'd be up and told her about the voicemail from Lisa. Or someone saying she was Lisa, except for the life of me I couldn't figure out why someone would leave that message if she weren't Lisa Morneau. I told her that the call had likely been placed by a burner phone. She'd told me to meet her and bring my phone with me. I told her I wasn't sure anybody had to be told that anymore, and that I was more likely to leave the house without lip balm. Or my gun.

Now we both had cups of coffee in front of us. She told me to try the challah French toast if I hadn't eaten yet. I politely declined, telling her I wasn't sure challah would improve French toast any more than micro-roasting could improve a good cup of coffee.

She put out her hand.

"Your phone," she said. "Don't make me shoot you."

She was in uniform. It was becoming harder and harder for me to think of her out of uniform. She was all cop, and always had been. I believed she would have been a star whatever lane she'd chosen at BPD. Human trafficking had become her crusade. I wondered if her name being in the papers as often as it was, and Darcy being on television as often as she had been, helped her with her bosses. Or maybe made them see her as some kind of threat.

Men seeing a strong woman as a threat.

Where had I heard that one before?

She held my phone in the palm of her hand, swiped it, then tapped it. The next thing we both heard was the woman who'd identified herself as Lisa.

"She sounds legit scared," Darcy said.

"It has to be her," I said.

"But you've never heard her voice."

"Nope."

"But if she is as scared as she sounds, why wouldn't she tell you where she was so you could go find her?" Darcy said.

"I'll ask her, first chance I get," I said. "Is there any kind of techy voodoo you guys have that might be able to track where the call came from?"

She'd had plenty of cases, she said, that involved search warrants and subpoenas and VOIP devices. I asked what a VOIP was. She said, "Voice over Internet protocols."

"Oh," I said, "*that* VOIP."

Then she was telling me about devices, even burners, registering with provider services, and enabling the provider to locate IP addresses.

"You know what an IP address is, right?" Darcy said.

"I'm not a complete idiot," I said, "as long as you don't go too fast."

She said, "When a call is placed, the device has to connect to the provider's network. Then it's routed through a proxy server, which then figures out where the other end of the call is located. *Then* the call is sent across the net to you."

She grinned.

"Still with me?" she said.

"Barely," I said.

"Only the VOIP knows the IP address of the phone that placed the call," Darcy said.

"Does that mean you can figure out the general area

from which the call was placed?" I said. "Like pinging it after the fact?"

"I honestly don't know if that's possible without a search warrant or a subpoena," she said. "But I can ask."

"Can you ask someone who doesn't talk?" I said.

"This is me *you're* talking to," she said.

"Sorry," I said.

"You obviously forgot we're practically partners again," she said.

"Got a lot on my plate," I said.

"Not challah French toast," she said.

Then she said, "I'm gonna need to take your phone with me to VOIPville for a few hours. You actually caught a break that I'm at headquarters today. You okay leaving it with me?"

"Gonna have to be."

She finished her coffee, pocketed my phone, stood up. She had paid for the coffee this time.

"By the way?" she said. "Anything in your phone that might embarrass you?"

"Would you count shirtless pics of the guy who played Black Panther?" I said.

"Hope they're some I don't have," Darcy said, and left me there, phoneless.

21

I THOUGHT ABOUT BUYING a burner phone myself, maybe as another form of sisterhood with Lisa Morneau. But then I decided it might actually be liberating to be off the grid for a little while, even if it meant Lisa wouldn't be able to reach me if she tried again before Darcy gave me my own phone back.

For the next few hours the only people who'd know where I was would be the ones following me, if I was still being followed, and Dr. Susan Silverman, when I showed up in Cambridge for my one o'clock appointment.

It was another January day the color of cement, the sky once again appearing to be full of snow. Lisa had now been on the move and off the grid for over a week. More likely than not, if she were still able to elude the people she said wanted to kill her, she was on the move again.

I decided to walk for a little while to try to clear my head.

I took Tremont to Columbus to Seaver Street and passed Southwest Corridor Park. I kept hearing the message she had left on a constant loop inside my head. Since she'd called me, it meant somebody had given her my number and told her I was looking for her. It could only have been Callie or Laura or Kourtney with a *K*.

When I finally tired of walking aimlessly, having made it all the way to the Franklin Park Zoo, I managed to hail a cab.

"Where to?" the driver said.

"Not entirely sure," I said.

"It will slow the whole process down if you make me guess," he said.

I still had plenty of time before I planned to drive over to Susan Silverman's office, so I told him to take me to River Street Place.

When I got there, Bradley Cooper was sitting on my front step, grinning at me.

22

HE WASN'T REALLY Bradley Cooper.

Spike said that there were two categories of people when you were comparing somebody's face to a celebrity's: They were either a Looks Like or a Reminds You Of.

The guy getting up off my step, long hair and blue jeans and old Timberlands and bomber jacket, reminded me of Bradley Cooper, whom I hadn't been able to save, despite an embarrassing amount of tears, in *A Star Is Born*.

As he came toward me I said, "I have a gun."

"Makes two of us!" he said, putting up his hands in surrender. "May I show you mine?"

"Slowly," I said. "I've had a rough couple of days."

The bomber jacket was open, despite the cold. He

pulled it back to show me the shoulder holster he was wearing and the badge around his neck.

"My name is Jake Rosen," he said.

"What division?"

"What is this, a job interview?"

"Think of it that way."

"Kind of my own division," he said. "General investigator."

"Reporting where?"

"Superintendent of the General Investigations Unit," he said.

"Focusing on?"

"You know it's cold out, right?" Rosen said.

"Humor me."

"I call it the three *G*'s," he said. "Gangs, girls, guns."

It was the unit Darcy had described.

"I'm a girl and I have a gun," I said. "But my only gang is at yoga. Not that you'd ever want to pick a fight with us."

"Good one," he said.

"What are you doing here?" I said.

"I tried to call," he said.

"My phone is in the shop," I said. "Tried to call about what?"

"Your friend Mr. Marcus."

"Not my friend."

"Not mine, either," he said. "Hey, could we go inside?"

I told him we could, and walked past him and

opened the door. I still had plenty of time before my appointment with Susan Silverman.

And he was definitely cute.

ROSEN AND I sat across from each other at the kitchen table. Rosie had finally stopped barking at him, and was now in the living room pouting and emitting an occasional low growl. I had made us coffee. Rosen didn't seem to mind that it wasn't micro-brewed.

I asked if he knew Darcy Gaines.

"Everybody knows Darcy," he said.

"You two get along?"

"Kind of," he said.

"Kind of?"

"We kind of got in each other's way on a thing a few months ago and I got on her bad side," he said.

"Not where you want to be with her," I said. "I know from experience."

"I think we're good now." He grinned. "I kept telling her I was too cute for her to stay mad at me."

"And that worked?"

"It was more a feeling I got," he said.

"Get it a lot?"

He grinned. It was a tiny bit lopsided. But it seemed to be working for him. "You bet."

I looked at the clock behind him.

"What about Tony Marcus?" I said. "I know his business is girls. And he talks about dabbling in guns. But gangs?"

"He's always looking to expand," Rosen said, "especially with foot soldiers looking to move up in the world."

"So now he's checking all your boxes?"

"Including ways I'm not really at liberty to discuss," he said.

"Then why are you at my kitchen table, drinking my coffee, acting like you're afraid of my dog?" I said.

"I am *not* afraid of your dog," he said.

"Easy to say when she's out of the room."

He toasted me with his cup and smiled. Blue eyes like Bradley's, too. I was starting to think that I needed Rosie back in here to protect me. Mostly from myself.

"Why are you here, really?" I said.

"Because you're working for Tony," he said.

"Who told you that?"

He was still smiling.

"Are we really gonna do this?" he said.

"Probably not."

"I just want to give you a heads-up that this might not be the best time to be in the Tony Marcus business," he said.

"Thanks," I said. "But I'm good. And not really in the Tony Marcus business." I put air quotes around "business."

"Listen, I know who your father is," he said. "Everybody in the department knows who your father is. Think of me being here as a professional courtesy."

"How much of what you're not at liberty to discuss has to do with Tony and Gabriel Jabari getting ready to go all *Game of Thrones*?" I said.

"Some," he said.

"Who wins that one in the end?" I said.

"If we play it right, neither one of them does," he said. "You don't mind me asking, how'd you come to work for a jackwagon like Tony?"

"Not at liberty to discuss," I said, and smiled.

"How about this?" he said. "How about if you find Lisa Morneau you tell me and not Tony?"

"Who's Lisa Morneau?"

He put his elbow on the table and leaned down so he could run his hand through his hair. How old was he?

"We still doing this?" he said.

"Not showing you mine if you won't show me yours," I said.

There was no point in telling him that Lisa had called me. Maybe he already knew. Maybe somebody at headquarters had said something to somebody, even though Darcy had said they would not.

"There's a chance we can help each other here," he said.

"That's only assuming you have something I want," I said.

The cocky grin again. I could see why he didn't think anybody could stay mad at him for long. *Yeah. Definitely cute.*

"Could you be a little more specific?" he said.

I looked at the clock again. It was past noon by now. Time to go.

Jake Rosen said, "I just want you to know that if your pursuit of Lisa gets in my way, then maybe shit happens and I don't take those *two* jackwagons off the street who need to be taken off."

Now he was the one taking a card out of his wallet and placing it on the table between us.

"Working together would be a lot more fun than working against each other," he said. "I've managed to inflict some serious pain on some serious bad guys over the past few months, but Tony's the one I want."

"I'll keep that in mind."

"Lot of moving pieces here," he said.

"Tell me about it," I said.

He said he'd be in touch. Rosie then barked him all the way to the front door. I watched him walk down the walk, careful not to slip on the snow, telling myself that only a cynical person would suggest that I was looking at his butt.

23

I USED MY LANDLINE to call Darcy Gaines before I left for Cambridge. She said that they were still working on the phone. I asked if the phone could still accept a call while they tried to work their magic on it. She said it could, and that if Lisa called back, Darcy would talk to her—not tell her she was a cop, just tell her she was a friend that I'd left my phone with—and try to find out if she was safe, and where she was.

"Or," I said, "you could just try to keep her talking while you traced the call."

"You watch too much television," Darcy said.

Now I was with Susan Silverman. Today she wore a gray cashmere turtleneck sweater, black slacks, and black zippered ankle boots. Her lipstick was plum-colored. It matched her fingernails. Her black hair was gleaming, as always.

"Do you mind if we talk a little about my case today?" I said.

"I always want to talk about what you want to talk about," she said. She smiled. "It's in all the handbooks."

"I just thought you might help bring some clarity to it," I said. "And structure."

I tried to catch her up as quickly as I could, about everything that had happened and everything I knew, except the part about staring at Jake Rosen's butt. By the time I finished I knew I had used up a fair amount of my time.

"And did I mention that I have quickly developed an attachment to Richie's little boy?" I said.

"It all sounds a little overwhelming," Susan Silverman said.

I sighed, and loudly. "Tell me about it," I said.

"But you said you wanted to begin with the missing woman."

I nodded.

"You know that I've had to immerse myself in the world of prostitution before," I said. "The last time before this was on a case up in Paradise, with young women who were part of a religious cult."

"It began with one girl," she said, "and expanded to all of them."

"I wanted to save them," I said. "And while I feel a

similar motivation this time, my feelings involve a woman I haven't even met."

"But you met the woman who was murdered," Susan Silverman said.

"Whose story was heartbreaking," I said.

"Aren't they all?" she said.

"I couldn't help her," I said. "Or save her."

"You couldn't save her and now are unable to find the woman you were hired to find," she said.

"I don't know if I'm more frustrated by my lack of progress or that I took the case in the first place," I said.

"Tell me more about the missing woman," she said. "Lisa."

"Somehow she achieved a position of at least some power in a world where brutal men form their own autocracy," I said.

"Well put," she said.

"I have my moments," I said.

"And what happens if and when you do find her?" Susan Silverman said.

I smiled now.

"Why, save her, of course," I said.

"On your last big case," she said, "the damsel in distress wasn't even a damsel."

"It was Richie," I said.

"You had a far easier task distinguishing the good guys from the bad guys," she said.

"This time I've only got bad guys and worse guys," I said, "until I find Lisa."

"You mentioned Richie's son before," she said. "But how are things between you and Richie?"

I smiled again.

"Wow," I said.

"That good?"

"No," I said. "Wow because this was effectively a Richie-free session until now. When have we ever had one of those?"

"Never?" Susan Silverman said.

"Is that a sign of progress," I said, "or my ability to compartmentalize like a champion?"

"Perhaps a little bit of both," she said, and said she would see me next week.

DARCY CALLED A couple minutes after I was back at River Street Place. She said she was on her way out the door and would drop my phone on her way home.

"But there's good news," she said.

"Tell me."

"We managed to thread the needle," she said. "Not quite sure how Sergeant Loomis did it, but she did."

"You found out where the call came from," I said.

"Well, Loomis did," she said.

"Where?" I said.

"Paradise," she said.

I laughed.

"Something funny about that?" Darcy said.

"I have an old friend up there," I said.

24

OFFICER MOLLY CRANE was sitting at her desk outside Chief Jesse Stone's office when I walked into the Paradise Police Department a little before six o'clock that night.

"Deputy Chief Crane," I said.

"From your lips," Molly said.

"You never age," I said.

"Neither do you," she said, standing to give me a hug.

"Liar," I said.

Molly pulled back and said, "You started it."

I looked past her and saw Jesse standing in the doorway to his office, grinning at us.

"Did you check her for concealed weapons?" he said to Molly Crane.

"You're the chief," she said. "If she needs frisking,

you handle it." She winked at me. "It's not as if he doesn't have experience in that area. Or various other areas, for that matter."

"Dirty job," Jesse said. He lifted his shoulders and dropped them. "Somebody had to do it."

He motioned me into the office and shut the door. Now he was the one giving me a hug, one that I felt had far more follow-through to it than Molly's had. I did not offer much resistance. But then I rarely had with Jesse Stone, with whom I had once made love standing up in a changing room in a boutique in Beverly Hills.

We finally pulled back from each other. He walked around his desk and sat down. He was wearing a zippered blue sweatshirt and jeans and looked older than he had when I had last seen him a little over a year ago. We had stayed in touch even after ending what had been, for me, the most serious relationship of my adult life other than the one I had shared with Richie. I knew Jesse had stopped drinking. I knew a woman with whom he had been deeply involved had been previously murdered by a serial killer. I knew a grown son, one he had not known existed, was now a part of his life, and living in Paradise. Cole, his name was.

"You look good," he said.

"So do you."

"Older," he said.

"And wiser?"

"Hard to tell."

"Little grayer, too," I said.

"Comes with being wiser, pretty sure," he said. "Maybe I need your colorist."

"Hey," I said.

"Okay, enough small talk," Jesse said. "How're things with Richie?"

"His ex-wife has moved back to Boston with their son," I said.

"Permanently?"

"Unclear," I said.

"But getting a place of their own?"

I nodded.

"So we're both learning to be parents," he said.

"You're an actual parent, even if you're getting a late start," I said. "Right now, I'm a glorified babysitter. But he's a cute kid."

"Lucky one, too," he said. "If he's got you as a babysitter."

"The whole situation is somewhat out of my control," I said.

"Uh-oh," he said. "That's never what we're looking for."

"Exactly."

I had walked to the Four Seasons after Darcy had dropped off my phone, left through a service entrance, and requested the Lyft car that had picked me up around the corner from the Park Plaza hotel. If someone were still following me, I did not want them coming to Paradise if there was even an outside chance that Lisa Morneau was still here and an even more remote chance that I could locate her.

I had called Jesse to tell him I was on my way. I told him some of the backstory in the process. Now I told him the rest. The last time we had worked together on a case had been when I had helped him bust the cult known as the Bond of Renewal, run by a smooth-talking grifter who called himself The Patriarch. At the time, Kathryn had just given birth to Richard, and I had convinced myself that Richie and I would never again be together as a couple. And thought that Jesse and I might stay together, despite his lingering feelings for his own ex-wife.

I had been wrong on both counts.

I saw Jesse smiling at me.

"What?" I said.

"Just thinking of your song," he said.

"It's *not* my song," I said.

Bobby Hebb's old song, "Sunny."

"You're dating yourself," I said.

"Always liked the part about nature's fire," he said.

"You really remember all the lyrics?"

"I remember everything," he said.

I said, "Are we going to flirt, or talk about my case?"

"What," Jesse said, "we can't do both?"

"I'm going steady," I said.

But remembered everything he remembered. Maybe even more. *Down, girl,* I told myself. First Jake Rosen. Now here I was with Jesse. Somehow, even with everything going on, I suddenly felt as if my day had turned into a hormone festival, with everything except floats and marching bands.

I played the message Lisa Morneau had left, then played it again.

"You got a picture of her?" Jesse said.

I took the one I had out of my purse and slid it across the desk. There was a file cabinet next to him. On top of it was a baseball glove. I knew he still played softball in the summer, and had been a star player in the minor leagues before getting hurt. I wondered if he still had the poster at home of the shortstop he said had been his hero, one he called the Wizard and talked about as if he were some kind of baseball holy man.

"So somebody could have tracked her here before you did," Jesse said. "Hard as that is to believe."

"Practically unthinkable," I said.

"You know any possible connection she would have to Paradise?"

"I do not."

"But despite the way the message ended," he said, "she still could be here."

"Why I'm here," I said.

Jesse said, "I was hoping it was at least partly because you missed me."

"I do miss you," I said.

"Even though that was the old me?" he said.

"Even though," he said.

He smiled again. I smiled back. I didn't know what there was still between us. Something. He had never been Richie. But he'd come the closest.

"I'd like to ask around about her," I said. "But I don't want to spook her if she's still here."

"You thought about how you'll handle it with Marcus if you do find her?" Jesse said.

"I just want to hear her story," I said.

"But you're still working for Tony," Jesse said.

"Sort of," I said.

"Care to talk about that?"

"Later," I said. "For now, I want you to help me find Lisa."

"I can do that," he said. "I'm the chief of police. We know practically everything. And what we don't, we find out."

There was a silence now in the office. It had never made him uncomfortable. He was like Richie that way. But there was more darkness in him, or sadness, or pain. Maybe all of those things. As close as we had been, as well as we had understood each other, and as much of a bond as we had shared because of failed marriages, there were places inside him that I knew I had never come close to reaching, places I'm sure even his ex-wife had never reached.

"How's Jen?" I said.

"Still married," he said. Grinned. "I think if she stays at it another year, it might be a record for her."

"She happy?"

"Happy as Jen can be," he said.

"How's it going with Cole?" I said.

"We're getting there," he said. "Work in progress. Like his old man."

He took the photograph of Lisa Morneau out to Molly and asked if she would make some copies. He said that he and Molly and Suitcase Simpson, a young guy on the force whom Jesse had treated like a son before his real son showed up, could discreetly distribute them around town in the morning.

"Is Spike's still the most popular restaurant in town?" I said.

"I assume you're referencing the Gray Gull," Jesse said.

"He thinks of it as Spike's North," I said.

"He would," Jesse said.

"Why don't we go over there and grab a bite to eat and ask if anybody there has seen her?" I said.

Jesse said that sounded good to him. He grabbed a blue baseball cap with *PPD* on the front, stuck it on his head. As we walked past Molly's desk she said, "See you for coffee in the morning, Sunny?"

"Funny," I said.

"Who's joking?" she said.

"Like we used to say when I was playing ball," Jesse said as we headed for his Jeep. "You can't stop Molly. You can only hope to contain her."

WE SCORED A corner table that we'd had plenty of times before. There had been a night, after Spike had bought the place, when he'd described Jesse and me as "fooling around." Jesse had corrected him, saying we weren't fooling around because we were serious. Which we most certainly had been.

I hesitated briefly when the waitress asked for our drink order. Jesse noticed and told me I was of a legal age and allowed to have an adult beverage. I ordered a white wine. He ordered iced tea.

When she left I said, "Do you miss it?"

"Every damn day," he said, then added, "at a time."

When she brought our drinks back we clicked glasses.

"Did I mention you look good?" he said.

"Tony referred to me as a woman of a certain age," I said.

"What does he know?" Jesse said. "He can't even hold on to women he's paying."

I told him why I'd taken the case. And about Jabari. Even about the kid at Harvard Stadium.

"You got the drop on him," Jesse said.

"Did I ever," I said.

He raised his glass of iced tea in a toast.

He said that tomorrow he and Molly and Suit would circulate Lisa's picture. They would work the downtown area and the bed-and-breakfasts that he said still did a pretty good business, even at this time of year.

"It's still a small town," he said. "If she's been here, somebody saw her. We'll find her."

"Like the old days," I said. "We did make a pretty good team."

"Not just as crime-stoppers," he said.

"Stop," I said.

"Right," he said. "You've got a boyfriend."

"Keep that in mind," I said.

"Just making conversation," he said.

I smiled at him again. "The hell you are," I said, and he laughed.

We both ordered salmon. While we were eating it Jesse said, "You think there's any possibility she's trying to shake him down?"

"I'll ask her when we find her," I said. "But if she lived with Tony and worked with him, she knows him. And knows what generally happens to people who cross Tony Marcus."

"I know," he said.

"Do you?"

"Like I said," Jesse said. "I'm the chief of police. Guys like us know all kinds of shit."

"Then tell me why we didn't end up together even when Richie and Jen weren't in the picture."

"Damned if I know," Jesse said.

We passed on dessert and coffee. Jesse asked for the check. I told him I was going to Uber back to Boston, or Lyft, whichever one could get here first. He said he'd drive me.

"Not like the old days," he said. "I can be a designated driver now."

I told him I didn't think that was the best idea in the whole world.

"Don't trust me?" he said.

"Don't trust either one of us," I said.

"Even though you've got a boyfriend?" he said.

"Even though."

As we made our way past the bar, I got the bartender's attention. He was young, but then who didn't look young to me these days? He was wearing a tight black T-shirt that was like an advertisement for whatever time he'd been putting in at the gym. He had a full array of tattoos up and down both arms. Spike had informed me they were now called sleeves. I'd asked if guys preferred puff, or raglan.

He nodded at Jesse, who said, "Hey, Andrew." I showed Andrew the picture of Lisa Morneau.

"Have you seen her around here?" I said.

"Yeah," he said.

Boom.

"You did?" I said.

"Last night," he said.

"She was here last night?" I said.

"Sat down at the end by herself," Andrew said. "Paid with cash."

"You talk to her?"

"She was a good-looking woman drinking alone at my bar," he said. "It was practically my sworn duty to talk her up."

"How did she seem to you?"

"Nervous," he said. "Every time the door would open she'd whip her head around. I finally kidded her and asked if she was on the lam or something. And she said, 'Or something.'"

"What time did she leave?" I said.

"Not sure," he said. "Maybe around eleven?"

The message on my phone had been left at ten minutes after eleven o'clock.

"Anything else?" I said.

"She ordered one more, for the road," he said. "I told her it was on me. Then she said she was going outside to make a phone call and never came back."

25

I WAS AWAKENED FROM a deep sleep by the old-fashioned ringtone of my cell phone. The phone was on the nightstand. When I touched the screen I saw that it was 2:12 in the morning.

UNKNOWN CALLER again.

I sat up in bed, switched on the light, as wide awake as if an alarm had just sounded. I touched the screen to accept the call.

"Sunny Randall," I said.

I could hear breathing at the other end.

"Hello?" I said.

"It's Lisa Morneau."

"Are you all right?" I said. "I was up in Paradise tonight looking for you."

"How'd you know I was there?" she said.

"Tracked you off my phone," I said.

"Mine and not yours? You can do that?"

"Cops helped."

"No cops!" she shouted.

"Where are you right now?" I said.

"Boston."

"Tell me where, and I'll get dressed and meet you," I said.

"I don't know why I should trust you," she said.

"Lisa," I said. "You've now called me twice."

"I don't even know why I did," she said. "All I know is that you're helping Tony right now. Find *me*."

"I want to help you," I said. "But I can only do that if you'll let me."

"Running out of options on people I can trust," she said.

There was another silence, longer than before.

"See, the thing is, nobody has to be afraid of me," she said. "But now it's me that's afraid of them." I thought I could hear traffic sounds in the background. "They didn't have to kill Callie!"

"Lisa," I said, keeping my voice calm, not wanting to agitate her any more than she already was. "Who's *they*? *Who* killed Callie?"

"Fuck!" she yelled.

Keep them talking, my father had always told me.

"Why would Tony hire me to find you and then come for you himself?" I said. "How does that make any sense?"

"I won't tell!"

She sounded out of breath.

"Won't tell *what*?"

Another pause.

"Talking to you got Callie killed," Lisa Morneau said. "What do you think will happen to me?"

She was shouting again, in circles now.

"Did she know where you were?" I said.

"I never should have told!"

I knew she wasn't going to give me the answers I wanted over the phone.

"I can come to you," I said. "Tell me where you are."

"I just wanted to get out," she said. "I just couldn't take it anymore. Girls dying like that. Those girls could've been *me*."

Before I could even respond to that she said, "I'll call you back."

"Don't hang up," I said.

She did.

Now I was the one yelling "Fuck!"

Rosie, who didn't like loud noises of any kind, jumped up at her end of the bed, staring at me. But we both knew she'd heard worse.

26

I SOMEHOW GOT A few hours of sleep. When I was up early and showered and caffeinated, I called Spike, who had turned into an early riser despite the hours of owning a restaurant, and told him I needed to talk. He suggested we meet for coffee. I suggested a walk along the Charles. He said it was too goddamn cold for a walk along the Charles. I told him he was a wimp.

We compromised on a walk down Commonwealth that would end at the Eliot Hotel on Mass Ave, where I promised I would buy him a hearty breakfast at Uni.

"I liked the Eliot better when they still had the Eliot Lounge and Tommy Leonard was the bartender," Spike said when we met at the top of the walking mall at Comm Ave and Arlington.

"Before my time," I said.

"Tommy died last year," Spike said. "But, man, back in the day when the Marathon was starting to get really big, the Eliot Lounge became like the capital of running. But it wasn't just runners. One time Bill Lee got into a fight with the Yankees at Fenway and got beaten up pretty badly. When the writers asked if he was going to the hospital he said, no, he was going to the Eliot Lounge."

"Who's Bill Lee?" I said.

"They called him Spaceman."

"Boy," I said, "those really were the days."

The temperature was back down into the twenties. Wind chill made it feel colder than that. Spike was still dressed as if he was driving dogs in the Iditarod. His parka made him look as big around as the Michelin Man.

As we walked, I caught him up on everything that had happened since we'd talked last, including the trip to Paradise and all the way through getting another call from Lisa Morneau, this one in the middle of the night.

"I heard you and Jesse were communing," he said.

"Who told you?"

"Multiple sources," he said. "It's my joint, remember."

"Strictly business."

"Funny business?"

"Focus," I said.

"It's hard when it's cold as fuck," he said.

"You can do it, Nanook," I said. "I need to talk this out."

"Okay," Spike said. "But please walk faster."

"I'll ask you what I asked Lisa," I said. "Why would Tony chase her up to Paradise himself, if it was Tony?"

"Maybe he was displeased with the, uh, pace of your investigation," he said. "I know we keep circling back to the same place. But whatever she has is scaring the piss out of a guy who doesn't scare very easily."

"She thinks somebody is willing to kill her to get it, or to stop her from revealing it," I said.

We crossed Dartmouth. For the first time I looked back over my shoulder.

Spike said, "If somebody is still following you, they're very good."

"Maybe they got tired of watching me chase my own tail," I said.

"Ah," he said, "but such a cute tail it is."

We finally moved to the Newbury side of the street, Spike theorizing that getting closer to some buildings, the wind wouldn't be as bad. I told him the wind was coming from the river. He said I should humor him.

"Ask yourself something, before I pass out from hunger," he said. "If leaving him and going on the run has made her this frightened, what does she do now? And where does she go?"

I looked at him and smiled. By now, his cheeks were the color of a STOP sign. His knit hat was pulled down close to his eyes.

"Maybe Tony does think she's going to use something she knows against him," I said.

"And whatever it is, maybe Jabari wants to use it against him first," I said.

"Him being the only other big piece on the board," Spike said.

"That I know about," I said. "But who the hell knows, there could be others. A lot of people in town would like to see Tony go down. Or at least become marginalized."

"Let me ask you another question," Spike said. "How much do we really know about Mr. Jabari? Other than him owning or running or fronting a high-class titty bar?"

"Good question," I said.

"No shit," he said.

"We know very little about him," I said. "But you knew that before you asked."

"I watch the same lawyer shows you do," he said. "They say never ask a question you don't already know the answer to."

"Maybe it would be in my best interests if I could find out a little more about him," I said.

"Our best interests," Spike said.

"You're a good wingman," I said.

"Even this cold and this hungry," he said.

"Maybe we could follow him around," I said, "as opposed to the other way around."

"I like it," he said, then said we could discuss it further after we'd had breakfast and feeling had returned to his fingers, whichever happened first.

27

TONY MARCUS WASN'T answering his phone. Either he was sleeping even later than usual or he didn't want to talk to me today. I said in my message that I had spoken to Lisa and to call me when he could.

When I had worked cases in the sex trade before, everything had started with the victim. Once it had been a teenage girl named Millicent Patton. In the Paradise cult it had been Cheryl DeMarco. Was Lisa, a grown woman who'd existed in Tony's world for a long time, the victim here? Or had I simply defined her as one as a way of justifying my search for her?

I had taken a car back to River Street Place. I had just shut the front door behind me when Richie called and asked if he could stop by.

"It's important," he said.

He never said it was when it wasn't. Neither did I.

"What?" I said.

"Kathryn doesn't know if she wants to stay," he said.

"Meaning stay here," I said.

"Yes," he said, then said he would tell me more about it when he arrived. Twenty minutes later he walked through the door and I kissed him even before Rosie did, and told him I had put on the strongest tea I had.

"Wish it was stronger than that," he said. "Maybe, as my father likes to say, just a wee bit of Irish."

"Pretty early in the day," I said.

"Not in Ireland," he said.

I poured enhanced tea for both of us and brought it to the living room. He asked how the case was going. I didn't think he was merely being polite. He seemed genuinely interested. So I quickly caught him up, without telling him about my dinner with Jesse Stone. Richie had never known the complete extent of my relationship with Jesse. Just that there had been a relationship that had persisted, before we finally drifted away from each other. But today was not the day to travel back to that stretch of road.

"So Kathryn has now decided she doesn't want to put roots down in Boston?" I said.

"It's more than that," he said. "She says she wants to be alone for a while."

"Alone meaning without her son?"

Richie nodded.

"Wait," I said. "She wants to leave the boy with you?"

"She does," he said. "She actually referenced you as she tried to explain her feelings to me. She spoke of how self-sufficient you are, and how envious she is of that."

"Oh, ho," I said.

"'Oh, ho'?"

"It's an expression my therapist uses," I said. "She says she got it from the man of *her* dreams."

"I've maintained that status with you?" he said. "Even with everything that's going on?"

"Yeah," I said. "You have."

"She says she tried to define herself through me," he said. "Then through our son. Then through the next man in her life. And then said she needed to be by herself."

"You won't be by *your*self," I said.

He sipped tea.

"He's my son," he said. "I've always wanted him in my life. She was the one who removed him from it."

"And now she wants to remove her own self-absorbed self from it," I said.

"At least temporarily."

"She was originally going to London temporarily."

He sipped more tea. He wasn't usually a tea guy. I was pretty sure it was the enhancement, even though I hadn't overdone it. Usually when Richie Burke drank in the afternoon, he wanted to go somewhere and take a nap.

"Are you ready to be the single parent now?" I said.

"I don't have much of a choice," he said. "And he's such a spectacular kid."

"I know," I said. "Already got a little sneaker going for him myself."

"He really likes you."

"Think he likes Rosie more."

"Don't be so sure," Richie said.

"I can't control the power I have over men," I said. "Of all ages."

"Tell me about it," Richie said. He gave me a long look and then said, "I can't do this alone."

"I will help you," I said.

"Gonna need some kind of nanny, too," he said. "Can you help me pick one?"

"As long as she doesn't look like the one Tiger Woods married back in the day," I said.

"Thought you didn't follow sports," he said.

"I followed that one," I said. "Mostly checking out at the supermarket."

"I thought looking for apartments was the beginning of the process," Richie said. "Then she changed the process."

He sighed and leaned back and closed his eyes, as if he suddenly did need a nap. I felt myself smile at the sight of him in repose. Things really had been better between us than they'd been at any time since he had married Kathryn. Even though Richie would occasionally raise the idea of us once again trying to live together, and even raised the subject of remarriage once or twice, we had stopped obsessing about the future. The experience of saving his father, even if we couldn't save his uncle Felix, had only reinforced our bond. Or perhaps made us stronger than ever at what had once been broken places.

Richie said, "We can do this."

"I'm not looking to be a mom," I said.

"He already has one," Richie said.

"Not if she goes off on a journey of spiritual fulfillment," I said.

Now I drank tea.

"My father raised me after my mother died," he said.

"Felix raised you," I said.

"Neither one of them had you," Richie said.

"Goddamn her," I said, "all to hell."

"We *can do* this," he said again. "You know I love you. And I know you love me."

"And if we'd wanted to have a child together," I said, "nobody was stopping us."

There was another silence between us. But, as always, all the way back to the time when we were first in each other's lives, it was as if the conversation were continuing.

"Is this a done deal?" I said. "Her leaving, I mean? She's changed her mind before."

"She says she wants to have the chance to find out what her life is like unencumbered by the past," he said.

"She said that?" I said. "For real?"

"She did."

"Sounds like shrink talk to me," I said. "Or a fortune cookie."

"She's not as bad as you think."

"Low bar."

"Maybe when you get some free time, you and Richard and I can go off and do something together," he said.

"As I mentioned before, things are starting to percolate somewhat with this case of mine," I said.

"Can I help?" Richie said. "Or can Desmond?"

"If it comes to that," I said, "you will be the first to know. Then him."

"Any chance at even a quick dinner tonight?" Richie said.

"Tonight," I said, "I will be doing something you would not want me doing."

"Any point in me asking what that might be?"

"Nah," I said.

We stood. He hugged me. I hugged him back. Yesterday it had been Jesse. Today Richie. I couldn't unencumber myself from my own past with a court order.

28

I HAD CONSIDERED GOING to Suite alone and waiting outside long enough to follow Gabriel Jabari home, wherever home was for him.

It was a place to start with him, and working my way back or forward to find out who he really was and where he had come from. I was good at following people. It had become part of a skill set I could never have imagined for myself when I was majoring in fine arts at Boston University. I liked telling myself that there were all sorts of fine arts, whether you studied them in college or not. I wondered if any of the women who'd been in my Post-Impressionist class could follow anybody as well as I could, or shoot a gun.

But if somehow I ran into trouble tonight, I did not

want to be alone. So I called Spike at Spike's in the early evening and asked if he wanted to come along.

"I had set up a thing that could turn into more of a thing after closing time tonight," he said.

"Who with, if you don't mind me sounding like a professional snoop?"

"You *are* a professional snoop."

"There you go," I said.

"It's the weather guy," he said. "Would be after he does the late news."

"You'd rather have a date with him than sit outside a strip club with me?" I said.

"Well," he said, "when you put it like that. But how do you know Jabari's there?"

"He told me he's there pretty much every night," I said. "Hands on, so to speak."

"Maybe he won't go straight home."

"But maybe he will," I said. "I keep thinking that as much as Jabari says it's just business with him and Tony, it seems a hell of a lot more personal to me."

We agreed to meet at his place at a little after eleven. If I were still being followed, I didn't want to make it easy for them. Whoever they were. So I walked over to Mount Vernon Street and went inside the Beacon Hill Hotel, where I knew the bartender. He directed me to the service entrance and I made my way to Mount Vernon, then worked my way up to Joy Street. The Uber app took care of the rest.

When I got to Spike's, we had one drink at the bar.

He'd driven his Mercedes to work tonight, saying he was going to drive over to the station and pick up the weatherman before somebody blew *that* shot at romance sky high.

By midnight we were parked halfway up Tremont from Suite, with a clear view of the front door. Despite the cold, and the hour on a weeknight, there was still a steady stream of customers heading into the club. Parked directly in front was the black Navigator in which Gabriel Jabari and I had taken our ride.

"There are a lot of black Navigators," Spike said. "Doesn't mean that one is his."

"I remember the plate from when he dropped me," I said.

WBOS, Spike's favorite rock station, was playing softly on the car radio. He was dressed all in black: leather jacket, jeans, boots, even the black horn-rimmed glasses he wore when driving. He had his own Glock, too, permit in the glove compartment.

"Tell me again what we really hope to accomplish?" he said.

"He knows where I live, I ought to know where he lives," I said. "Might be as simple as that."

"You don't like this guy," Spike said.

"Not so much."

"You ever give much thought to why you like Tony more?" he said.

"*Like* is a strong word," I said. "Sometimes I just tell myself that if Tony is a pirate, he's my pirate. Even in a disgusting line of work. And we have done each other favors in the past."

Two big guys, walking unsteadily, got out of a limo and headed for the front door. One slapped the other on the back and nearly knocked his friend down. Then the first guy put his arm around the second guy and they disappeared into Suite. Maybe this was their idea of an expensive frat house, just with naked pole dancers and a champagne lounge.

"Tony's a killer and a pimp," Spike said. "All we know for now is that our boy Gabriel is some form of pimp."

"Devil you know?" I said.

We sat in the front seat of the car and listened to music. Spike asked me more about being with Jesse again. He wanted to know if I really thought I could even be a part-time parent to Richard.

"Been thinking a lot about that," I said. "And what I think is that I don't know."

"You scared?" Spike said.

"Yes!" I said in a loud voice, and we both laughed.

Spike said, "I've got more comedy gold about you and Jesse."

"Save it for our next stakeout," I said.

I asked him whatever happened to Charles Laquidara, who was the most famous rock 'n' roll disc jockey at WBCN when I was a kid. Spike said he was living in Hawaii now, but you could still catch him online. I asked him how he knew stuff like that. He said he wasn't just beefcake. I asked Spike why he thought Lisa was calling me.

"Protection?" he said. "Maybe she has run out of better options. If she even has any options left."

"Only she won't let me protect her," I said.

"Ay," he said, "there's the rub."

"*Hamlet,*" I said.

"Comes right after the part about to sleep and perchance to dream," Spike said.

"Marry me, you silver-tongued devil," I said.

"Even though I don't have kids?" he said.

"Screw you," I said.

"Can't," he said.

At fifteen minutes past one o'clock Gabriel Jabari and Gled appeared on the street. Jabari reached into his pocket and tipped the doorman. There was a woman with him, but Jabari and Gled blocked our view of her. Before we could catch a glimpse, she got into the backseat and Jabari followed her.

"Be cool," I said as Spike put the car silently into gear with that Mercedes whisper.

"As you know from vast personal experience," he said, "I am the coolest."

I reminded him then that the lines right after "ay's the rub" in *Hamlet* were the ones about shuffling off this mortal coil, and how we should try to avoid that tonight if at all possible.

Spike was very good at tailing cars, too. We made our way around from Tremont and then were heading toward the water, passing the Boston Harbor Hotel and

Rowes Wharf. I knew that cruise ships docked right behind the hotel. Sometimes Richie and I would have dinner at The Wharf Room, which had good food and an even better view.

"If Gabriel has digs over here," Spike said, "the hell with Spike's, *I'm* opening a strip club."

We circled back around and finally came up on the Vintage restaurant at Franklin and Broad as the Navigator made the turn on Broad and came to a stop in front of what looked like a smallish apartment building.

"The Folio," Spike said. "I looked at a place here one time."

"Not as expensive as living on the water?" I said.

"Still ain't cheap, blondie," he said.

Spike had kept his distance. He had time to park the Mercedes at the corner, in front of the Vintage. We both got out.

"Where else could he be going except inside?" Spike said.

"We've come this far," I said.

The lighting was good on the street. Gled got out and opened the rear door on the driver's side. The woman got out first. As she did, she turned and looked up the street so quickly I was afraid she'd seen me. If she did, she gave no indication.

But I had seen her.

"What the hell?" I said.

"What the hell *what*?" Spike said.

"I know her."

"Tell me it's not Lisa," he said.

"It's not," I said.

"So who?" I said.

"Natalie Goddard," I said.

"Who?"

"The former Natalie Marcus," I said.

Tony's ex-wife.

29

I HAD FIRST MET the former Natalie Marcus when on a case involving a client named Mary Lou Goddard. Mary Lou was being stalked, and I'd eventually found out who was doing the stalking. It was more complicated than that—they all are—but before she fired me, I found out Mary Lou had been in a relationship with Natalie. As far as I knew they'd never made their union official. Natalie had still taken her name, and kept it after they'd broken up.

Along the way, I had further discovered that Natalie's *real* name was Verna Lee Lister, and that she was the sister of Jermaine, the pimp Tony had killed in prison.

On the day I'd been the one to tell Natalie what had happened to Jermaine, she and I had even shared a moment during which she tried to kick me in the groin and punch my lights out. And called me a honky bitch.

I reminded Spike of that, after reminding him just whom Natalie had been in her previous incarnations.

"Your way with people has always been a rare and magical gift," Spike said.

Now it was the next morning. I very much wanted to speak with Natalie about her association with Gabriel Jabari—or liaison?—even knowing that if I did track her down and show up on her doorstep she would be about as happy to see me as she would a process server.

When we had first crossed paths, if unpleasantly, she had been living in a Beacon Hill apartment on Revere Street, but that was well over a decade ago. I had no idea if she might still be there, but if she were, we were practically neighbors. To get to what had been her building at the time, all I had to do was walk a couple blocks and take a left on Charles and then another left before walking the few blocks to Revere.

The night before, Spike had asked how Natalie might get me to where I wanted to be with Lisa.

"All I know," I'd said to Spike, "is that we just saw the woman who used to be married to Tony with a guy Tony considers to be his nemesis, and perhaps even competition for his missing sweetie. Don't you think we should treat that as a clue?"

"We'd be fools not to," Spike said.

There are moments from your life that remain with you, with great clarity, no matter where you have stored them and how infrequently you have accessed them. One was the first time I had shown up at Natalie's residence on Revere Street unannounced and told her everything I knew about her. What I remembered more than her trying to attack me was her genuine grief when I told her about her brother.

Now, all this time later, my life had once again intersected with Natalie's, though she didn't know it just yet.

All I knew for sure was that she and Jabari had left Suite together and arrived on Broad Street together. Tony's ex-wife. Spending time with Gabriel Jabari, who wanted me to find the same woman Tony had hired me to find. The same Jabari whose stated mission was to take down Tony Marcus. My father had once said that while coincidence might exist, you could go broke relying on it.

Maybe I would get lucky. I could use some luck. Maybe she still lived on Revere Street, which was a very nice address in a very nice part of town. Maybe if you'd had enough luck to score a place there you didn't easily give it up.

I didn't remember the exact address but did remember the building as soon as I saw it.

I walked up some steps to the front door. The name *Goddard* was still there.

I rang the bell and waited.

From the speaker I heard a woman's voice say, "Who is it?"

"Sunny Randall," I said.

I waited. No response. It was as if the speaker had gone dead.

It had not.

"Go the fuck away," she said.

"We need to talk," I said.

"I never needed to talk to you," she said. "Not for one damn second."

"We need to talk today," I said. "About Gabriel Jabari. With whom you walked out of Suite last night and then accompanied to a condominium on Broad Street."

There was another pause, longer than the first, as if she were reviewing her options.

Finally she said, "You got ten minutes."

Then I heard the buzzer and the click of the door.

"Missed you, too," I said.

I opened the door and headed up the stairs.

30

SHE WAS STILL quite attractive, hair still cropped short. Not a Halle Berry look-alike, more a Reminds You Of. She had to be in her fifties, at least, but her face was still remarkably unlined. It was either good genetics or the joys of Botox, a subject about which I knew I was becoming far less judgmental as time passed.

She was waiting with the door open, wearing a pale-blue crewneck sweater, cargo pants, and old-fashioned high-top sneakers. Spike would have known the brand instantly.

"Ten minutes," she said again, gesturing me into the apartment.

"Does that count stair time?" I said.

She sighed, and showed me in.

The living room had the look and feel of a place that

had been lived in for a long time. The wall behind the couch, which I thought might be a Thessaly, featured a floor-to-ceiling bookcase. There were a lot of plants, and a chair that seemed to match the couch, and a flat-screen television. As far as I could see, there was not a single photograph in the room.

She took the couch. I took the chair. There was no offer of refreshment of any kind and, I was fairly certain, none forthcoming.

"You were staking out a strip club?" she said. "For real?"

I smiled. "Kind of," I said.

"You followed me there?" she said.

"I was more interested in Gabriel," I said. "So, technically, I followed him out of there. I didn't know you were with him until later."

"Why were you following him?"

She crossed her arms in front of her, waiting. There was a faint scent of jasmine from a lit candle on a small table on the other side of the room. Or was it gardenia? I could never keep them straight.

"He's involved in a case I'm working," I said. "Perhaps he mentioned it."

"A case involving the asshole to whom I was once married," she said.

"Yes," I said.

She said, "I had my reasons for turning tricks for him. What's yours?"

"I've worked for a lot of assholes," I said. "Mary Lou Goddard comes almost instantly to mind."

She almost smiled.

"Well," she said, "you got me there."

"You two still stay in touch?" I said.

"As far as I know," Natalie said, "there's no cell service in hell."

"I know how *my* business could involve Gabriel," I said. "What I'm trying to figure out is what business *you* might have with him."

She tilted her head to the side. Her face was still all hard angles and planes. But she was pretty, no getting around it.

"There's no business," she said. "We've just known each other a long time."

"Tony clearly sees him as a threat," I said.

"Tony sees almost everyone as a threat," she said. "Inside his organization and out."

"But how much of a threat might Gabriel present?"

"I forget the color schemes for threat levels," Natalie said. "But what's the highest?"

"Red," I said.

"Go with that," Natalie said. Again she almost smiled. Maybe it was the best she could do.

"Why?" I said.

"Just say they go way back."

"They have history, then," I said. "Gabriel never mentioned that."

"What's the old saying?" she said. "The friend of my enemy is my enemy?"

"It's actually the enemy of my enemy is my friend," I said.

She shook her head. "You're still a smart-assed bitch," she said, "aren't you?"

"But I'm making progress with you after all this time," I said. "You used to call me a honky bitch."

She wore a big watch on her wrist and made a show of looking at it now.

"What do you really want?" she said.

"I want to know if you might know something that might help me find the most recent woman in Tony's life," I said.

Natalie laughed, somehow managing that without changing expression, the sound harsh.

"You mean his latest whore?" she said. "At least she wasn't fool enough to marry him the way I did."

"You don't think he could possibly have real feelings for her?" I said.

"You mean other than in his pants?" Natalie said. "He's probably just worried she could fuck him over the way he's been fucking people over his whole life."

"Is that why your friend Gabriel wants to find her first?" I said.

"If she can help take Tony down, I hope he does," she said.

"Are you and Gabriel somehow involved in this together?" I said.

"Involved how?"

"However."

She sighed. "Now you do sound like a *dumb* honky bitch," she said.

"You know," I said, "it was Abraham Lincoln who said that knavery and flattery are blood relations."

"You really do talk a lot of shit, don't you?" Natalie said.

"I'm trying to quit," I said.

"Are we done yet?" she said. "I've let you stay here longer than I intended."

"How do you and Gabriel know each other?" I said.

"I told you," she said. "We go way back."

"Could you be more specific?"

"No," she said. "Anything else?"

"Yeah," I said. "I'm thinking that if you were really picking a side here, it might be the missing woman's. Because in a lot of ways, you were her once."

"Before Tony became *my* enemy," she said.

She stood. I stood. She walked around the couch and opened the door, standing there with her hand on the knob.

"Gabriel," she said, "is going to take Tony down with or without Lisa Morneau. He just feels that having her on his side will make it more enjoyable for him. And perhaps streamline the process."

"A lot have tried to put Tony out of business," I said.

"They were likely not as motivated as Gabriel," she said.

"Why?" I said.

"Good talk," she said.

As I walked past her she said, "I know Tony has threatened to kill you in the past. But if you get in Gabriel's way on *his way* to Tony, Gabriel just might."

"He told me he's not a killer," I said. "But thanks for the heads-up."

"I were you?" Natalie Goddard said, "I'd think twice about following him again."

There was nothing for either one of us to add to that. So I walked back down the stairs and out onto Revere Street, into a bright winter sun.

Yeah, I thought.

Good talk.

31

A FEW HOURS LATER Richie and I took Richard to the New England Aquarium.

Tony Marcus was still not returning my calls, which bothered me. Lisa still hadn't called me back. I had a plan for finding out more about Gabriel Jabari. But I knew the plan would require more preparation, even if it happened to be a variation of something that had once worked quite well with Natalie.

If somebody were still following me, all they were doing was what I was doing, bouncing around as randomly as a pinball, from a strip club to Callie Harden to Olivia Hewitt's home for wayward girls to Harvard Stadium to Paradise to Natalie's place on Revere. Maybe if I ever did find Lisa, it would all make sense.

Just not yet. And not close. I kept telling myself I had found my way out of the deep, dark forest before.

For now, though, a trip to the aquarium, one that included a six-year-old boy, seemed almost therapeutic. We spent an hour with the penguins. Richard said that he'd never seen a real one before, the only penguins he'd ever seen were in books and a movie he'd watched with his mom one time.

He loved the penguins. But, I thought, who didn't? Richie and I had come here early in our dating life. I'd loved them then and still did. We wandered around after that. We had lunch. After lunch Richard asked if he could see the penguins one more time. We did that.

Finally the boy looked at his father, plaintively, and asked if he had to go back to the hotel yet.

Richie looked at me.

"I'm good," I said.

Then I knelt down and looked at Richard and said, "Would you like to go back to my house and play with Rosie?"

"Yes!" he said.

"I know it's cold out," I said. "But we could even take her for a walk in the park."

"This is the best day ever!" he said.

Rosie wasn't much of a cold-weather dog. She didn't seem to mind the conditions much today. But by now I had reached the conclusion that a nuclear attack wouldn't bother her as long as she was with her new friend.

Richie had stayed behind at the house, saying he was

getting jammed by a couple of his delivery companies, and was desperately trying to unjam himself.

So Richard and I walked past the now-frozen lake that the swan boats toured in the summer, past the statue of George Washington, and then circled back so Richard could see the small duckling statues on the Beacon Street side of the Public Garden.

At one point the boy reached over and placed his hand in mine.

"My mom is going away," he said.

"I heard," I said.

"It scares me," he said.

"Would scare me, too," I said.

"But I try not to show it," he said. "I don't want my dad to worry about me."

"I think your dad is pretty proud of the way you're handling all this," I said. "For being as strong as you're being."

"I want to be strong like him," he said.

Boys and their fathers.

"You're doing just fine," I said.

"I want to be like him," Richard said. "I only knew how much I missed him until I got to be with him again."

I feel the exact same way, I thought.

I waited for him to take his hand out of mine. But he did not. All the way home.

When we got back to the house I made hot chocolate for everyone. Rosie frolicked with Richard. Richie and I drank hot chocolate and watched them.

Reluctantly, I asked how Kathryn was doing. He said she was a mess, that she'd come to Boston hoping that it might become some sort of new beginning but that now it seemed like just another dead end.

"I don't care how much of a mess she is," I said. "On what planet could she leave this kid for any extended period of time?"

"I think she views it as a vacation from the responsibilities of being a parent," he said.

"Not sure it works that way," I said. "The vacation part."

"I'm aware how self-absorbed she can be," Richie said, "even at her best."

I grinned. "Who the hell would marry someone like that?" I said.

"Not funny," he said.

"Is too," I said.

"Let's change the subject," Richie said. "Anything good happening in the case?"

"It just gets more confusing," I said, and told him about our adventure with Jabari the night before, my latest call from Lisa, my meeting with Natalie.

"Jabari and Tony have history?" Richie said.

"According to Natalie."

"That come up before?" he said.

"Nope," I said.

"Could this be a whole new grudge match?" he said.

"Yup," I said.

There was a squeal from the kitchen.

"Was that Richard or Rosie?" I said.

"Hard to tell," Richie said.

"Tony doesn't want to talk to me right now," I said.

Richie smiled at me. "When has that ever stopped you?" he said. "And maybe the junior pimp is a better way to go, anyway."

"He sees himself as more an entrepreneur," I said.

"So did my father," Richie said.

"Desmond was never a pimp," I said.

"So he says," Richie said.

"Tony says he didn't know anything about Jabari until he showed up in town," I said. "Do you think it's possible he might have screwed him over in the past and doesn't even know he did?"

"Be good to know," Richie said. "But would it help you roll things up with Lisa?"

"Beats the hell out of me," I said.

"Find the woman," Richie said, "find out what she has."

"Yes, sir," I said, and leaned up and kissed him on the mouth.

"Find out once and for all," Richie said, "if he really is more scared of losing her, or what she might have on him."

"Tony doesn't scare easily, we've long since established that," I said. "So what could scare him that much?"

Richie said, "Didn't you tell me that he might have more to fear from the cops right now than from anybody else?"

I had told him about my conversation with Jake

Rosen, if not about Rosen's flirtatiousness. And all-around cuteness.

"Maybe you should circle back to him," Richie said.

I told him that was such a good idea it was worth another kiss, and gave him one, longer than before. It might have lasted longer than it did if we hadn't heard another squeal from the kitchen.

"Not in front of the children," he said.

32

JAKE ROSEN AND I were having a drink at Shea's Tavern in Southie, on the corner of West Broadway. It looked like one of those places out of the fifties, or even before that, next door to Al's Bottled Liquors. We sat at a small table against a wall opposite the bar, right next to the shamrock stenciled into the floor. We were at Shea's because Jake said he had to meet a guy in Southie in about an hour.

"A guy?" I said.

"Who knows a guy," he said.

"Oh," I said. "*That* kind of guy."

"We never close," he said.

He was drinking Budweiser beer out of a bottle. I was nursing a Black Bushmills, having decided that ordering a pleasant chardonnay was pretty much out of the question at Shea's.

He was wearing the same basic uniform he'd been wearing when he'd showed up at my house: bomber jacket, jeans, and boots. This time he didn't have his badge hanging around his neck, perhaps not wanting to scare the customers. Still had the cool Bradley Cooper vibe going for him.

Still cute as hell.

Just because I was in a committed relationship didn't mean I couldn't look.

Or wonder what kind of kisser he might be.

"Could somebody besides Jabari be looking to make a move on Tony?" I said.

He drank some beer and wiped his mouth with the back of his hand, grinned, and leaned forward, focusing all of his attention on me.

"Everybody is always looking to make a move on everybody," he said. "It's why none of these guys wants to leave anything to chance."

"Like Lisa," I said.

"Anything new with her?" he said.

"Talked to her on the phone," I said.

"Where?"

"I was in bed."

"I meant her," he said.

"She said Boston."

"This may sound off-point," Rosen said, grinning. "But were you *alone* in bed when she called?"

"Wouldn't you like to know," I said.

Feeling a little flirtatious myself, despite the subject being discussed.

"A lot I'd like to know about you," he said.

I let it go.

"She sounded scared," I said.

"Of Tony?"

"I honestly couldn't tell," I said. "It sounds like she knows something she wasn't supposed to know."

"She say what it was?" Rosen said.

I shook my head.

"Tell her to come in," he said. "We can protect her. *I* can protect her."

"I was sort of thinking that might be my job," I said. "Bringing her in."

"Maybe you don't know what you're up against," he said.

"That's what they're saying," I said, "all over town."

He finished his beer and waved at the bartender for another. He looked at me. I put my hand over my glass. The bartender brought Jake his beer.

"So who's looking to make a move on Tony, if it's not Jabari?" I said to him.

"It could be somebody from what's left of Jackie DeMarco's outfit, even if I've been up in their shit lately," he said. "Or Eddie Lee, the king of Chinatown. I hear old Eddie's not too thrilled that Tony is getting into the massage-parlor business. Could even be some of the headbangers still working for your former father-in-law. I've had to take a crash course in the various factions. What I know is that a lot has changed. You know a lot of this. Joe Broz died. Somebody took out Gino Fish. Things aren't the same as they were with the Burkes now that Felix is dead. Bottom line? Tony thinks he's positioned himself to be the biggest guy in town. But that doesn't mean he's there yet, even with a lot of the competition falling back."

"So Lisa could be a threat, depending on what she might know," I said.

"Bet your ass," he said.

He smiled. I smiled.

"Not yours to bet," I said.

"Not yet," he said again.

He winked. Not all guys could carry off a solid wink, no matter how cocky they were. He could. And we were both quite aware that I was egging him on. Or just flirting with him as much as he was with me.

"Do you ever turn it off?" I said.

"When I'm dead," he said. "And maybe not even then." He reached over and tapped my glass with his bottle. We both drank. He pointed at my glass when I put it back on the table.

"If I'm trying to ply you with liquor," he said, "I seem to be doing a crap job."

"But you're showing a lot of heart," I said.

"Tell me you don't feel at least a little chemistry between us," he said.

"Not happening," I said. "No offense."

He grinned again. "None taken," he said.

He finished his beer in a long swallow.

"Listen," he said. "You and I, we're on the same side

of this. I know Tony got you into this in the first place, and I think I know why you got into this. But we both know this goddamn city would be a better place with him off the streets, same as your old man knew before us."

"I'm not my father," I said.

"Yeah," Jake said, almost sadly. "Me neither."

"I just don't want what happened to Callie to happen to Lisa," I said.

Rosen looked at me and shrugged. "Cost of doing business," he said, "when you know too much."

"Tough guy," I said.

"Can't survive if I'm not," he said. "Listen, I've got a chance to take Tony out of play here. And maybe Jabari at the same time. What I'd mainly like to do is head off a bunch more people getting killed and find out what Lisa Morneau knows. Knowledge is power."

"I've heard that one," I said.

"These guys think they have all the power," he said, "until they run into me."

"How do you think Jabari really fits into all this?" I said. "Last time I checked, he's just running a fancified strip club."

"It's more than that," he said. "He's picked off a few of Tony's girls, just to fuck with him. Opened a house a couple of blocks from where Tony's got that one over by Symphony Hall. And Tony's not the type to just let shit like that go."

"My ex-husband says that sometimes it's best to just get out of the way and let God sort things out," I said.

Jake said, "You don't think that way and neither do I. Or you wouldn't have your job and I wouldn't have mine."

He leaned forward one last time, put the blue eyes on me one last time, grinning again. Maybe there was a little chemistry going on here, not that I was going to tell him that.

"Tell you a secret?" he said.

"Sure."

"When it comes to *my* job, and the way I look at these assholes?" he said. "The one with the God complex is me."

33

I THOUGHT ABOUT STOPPING by Buddy's Fox to see if Tony might be around and willing to once again start speaking with the person he'd hired to find his missing girlfriend. But I was tired. Jake said he would have given me a ride home if he had more time, but did not.

"You have to see a guy," I said.

"A guy I actually needed to see more than you tonight," he said.

"Not sure *need* is the word you're looking for here, at least not where I'm concerned," I said.

"Speak for yourself," he said.

He said he'd be in touch. He'd parked his unmarked at a hydrant in front of Shea's. Clearly, cops got all the good parking spaces, even when they weren't spaces. I'd parked in a small lot behind Al's Discount, and experienced a thrill of excitement that my car was still there. I got in and cranked up the soundtrack from *A Star Is Born* and listened to it all the way home. How had Lady Gaga gotten to make out with the real Bradley and not me? Life wasn't fair. But I already knew that.

I turned off the alarm when I was through the front door and was promptly greeted, and quite enthusiastically, by Rosie the dog. If Tony didn't want to see me, at least she always did. I grabbed her leash and a waste bag and my gun out of my purse and took her out for her last walk of the evening. Poop bag and gun. I knew there was symbolism in there about the life I had chosen, the need to be packing when I walked my dog on the periphery of Beacon Hill. I wondered if any of the swells did the same over at Louisburg Square.

Rosie took her sweet time tonight. I reminded myself not to get impatient with her, that as wonderful and indispensable and even as humanlike as she could be—but only in the good ways—she was still a dog. Spike also reminded me of that all the time, especially when I would chastise him for saying hurtful things in front of the baby.

The first Rosie had been one kind of child for me. This Rosie felt the same way, only now there was a real child in my life. And as much as I told myself that the little boy was Richie's and Kathryn's, I knew he was going to be mine, too.

Rosie and I walked around back to what was known in the neighborhood as the Poop Loop. She still gave off none of her usual signs about getting busy anytime soon, so we walked up River Street a bit and then back. The street was empty except for the cars parked on the west side. We returned to the back of my building. The area was well lit back here. And I was armed, after all. Sunny and Rosie, Neighborhood Watch Patrol.

I heard a noise to my right near the basement art studio belonging to the woman who lived directly behind me.

We stopped. Maybe it had been my imagination. Maybe it had been the wind and the snow and the night and my own jangled nerves.

Or not.

Rosie did not growl, but the sound had gotten her full attention. And mine. I already had the .38 out of the side pocket of my vest. Maybe it really was my imagination. Or it was my friend from Harvard Stadium back for Round 2.

A figure stepped away from the shadows, out from behind the shelter of two SUVs parked against the wall. Light shone faintly onto the street from windows at the dead end of River Street.

Now Rosie low-growled.

I had her leash in my left hand and the gun in my right, pointed and steady. The .38 wasn't much for shooting anybody or anything at a distance. But this wouldn't be about distance shooting, if it came to that, and I had to fire off a shot that would scare the neighborhood.

"I have a gun," I said.

"I can see that," she said.

Lisa Morneau, lowering her hands, stepped fully into the light.

34

DOES YOUR DOG bite?" she said.

"Neither of us does," I said, and put my gun back into my pocket. Rosie's ablutions would have to wait. She'd had her chances.

"How did you get here?"

"I walked," she said. "I don't think I was followed. But I can't be sure. Not sure of anything these days."

She hugged herself against the cold.

"I need help," she said in a small voice. "I didn't know who else to ask for it."

"I can help you," I said. "But only if you let me."

"Only if it's not too late," she said.

She took a couple steps back toward the SUVs. So did Rosie and I. A treat had made Rosie stop growling.

"How long have you been waiting for me?" I said.

"A while," she said.

She wore a black vest, as if trying to blend into the night, and running shoes. Even seeing as little of her face as I could, I saw that she was prettier in person than in the picture Tony had given to me.

But everything about her, the sum of her own jangled nerves, indicated that she could bolt at any moment.

"Who is after you?" I said. "Is it Tony?"

"I told him we have to end this," she said.

"End what?"

"All of it!" she said.

"You spoke to him?"

"Little while ago."

She looked to her left, and to her right, her eyes no less frantic than they had been since we had started talking.

"He said he wanted me to find you because he cares about you," I said.

"Only now I'm the one who found you," she said.

I thought of all the questions I wanted to ask her, as if I could see them, one after another, written on a page.

"It's freezing out here," I said. "Let's go inside."

She hesitated, as if conducting a brief interior debate, and said, "Okay."

We walked, Lisa and Rosie and me, around to my front door. I opened it. Lisa went in first. We followed her.

"I can make coffee," I said. "You look like you could use warming up."

"Okay," she said.

I led her to the kitchen. She sat down at the table. I got a cup, and filled it with water, and inserted the pods into my Keurig.

As I did, she began speaking, almost to herself, tapping both hands nervously on the table in front of her.

"I need to explain to Tony, once and for all, that I'm not the threat to him," she said.

"Then who is?" I said.

She suddenly seemed out of breath.

"I don't want to do this anymore!" she said.

Makes two of us, I thought.

Keep her talking.

"How did you end up in Paradise?" I said.

"I'd go there sometimes, this little bed-and-breakfast, when I needed to clear my head for a couple of days," she said. "Paid cash this time. But told them at the desk, here's my number, if anybody came around looking for me, call me right away. Few nights ago, somebody did. So I ran again. I didn't want to end up like Callie."

"Callie knew where you were?" I said.

She nodded. I thought she might cry.

"I told her just enough to get her killed," she said.

"What do they want from you?" I said.

Still having no idea whatsoever who *they* were.

"They want to know if I told anybody their secret!" she cried.

"What secret?" I said.

She looked down at her watch.

"I have to go," she said.

I wondered if she might be on something.

"Wherever you're going, I'll go with you," I said. "You shouldn't go anywhere alone. You said you came here because you needed help."

"It always comes down to being the man," she said. "Doesn't it?" She looked at me, almost pleading. "Now Tony thinks I care what he had to do to *stay* the man? He's always done what he had to do. Does he think I don't know that?"

She seemed out of breath again. I felt as if I should be, chasing her around the conversation this way.

"I didn't *care* what kind of deal he made!" She shook her head. "It's like Tony says all the time. We're *all* whores in the end."

"Why did you leave?" I said. "Can you at least tell me that?"

"It was the young girls," she said. "I told him he had to stop working girls younger and younger. You know? Even younger than I was once. Getting beat up. Getting used up. Killing themselves or getting killed. It was on me, looking the other way on that as long as I did. I tried to tell Tony he ought to get out rather than do that. But he said he didn't have a choice. Wasn't his call. I said, 'You're Tony Marcus. You're the one makes the calls.' He said, 'Not anymore.' But I told him there's *always* choices. Told him we could leave together, he already had more money put away than he could ever spend. Go to the islands someplace. Go to Hawaii. Far away from here as we could be. Cash out and go."

"What did he say?" I said, knowing the answer almost before I'd asked the question.

"Laughed right in my face," she said. "Right before he told me he loved me as much as he'd ever loved anybody. Told me it didn't work that way for people like us, that we were serving out life sentences, we just couldn't see the bars."

Now she was crying.

"I can protect you," I said.

She looked at me, her eyes bigger than ever, shook her head. It was as if she were standing on some kind of fault line. Maybe she had been on it since leaving Tony. Maybe it had only gotten worse since Callie had died.

"Be back in an hour," she said.

"Where are you going?" I said.

"Place over in The Fens," she said. "Told Tony I'd meet him there. Settle things. Maybe even settle his mind once and for all. Remind him he's the one who's supposed to be the man. Or tell him I'm leaving him for real and never coming back."

"It makes no sense," I said, "coming to me for help and then running back to Tony. You know that, right?"

"Know more than I ever wanted to know," she said. "More than I should have."

She stood, her chair making a loud noise on the floor as she pushed back from the table.

"You got a bathroom I can use?" she said.

I told her there was one off the front hall. I said I'd show her. But when we were in the front hall, she was at the front door and opening it, in a blink.

"Lisa!" I yelled. "Wait!"

But she was already out the door, out on River Street Place, sprinting away from me, as fast a runner as Tony had said she was. I could run, too. Just not like her. I tried to chase her anyway, but finally gave up at the corner of Charles. She was already pulling away, heading in the general direction of the Public Garden.

"Goddamn it," I yelled, but only Rosie could hear, and perhaps the neighbors, because by now Lisa was already gone. On the run again.

35

SHE WASN'T BACK in an hour.

She had talked about a lot of things before she had gone flying out the door. But I hadn't learned nearly enough. She had obviously confided in Callie about Paradise. What else had she confided to her? She had spoken of secrets but not told me what they were. She had indicated Tony might not be entirely in charge of his own operation, but hadn't indicated why. Or who was.

She was frightened and frantic. A friend of hers had been killed, probably because of her. Someone had tracked her to Paradise. There was the concept in fiction of the unreliable narrator, I knew from my college English classes. How reliable was Lisa Morneau narrating her version of these events? Trying to pin her down had been like trying to hold water in my hands.

I sat a long time at the kitchen table, finally allowing myself a glass of whiskey, staring at my phone, waiting for it to ring. It did not.

Past one in the morning by now.

I kept replaying the scene behind the house, then in the kitchen, wondering how I could have done things differently. What, put my gun on her? Tie her up?

But now I wished I had. Anything was better than having her and then losing her.

Maybe Natalie had been right all along. Maybe I was a dumb honky bitch after all.

I had been tonight.

I called Spike.

"I had her and lost her," I said.

"Lisa," he said.

"She was waiting for me outside," I said. "I got her inside. Then she ran."

"Shit," he said.

"Yeah," I said, that was my sentiment, exactly. Then told him I was all the way back to the beginning, brilliant sleuth that I was. I didn't know where Lisa Morneau was, or if she was ever coming back.

36

MY CELL PHONE finally rang at a few minutes after two.

The screen read UNKNOWN CALLER.

I hoped it was Lisa, using another burner phone, calling to tell me she was safe and on her way back.

"She dead," Tony Marcus said.

I felt as if all the air had come out of me, all at once.

"Lisa," I said.

"Fuck yeah Lisa," he said.

I did not tell him that she had come to my house. Or that she had told me she was going to meet him. I wasn't sure why. But for the moment I was more interested in what he knew. The questions I wanted to ask him about what she'd told me—about him—could wait.

"Where?"

"One to the forehead," he said.

"No," I said. "Where did it happen?"

"Does it matter?" he said, and then gave me an address in The Fens, saying it was near Fenway Park. So she had been telling the truth about where she was going. Tony said it was one of the apartments Lisa had convinced him to rent for their high-roller customers who didn't want to go to one of the houses, the kind Olivia Hewitt had described to me when I'd visited her house.

"She must've kept a key," Tony said.

"Did you have something to do with this, Tony?" I said.

"Killing her?" he said. "I fucking loved her."

There was no strut or swagger in his voice now, none of his street-corner brio. Nor the thug in him. The man who had run women his whole life was only talking about one now.

I was out of bed now, walking across the room to where I'd left my jeans draped over a chair.

"Who found her?" I said.

"I found her," he said. "Who the fuck you think found her?"

"Do the police know?"

"You know," he said. "I know."

"Are you with the body?" I said.

"Hell no," he said. "She called me, told me we needed to talk. Said something about wanting to settle things, whatever the fuck that meant. Told me to meet her over at The Fens, she'd be there 'round one o'clock. I get there and walk in and find her dead on the floor."

I had my phone between my shoulder and cheek and was getting into my jeans.

"Where are you now?" I said.

"Back home," he said.

"Who else knew you were going to see her?"

There was a pause at his end.

"Couple of my boys," he said.

"You told no one else?"

"No."

"I'm sorry, Tony," I said. "I really am."

There was another pause at Tony's end before he said, "So am I."

I tapped the speaker key briefly so I could pull a turtleneck over my head. Rosie stared at me from her end of the bed as if knowing this wasn't the time of night for me to be getting dressed. I should have known Tony would leave her, that he couldn't be anywhere near a crime scene, certainly not with a dead girlfriend the cops already knew he'd hired me to locate. Lee Farrell had already questioned him in connection with the death of Callie Harden.

"I'm going over there," I said.

"Why?"

"Because I am," I said, and asked if I needed a key. He said he'd left the door unlocked.

Before he ended the call he said, "Remember what I told you about clients and privileges? You remember that before you tell anybody about this call I just made to you."

There was one last pause and then he said, "If I did

it, I wouldn't've fucking called you," before he ended the call.

There had been nothing for me to say in my defense. He was right. I was having some week. I'd gone to see Callie and a few hours later somebody had shot her dead. I had finally gotten with Lisa and now somebody had shot *her* dead. As soon as I ended the call with Tony I should have called Olivia Hewitt and Laura and Kourtney with a *K* and tell them to watch their backs.

I knew I could call in Lisa's death anonymously. Or I could call Lee Farrell and wake him up and tell him that Lisa Morneau had been murdered and where he could find her.

But then he'd want to know how I knew all that.

I wanted to go to The Fens first. I didn't know what I could do there or what I might find, but somehow I wanted to do better for Lisa Morneau in death than I had in life. I wanted to see her. To somehow see this through. I felt I owed her that.

I *wanted* to be the one who found her killer, and nailed his ass.

I DROVE OVER to Peterborough and parked around the corner from the address Tony had given me. The door was unlocked, as he'd said it would be. She was in the living room, next to a coffee table, on the floor, on her back. One shot to the head, like Tony had said. A stain of blood that had spread out like a halo. Her running shoes were splayed. Her eyes were closed. I wondered if

Tony had closed them. She was still wearing her vest. I stared down at her. She was another who had tried to get out of the life and now had no life at all.

I knelt down next to her now and felt the pockets of the vest. Nothing.

I had brought crime scene gloves with me that I kept around the house for special occasions. I put on the gloves and carefully reached under her and felt something in one of the back pockets of her jeans. I turned her just slightly and pulled out the small, thin ZTE phone. Maybe Tony hadn't thought to search her. Or simply didn't care, just wanted to get out of there as quickly as possible.

I placed the phone into the back pocket of my jeans, then reached into the side pocket of my vest and pulled out my phone and called Lee Farrell and told him where I was, and commenced lying my ass off about how I'd gotten there, and why, holding things back from him the way I just had with Tony Marcus.

37

LEE FARRELL AND I were having coffee at the South Street Diner, near the Tufts Medical Center, at six o'clock in the morning. We had finally left the crime scene at the apartment on Peterborough Street and gone back to headquarters so he could take my statement. The South Street Diner, I knew from experience, was open all night, even though we were well into the next morning.

"You had her," Lee said. "And then she ran."

"Clearly," I said, "I've lost a step. In more ways than one."

"But she didn't tell you where she was going."

"If she wanted me to know, she wouldn't have run," I said.

"And then you got a call."

"I did."

"Going to say something again," he said.

"I know what it is."

"Going to say it anyway," he said. "You are so fucking full of shit. Pardon my French."

"My father often says that when he uses bad language in front of me," I said.

"Do you lie to Belson like this?" Lee said.

"I'm not lying," I said.

"You're just not telling the whole truth," Lee said. "And nothing but."

I shrugged.

"You're telling me that an anonymous voice on the phone told you she was dead and where you could find her?" he said.

"That's what happened," I said.

"Bullshit," he said. "You expect me to believe you've turned into a one-woman Crime Stoppers tip line."

"I need sleep," I said.

"We're supposed to be friends," he said.

"We *are* friends," I said.

"I need to know who called you," he said, "because whoever it is happens to be a prime suspect in a goddamn homicide. Involving a woman you were probably the last person to see alive. Like the last ex-hooker you talked to before somebody aced *her*. Jesus, you're on some roll."

The waitress had left the pot of coffee. Lee poured himself more. He nodded at me. I shook my head. If I drank more coffee I wouldn't sleep until Presidents' Day Weekend.

"She said she needed to see somebody," I said. "To set things straight."

"Tony?" he said.

"Somebody," I said.

"Do you like him for this?" Lee said. "Tony, I mean. I'm going to talk to him either way."

"I never assume anything with him," I said. "He's Tony Marcus. If he did it, he just used me the way he uses everybody else."

Lee spooned more sugar into his coffee. "Tony's the type who always has a Plan B," he said.

I poured myself more coffee. What difference was more caffeine going to make at this point?

"I think he cared about her," I said.

"He must've cared about his ex-wife once, too," Lee said. "Now if you put the two of them together in a room it would be like throwing a couple of cats in a sack."

I had not yet told him about my meeting with Natalie. It was like the coffee: What difference did holding back one more thing make at this point? It was just a variation of the games I'd been playing with Frank Belson for years, much to my father's disappointment.

"Can you keep Lisa's visit to me between us for the time being?" I said.

"So you keep secrets from me, but I'm supposed to keep yours?" he said. "Got it."

"Can you?"

"Until I can't," he said.

"Thank you."

"You know I love you," Lee said.

"Uh-oh," I said. "Nothing great ever comes after that. It's like 'all due respect.'"

"But as much as I love you," he said, "I don't want you fucking up my case. And I sure as hell don't want you putting the interests of Tony Marcus above the law."

"I won't," I said. "And wouldn't."

He sadly shook his head.

"Still full of shit," he said. "He's a bad guy, Sunny. But you already know that."

"Doesn't mean he's good for this," I said. "And if I find out he is before you do, I'll be the first to tell you to hang him by his balls from the top of the State House."

He finished his coffee, tossed money on the table, and smiled.

"Powerful imagery," he said.

"I may be full of it," I said. "But I *was* a fine arts major."

38

I SAT IN THE kitchen drinking another cup of coffee that I needed about as much as I needed more shoes.

The phone that I'd pulled out of Lisa Morneau's back pocket was on the table in front of me. It was more than just her phone, I knew, whether it was a burner or not. It was evidence in a homicide investigation, one on which one of my best friends was running point. I also knew that the woman currently in charge of Homicide at the BPD, a captain named Glass, had never approved of my friendships with Lee Farrell, or Frank Belson, and did not much like that I occasionally got favored treatment from both of them because my father was Phil Randall. She would approve of me far less if and when she found that I had removed evidence from Lee's crime scene and had not yet told anybody that it was Tony Marcus who had discovered the body and not me.

But I did not view this as being their case. I viewed it as mine. In some way that I did not yet fully understand, I was at least partly responsible for two women being dead. I promised myself I'd get to the bottom of it.

I picked up the phone. I had put my gloves back on. I didn't know if someone other than Lisa had ever touched the phone, so was just being careful, in case I did ever feel the need to turn the phone over to the police.

It occurred to me again that the phone felt about as small as a credit card. I did not know enough about phones like this one to know what kind of memory it had.

It did have a call log.

She had placed only two calls on it. The first, I saw, was to Tony Marcus's number, one I had been calling a lot over the past week with only occasional success. The second call was placed more than an hour before Tony had called me, and thus much closer to the time when she had to have been shot. Maybe Lee Farrell would eventually tell me what the ME had established as the time of death, if he was in a mood to share information. All I knew was that by the time Tony had called me he had found Lisa at The Fens and returned home. I did not know where his primary residence was these days. I wondered if anyone other than Junior and Ty Bop knew.

I did not recognize the second number.

But Lisa had apparently called somebody after she had called Tony.

The phone, I saw, had plenty of battery power left, and thus was still operational.

I sipped more coffee, feeling silly holding my cup while wearing crime scene gloves. I was thrilled to see that despite all the caffeine in me, my hands had only a small case of the shakes. Small favors.

It was seven o'clock in the morning by now. The person Lisa had called was likely still sleeping. Unless, of course, that person had gone on the run the way Lisa had been on the run.

There had been no phone on Callie Harden when her body had been discovered at Joe Moakley Park, nor had one been found at her apartment. So her killer had taken her phone with him. Or her.

This time the killer had left a phone in Lisa's jeans. Had the shooter simply not checked once she was dead and on her back? Or been careless. Or had to leave in a hurry?

It seemed a logical assumption that the same person had shot both of them, but I couldn't take that as fact yet. I remembered the joke from the old *Odd Couple* TV show, Tony Randall standing at a blackboard and breaking up the word *assume* in a courtroom scene.

"When you assume," he said, "you make an *ass* out of *u* and *me*."

It was now official that I'd had way too much coffee.

I picked up the phone again. I had already used a

SIM card reader I had once bought on another case, and USB drive, to copy any other information that might be on Lisa's phone. Spike was a gadget guy. He could check it out for me later, see if there was anything else useful in the phone's memory before I turned it over to Farrell and apologized for being a bad, bad girl.

For now, even wearing the gloves, I carefully tapped the last number Lisa had called, and soon was listening to one ring after another.

I waited to be sent to voicemail, perhaps a generic message that told me nothing about whose phone it was. Or maybe it would just keep ringing into infinity, and no one would ever answer.

Then someone did.

"This is Gabriel," he said.

39

I WONDERED IF HE could hear me breathing.

"Whoever the fuck this is better have a good reason for waking my ass up at this hour," he said.

Still I said nothing.

Finally he said, "Well, fuck you, Mr. Unknown Caller," and hung up.

That's Ms. Unknown Caller to you, I thought.

AGAINST ALL ODDS I then managed to get a few hours of sleep, having set an alarm for eleven o'clock. Then I called Gabriel Jabari back, this time from my cell. He asked how I'd gotten the number. I told him he'd given it to me when he tried to hire me that day in his car, even though he most certainly had not.

"Why are you calling me?" he said.

"To invite you to lunch," I said.

"Why would I want to do that?" he said.

"Because I want to share some information I have connecting you to the death of Lisa Morneau," I said.

Now I could hear his breathing.

"Wait," he said. "What? She's dead?"

"Somebody shot her in the head."

"When?"

"Early this morning," I said. "Over in The Fens."

"I don't know anything about that," he said.

"As I said, I have information that might suggest otherwise," I said.

"Well whatever information you think you've got is bullshit information, is what it is," he said. "I haven't seen the woman since the night she came to the club."

"Sea Grille," I said. "Almost right across the street from where you live."

He waited and then said, "One o'clock."

I'd wanted to get his attention, and knew I had succeeded. Now I wanted to see his reaction when I showed him my cards. *Look 'em in the eye,* Phil Randall had always said.

Before leaving for the Sea Grille, which was part of the Boston Harbor Hotel, I called Spike back. He let me tell him everything that had happened since our last phone call without interrupting. When I finished he said, "It's got to be one of them. Tony or Gabriel."

"Maybe it's as simple as Jabari wanting to hurt Tony as badly as he could by taking away something—or someone—Tony could never get back," I said. "What better revenge than that?"

"We still don't know revenge for what," Spike said.

"Maybe I can learn that at lunch today," I said.

"You're so good at drawing people out," he said, "at least until they threaten to shoot you."

"I still don't see Tony for this," I said.

"Unless he was lying to you all along about why he wanted her back," Spike said. "And she did have something on him. And was reckless enough or just plain dumb enough to think she could use it against him. Then he shot her. Or, more likely, Ty Bop did."

He paused. "I assume there was no bullet or casing found?"

"Nope."

"Let's say for the sake of this conversation he did do it," Spike said. "Why call you after he did?"

"Head fake? To give himself cover, at least with me?"

"Why leave the phone?"

"I've been asking myself that same question," I said.

"You think maybe you were supposed to find it?" Spike said.

"Been asking myself that, too," I said. "Maybe if it is Tony, he wanted to point the finger at the other guy."

"Or the other guy gets careless this time," Spike said. "Or didn't roll her over and check."

"In which case," I said, "it would be like Lisa pointing the finger at him."

I sighed, with feeling.

"Do you ever long for a simpler life?" I said.

"I actually used to have one before I started hanging around with you," he said.

We agreed to meet for a drink later at his place. Before leaving the house I took a picture of Lisa's call log with my own phone. Then I left Lisa's phone in the small safe on the top floor of the house, where I had my studio. The safe was now behind one of my paintings, of the Marblehead Lighthouse, from a photograph I'd once taken from Chandler Hovey Park when Jesse Stone and I had taken a ride over there.

When I got to the Sea Grille, Gabriel Jabari was already seated at a table near the window, facing the dock and the water. I passed Gled, who sat at a chair in the lobby near the hostess stand with a direct view of Jabari's table.

Jabari was wearing a tight-looking black blazer, buttoned, over a white shirt. I was business casual, dressed for success, black pants and a blue collared shirt, just slightly darker than a blue cable sweater vest. My .38 was in my purse.

The water and sky seemed to be the same color today. If you looked far enough out, it was almost impossible to distinguish where the ocean ended and the sky began.

When I was seated Jabari said, "Are we really going to eat?"

"I'm buying," I said.

"No shit," he said.

We ordered drinks and food at the same time. He ordered the Cobb salad with shrimp, and a spicy Bloody Mary. I went with the kale Caesar and sparkling water.

When the waitress left he said, "I didn't fucking do it."

"Didn't say you did."

"But you said you had evidence connecting me to it," he said.

"I do!" I said brightly.

I took my phone out of my purse and clicked on the picture I'd taken of Lisa's phone, one that showed only his number.

"That's your number," I said.

"I know my damn phone number," he said. "Doesn't prove nothing."

"She placed that call to your number not long before someone shot her in the head," I said.

"Proves nothing," he said again.

"Proves she called you while she was still alive," I said.

"*Somebody* called me from that phone," he said. "I was still at the club. I usually don't pick up when I see UNKNOWN CALLER. This time I did, for some reason. Only nobody says anything at the other end. I finally told them to fuck off and hung up."

"As you did with me when I called you early this morning," I said.

"That was you?" he said.

"I needed to find out whose number it was," I said.

"Somebody's trying to set me up," he said.

Our food and drinks came then. Again he waited until the waitress was gone.

"Natalie says that you have a long-standing grudge

against Tony," I said. "One you neglected to mention either of the previous times we spoke."

"Got nothing to do with somebody shooting Lisa," he said.

"You wanted me to find her for you instead of Tony," I said.

"Find her," he said. "Not kill the bitch."

I let that go.

"If you wanted to inflict the most possible pain on Tony, why not kill her if you found her yourself?" I said.

"Didn't."

"You say."

He was, I noted, an almost obsessively neat eater. He had lifted the shrimp out of his salad and lined them up on his butter plate. Then he had carefully cut up the lettuce. I wondered, if he'd wanted the salad to be chopped, why he hadn't just asked.

"Listen to me," he said. "You got to understand something, once and for all. It's Tony I want to fuck with here. I had no truck with her."

He pointed at my phone.

"You tell him yet that there was a call to me?" he said.

"No."

"That the truth?"

"I have no reason to lie to you," I said.

"You going to tell him?"

"Only if I think it gets me to where I want to go," I said.

"Might start a war, you do," he said.

"I was under the impression that's what you wanted," I said.

He drank some Bloody Mary, wiped the corners of his mouth with his napkin.

"I'll be the one to take it to him when the time comes," he said. "Not the other way 'round."

"What did he do to you?" I said.

"Doesn't matter what it was," Gabriel Jabari said. "Just *that* it was."

He seemed in no rush to work his way through his salad. Every few bites he would cut off a small piece of blackened shrimp.

"What is your relationship with Tony's ex-wife?" I said.

"What did she say it was?"

"She said you two go way back."

"That's a fact," he said.

"She hates him, too," I said.

He smiled. "Sometimes you can build a dream on shit like that," he said.

Then he took what looked to be a final sip of his Bloody Mary. He hadn't touched his celery stalk. It showed me an iron will. I could never resist.

"I'm done," he said.

"You haven't finished your food," I said.

"Meant that I'm done with *you*," he said. "At least for now."

He stood. I looked up at him and said, "I'll be in touch."

"Or," he said, smiling again, "maybe it will be the other way around."

He walked past the hostess stand and I watched as he and Gled made their way in the direction of the front lobby. When they were out of sight, I put on my leather gloves and reached across for the stem of his water glass and slid it to my side of the table. Then I looked around the room to see if anybody was watching me, leaned down, opened my purse, and placed my napkin inside it.

Then I turned slightly toward the window and the dock and the water and the gray afternoon, and gently placed Jabari's glass on top of the napkin before closing the purse.

If Gabriel Jabari were in the system, so were his prints. Which I now had.

No such thing as a free lunch.

40

I CALLED DARCY GAINES on the way back from the Sea Grille and asked if she had heard about Lisa Morneau. She said she had, but couldn't talk about it right now, she was swamped with actual police business of her own. She said she didn't know when she would have her head above water, but would call me when she did.

"I might need another favor," I said, "but I need to explain what kind in person."

"Until then," Darcy said, "I'll be sustained by even the chance that I might continue to serve and protect Sunny Randall."

I told her that sarcasm didn't become her. She said, "Become this."

When I got home I grabbed another pair of crime scene gloves out of the box of them I kept in the cupboard. Then I carefully removed the glass from my purse and placed it in one of those large Ziploc freezer bags. As I did, I remembered the time I had pretended to act clumsily and knocked a glass of Natalie's off a table, at a restaurant on Newbury Street. I had kept the glass, had the prints run, and found out that her real name was Verna Lee Lister. It was the beginning of what had become a less-than-beautiful friendship.

So now our lives had intersected again because of a prior relationship with Gabriel Jabari. So it turned out she was friends with a sworn enemy of Tony Marcus's, an enemy who was the only other suspect I had for Lisa Morneau's murder. Jabari said he hadn't done it. Tony said the same thing. One of them was lying. At this point in my life, even knowing more about Tony Marcus than I ever wanted to know, I found myself wanting to know a whole lot more about Gabriel Jabari.

I was boiling water for stress-relief tea that Spike had bought for me when I heard the chimes of the doorbell. When I pulled back the draperies in the front hall enough to look out, I saw Tony Marcus standing at the door. Junior and Ty Bop were behind him at the end of the front walk, standing near what I knew was an armored Cadillac Escalade, just because Tony had once bragged about owning one, as if the armor part would impress me.

I imagined how exciting this was for the neighbors.

"WOULD YOU MIND terribly asking the guys to wait in the car?" I said before showing Tony in.

"Neighborhood could use a little diversifying," he said, stretching the last word out as if it were made of taffy.

"If it's all just the same," I said.

He turned in the open doorway and made a swift motion with his hand that could have meant "get back in the car" or "storm the Charles Street Meeting House, guns blazing."

Tony was wearing a black topcoat. I told him I'd hang it for him. He said, "Wood hanger, you don't mind."

I told him I was having tea, and asked if he'd like to join me. He said, "Cream, two sugars." I went to the kitchen and came back with mugs for both of us. He took the couch. I took one of the chairs across from it.

High tea. Tony and me.

"You could have called first," I said.

"Had some business in the neighborhood," he said.

"This neighborhood?" I said.

He drank some of his tea. "One of these days, missy," he said, "you gonna come to the realization that you don't know nearly as much about my business as you think you do."

He wore a pale gray three-piece suit not much darker than its pinstripes, a blue shirt with a spread collar, and a navy silk tie with one of those knots that looked as big as a fist. His pocket handkerchief matched the tie. He crossed his legs. The shine on his cap-toed shoes nearly gave off a beam of light.

"Why are you really here?" I said.

"As a favor."

"To whom?"

"Whom," he said. He smiled. "Favor to you-m."

Now I smiled.

"What kind of favor?"

"I'm thinking that whoever killed Lisa wanted to know what she knew about me," he said. "And now they might think you know."

"I don't."

"But the killer don't know what you do or don't," he said.

"And I still don't know what the killer might have wanted to know about you," I said. "Which takes us all the way back to the beginning."

"Only now she dead."

"She didn't shoot herself in the head," I said.

"You really think I had her done?"

"Gun to *my* head?" I said. "I don't. But if you did, or had somebody do it, I'm going to find out."

"Are you sure that time you talked to her on the phone she never told you nothing it got out, it could hurt me?"

He still did not know she had come here. I still could think of no good reason to tell him. Lisa had her secrets. I had mine.

I shook my head and said, "She did not."

"You sure you telling me everything you know?" he said.

"You ever tell me everything *you* know?" I said.

"Let me take care of this now," he said. "Especially if it was Jabari had her done."

"Tony," I said, "if you actually think I'm going to drop this you know less about my business than you say I know about yours."

He leaned forward and put his face in his hands and rubbed the sides of it hard.

"You got to know that sometimes street justice is the only kind works," he said.

"You think it's Jabari?" I said.

"Don't you?" he said.

He reached into the inside pocket of his jacket and came out with a check and a Montblanc pen.

"Check all right to settle up?" he said. "Or I could have Junior come by later with cash."

"Neither."

"We need to close the books, you and me," he said. "Way I see it, we even now."

"I never actually thought of you as my client," I said. "I thought of her as my client. And now she's dead. So I don't want your money. I *never* wanted your money."

"You saying my money ain't good?" he said.

"Even if I ever did think about taking it, I didn't earn it," I said. "Turned out we both found her. Just too late."

"Have it your way," he said. "Just make sure what got her killed don't get you killed."

"Didn't know you cared that much, Tony," I said.

"Comes and goes," he said.

He stood.

"How come you didn't tell the cops was me found the body?" he said.

"The fact that I haven't yet doesn't mean I won't," I said.

"That a threat?"

"More of an observation," I said.

"Don't be looking to start up another grudge with me just when we about to clear the last one," he said.

"*That* a threat?" I said.

"Observation," he said.

"If we both want to find out who killed her," I said, "that puts us on the same side of this."

I got his coat out of the closet and handed it to him.

"I'm on my side," he said, "like always."

"What are you afraid of, Tony?" I said.

"My business," he said.

"A girl could take that a lot of ways," I said.

"Couldn't she, though?" he said.

41

IT WAS AFTER seven when Darcy Gaines got back to me. She was just leaving the Family Justice Center. She asked what the favor was. I told her about the glass and the prints. She said she had a friend at the lab, but since it wasn't a priority, the earliest they could run the prints was next week.

"You want to meet up in the morning so I can give you the glass?" I said.

"How about a drink right now?" she said. "Because I could goddamn well use one."

I told her I was on my way to Spike's. She said she kept a change of clothes at the office for situations involving emergency cocktails; that way, Spike's other customers wouldn't think it was a raid.

"My husband got to make the mac-and-cheese after my daughter's hockey practice tonight," she said.

"I didn't know she played hockey."

"She's the kind of player her mommy would be," Darcy said. "When she goes into the corner, she comes out with the puck."

Spike and I were at a corner table in the back room when Darcy showed up. By then I had told Spike about Tony's call and taking the phone off Lisa's body, and telling Lee Farrell about neither event. Spike said he promised to visit me at Massachusetts Correctional, but couldn't promise it would be every single Sunday, especially not during the pro football season.

Spike and Darcy had met a few times in the past. As he hugged her he said that the only times he'd broken any laws lately were because I had made him.

She sat down and told him she needed a martini, and fast, and it better be good. Spike waved over our waiter and told him the same thing, and that it was an official request from law enforcement.

Darcy wore a lavender pullover and jeans that were bad-girl tight. I told her she still cleaned up nicely. She said, "Blah, blah, blah. Where's the glass?"

I took the Ziploc bag out of my purse and she put it in her own.

"I'm thinking this guy might just turn out to be Tony on training wheels," she said.

"He appears to have a loftier vision of himself, and his professional pursuits," I said.

"Yeah," Darcy said. "Don't they all?"

The waiter came back with her drink. Dirty martini, four olives, Beluga Gold Line vodka, Russian, which Spike said was the best the mother country had to offer.

"Those mothers," Darcy said.

We all clicked glasses and drank. Darcy closed her eyes as the first taste ran through her. "But God bless America," she said in a husky voice.

"You look tired," I said.

"Thank you."

"That doesn't mean unattractive."

She grinned. "Thank you for that, too."

"Anything in particular?"

"It's not just one thing," she said. "Sometimes it just feels like everything. The last couple of months there've been a bunch of those skeevy massage parlors sprouting up like mushrooms. Providence police got a tip last week about one of those pop-up brothels that have become all the rage. And the guy who seemed to be in charge, it turns out, used to run women doing hotel work for Tony. So the guy immediately lawyers himself up with a local attorney who, shall we say, seemed to exist in a world slightly above this particular perp's means."

"Where is he now?"

"In the wind, as we like to say in the business," she said.

"Pop-up brothels?" Spike said. "Like vendors at the Public Market at Christmas?"

"They take short-term leases, or even go through

Airbnb," she said. "A week at a time. Maybe two. They generally stay until the neighbors wonder about the parade of assclowns going in day and night. But you do enough of them, you can make a very nice killing before moving on to the next."

"With young girls," I said.

"Goddamn it all to hell," she said. "I actually thought Tony had moved away from high school girls. Maybe not. I still haven't been able to get a legit ID for the kid who OD'd. I wonder if she was somebody else who was just collateral damage."

She drank more of her martini. She seemed happy to have it, happy to talk, happy to have us listen.

"Over the past couple of months," she said, "there has been an uptick, up and down the coast, of young girls disappearing from shelters and group homes, and a concurrent uptick in runaways." She shook her head. "And those are the runaways getting reported, because so often with these kids they're on the run from abusive situations."

"And then transition into the life," I said, remembering Millicent Patton.

"They recruit them in all sorts of ways," she said. "The pimps have charming young guys on the lookout all the time. They find these girls at the mall, at train stations and bus terminals and in the park when the weather is nice. They offer them a place to stay, they offer them drugs. Same old same old. Sometimes they move them back and forth between Boston and New York and Philly."

"High school girls," Spike said.

"Give the people what they want," she said. "These girls think there's never been anything good in their life, and now they're getting paid to do something they *are good* at. Or so they tell themselves."

"Until they figure out that they've just changed abusers," Spike said.

"Sometimes I don't just want to arrest the pimps," Darcy said. "I want to kill them all." She shook her head. "And, might I add, this is all going on while there's been a boom in trafficking of young girls from other countries."

I looked at her. Somehow, out of uniform, she looked as pretty as she ever had. And so much younger than she had in uniform. I wondered, and not idly, if she looked at me and thought I had aged as well.

I had been nursing my own martini. I drank some of it now. And was already debating whether or not to have another.

"If Tony really is skewing younger again," Darcy said, "I will make it my personal mission to fuck him up as badly as I can, whether I get in Jake Rosen's way or not."

"I'm just curious," Spike said. "When you two were with the cops, did you take swearing training together?"

Darcy said, "We just both come by it naturally."

"But if you guys do take down Tony, doesn't that leave the field open for an up-and-comer like Jabari?" I said.

"Unless I take the up-and-comer down, too," Darcy said.

She finished her drink, staring sadly at her glass as soon as she had, then asked Spike how much a bottle of Beluga Gold Line cost. He told her she didn't want to know.

Darcy looked at me. "You think Tony and Jabari are getting ready to fight for the title?" she said.

"It's a boxing reference," Spike said, grinning.

"I know what it means," I said. "What I don't know is the title of what."

42

JAKE ROSEN CALLED and woke me up at eight the next morning.

"Too early," I said.

"You know how New York is supposed to be the city that never sleeps?" he said. "Well, last night it was Boston."

"Do tell."

"Somebody took a shot at your pal Gabriel Jabari around five hours ago," Rosen said. "Sadly, they missed."

"Where?" I said.

"Getting out of his car near where he lives," he said. "Franklin and Broad."

"I know where he lives," I said.

"Anyway," Rosen said, "the big Russian guy who drives him around and acts as his body man—"

"Gled," I said.

"You gonna let me tell this?"

"Sorry," I said. "My manners aren't fully awake."

"So Gled the Russian guy gets out on his side and walks around to Jabari's side. Shooter steps out from behind a couple of cars parked in front of the Vintage. Somehow the Russian guy spots the shooter, shoves Jabari back into the car. Takes one to the shoulder, but still manages to fire off a couple of rounds himself before the guy takes off. He's gonna live. The Russian. Doesn't know whether he shot the shooter or not."

"And you wanted me to be the first one to know," I said.

"Well, the first one who happens to be the one who found Lisa Morneau's body," he said.

"I take it you'd like to talk further about this?" I said.

"I'm at headquarters," he said. "But could come to you."

"No," I said.

"If you're worried about being alone with me," he said, "remember you've got that attack dog to protect you."

"Let me get ready for the day, and then meet me at George Washington in an hour," I said. "I could use exercise, and some air."

We met at the statue of George Washington in the Public Garden at a little after nine on a sun-splashed morning trending far more toward spring than winter. Jake Rosen was dressed as always. It was impossible to imagine him wearing anything other than his bomber jacket, even if we met here in a heat wave on the Fourth of July.

"How come you didn't bring your dog?" he said.

"She hates you," I said.

"She's a girl dog, right?"

"She is."

"Then she couldn't possibly hate me," he said. "She just doesn't know me well enough yet."

We headed for the bridge from which you could stand and watch the swan boats in summer. Rosen was wearing aviator sunglasses today. They looked cool on him. He had one of those day-old growths of beard that looked exactly the same as the day-old growth he'd had the last time we had been in each other's presence. I wondered if people passing us as we made our way toward Charles Street and the Common thought us a couple.

"Gotta be Tony," Rosen said.

"As if wishing could make it so," I said.

"Hell yeah," Jake Rosen said, and gave me the lopsided grin.

"I'm sure you know that Darcy thinks Jabari is starting to traffic in young girls," I said. "He could have other enemies other than Tony. As Tony has far more than just him."

"Come on," he said. "Tony's the enemy whose girlfriend got shot dead two nights ago. What I'm trying to figure is why Tony would think Jabari had something to do with it." He turned to look at me while we waited for the light at Charles. "Got any theories on that?"

"They both wanted me to find her," I said. "If Tony didn't kill Lisa, maybe he thinks the only one who could have is Jabari. As you can imagine, Tony's big on street justice."

"Who isn't?" Rosen said.

"Aren't you sworn to enforce the law?"

"Yeah," he said. "Mine."

We crossed Charles and angled toward the playground tucked up near the corner of Boylston and Tremont. My father used to take me here as a child, when we would have one of our father-daughter days in the city, when the whole city felt like a playground to me. But inevitably we would spend time in this part of the park.

"I have to find out what finally got her shot," I said.

Rosen said, "Maybe it's better that whatever secrets she had, she died with them."

"I need to know," I said.

"You know what I don't need right now?" he said. He ran a distracted hand through his wavy hair. "A shooting war with these assholes, not when I've been slowly picking them off left and right."

"You still haven't picked off Tony."

He grinned again. "Getting there."

We were underneath the monkey bars by now. I pictured myself jumping up and grabbing hold of one of the bars and making my way from one end to the other as quickly and effortlessly as I had when I was ten, wondering if Jake Rosen would be impressed.

He pushed his sunglasses to the end of his nose and looked over them at me with amazingly blue eyes.

"There's shit you're not telling me," he said.

"You should actually be flattered."

"How do you figure?"

"Usually I have to know a cop much longer than I've known you before I hold shit back," I said.

I smiled at him.

"Maybe Tony thinks Lisa might have told Jabari something damaging about him before he killed her."

"Got any theories about what it might be?"

"Nope," I said.

"Would you tell me if you did?"

"I will tell you this," I said. "I'm going to find out everybody's goddamn secrets before I'm through. Somebody broke into my house already. I already pulled a gun on a guy following me."

"What guy?" he said.

"Almost doesn't matter," I said. "What mattered was the threat. I'm going to tell you something I never say out loud, because it sounds like I'm trying too hard to be a tough guy. But you don't run me off by threatening me. You better come at me with something better than that."

"I believe you," he said.

"I'm going to find out who killed her," I said. "This

all happened on my watch. I'm going to find out who killed her and who killed Callie Harden."

"You're a tough goddamn out."

I told him that I usually didn't care much for baseball analogies, but that he happened to be right this time.

I *was a* tough goddamn out.

43

IF TONY MARCUS did send somebody to shoot Gabriel Jabari, it raised the question of why the shooter missed. Because Ty Bop, from everything I knew about his résumé, missed what he was shooting at about as often as he read James Joyce.

I called Vinny Morris, the best shooter since Wild Bill Hickok, and asked if he thought Ty Bop could have missed from where the shooter stood in front of the Vintage to the sidewalk in front of Jabari's building.

"You said the bodyguard turned and saw something?" Vinny said.

"Apparently."

"That's one thing could've thrown him off," Vinny said.

"And the other being?" I said.

"Whatever Ty Bop might have ingested before the festivities began," Vinny said.

"Ingested?"

"I listen to that Doctor Radio on the satellite when I'm riding around in the car sometimes," he said.

So I guessed I still couldn't rule out Ty Bop as the shooter.

Two nights later, the cops hit two brothels not unlike Olivia Hewitt's, one in Cambridge, one in Charlestown. Each had sixteen-year-old girls working at them. A state senator was arrested at the place in Cambridge. They clipped a radio talk-show host in Charlestown. The women in charge were instantly represented by high-powered lawyers I knew had done work for Tony Marcus before. His name didn't show up in any of the news coverage, but I had no doubt that the places were his. I had even less doubt Jabari had somehow tipped off the cops, not only as to the locations of the houses but who was working there, and what caliber clientele would be on the premises when the cops showed up. He couldn't have done more damage to Tony with pipe bombs.

I called Jake Rosen when I heard about the raid.

"That's all Darcy," he said. "I think she's the one who got the call about the ones to watch. That's how they got the senator and the radio dude."

"Does this help you or not with Tony?" I said.

"All it does is make Tony more careful," he said, "and make my job harder. There wasn't a single scrap of paper tying Tony to any of these places." There was a pause and then he said, "You know who this really helps? Your friend Darcy. Her name and her picture are back in the news. That's like porn for her."

"I thought there was no *i* in *team*?" I said. "Isn't that what you guys always say?"

"Yeah," he said, "but there's still one in *bitch*."

He was right about Darcy being back in the news. There she was, in uniform, on all the six o'clock local news shows, being introduced by the chief in front of police headquarters despite the cold. Darcy was quick to point out that the story here wasn't the boldfaced names who'd been charged, it was the ages of some of the girls involved.

"But the story is as old as the world's oldest profession," Darcy Gaines said. "If men don't buy, pimps can't sell."

I shut off the television and once again wondered how Natalie fit into the looming war between Tony and Jabari. Was it possible that she somehow still knew enough about Tony's operation—or knew someone who did—to have jammed him up this way by tipping off Darcy Gaines on where she could catch a couple big fish?

When I thought Darcy had finished with her close-ups I texted her and congratulated her on being a television star. Her answer was for me to shut up.

I typed back:

Prints?

Her answer was that she still didn't have them, but when she did, I would.

I was about to make myself an amazing Cobb salad for dinner when Richie called.

"I'm having dinner with Kathryn," he said.

"Good to know," I said.

"She's really doing it," he said. "Leaving Boston."

"And leaving you with your son," I said.

"Yes."

I reached for the glass of white wine on the counter and drank some, only because the bottle wasn't close enough for me to drink out of that.

"Where's she going?" I said, hopeful that he might say the moon.

"Los Angeles. Her best friend from college just got divorced."

"Now you're the single parent," I said. "Does Richard know all of this?"

"Most," Richie said.

"How's he taking it?"

"He's acting pretty brave," Richie said.

"He *is* brave," I said. "And good. And kind of perfect, all in all."

"I know," he said. "I'm lucky to have him."

"He's lucky to have you," I said. "But just because he's acting strong doesn't mean that he is. They leave London. They come here. New school. New friends. Almost like a new dad, considering how little time the two of you spent together before this. Now she's going to leave him behind. He might need you right now as much as he ever will."

He waited. I waited. I drank more wine.

"I can't do this without you," Richie said.

"Yes," I said, "you can."

"It's something we need to do together."

"That has become a rather familiar theme," I said.

"I believe it," he said.

"When is she leaving?"

"Day after tomorrow. I told her I'd drive her to the airport."

"Let me," I said.

"It really is going to be you and me and Richard now," Richie said.

"Like a team," I said.

"If you want to put it that way."

Then I told him that while there was no *i* in *team* there was one in *bitch*, I didn't know if he'd heard that one.

44

I HAD AN APPOINTMENT scheduled with Susan Silverman the next morning, and was glad for it.

The temperature was back in the low thirties. I decided that it was just warm enough—or not cold enough—that I would walk to her office.

It was, I knew from having made this walk a few times before, four miles or so from my house to hers. I left myself an hour and a half. If I gave up and decided to call for a car, I had time for coffee before my appointment. On the way I thought more about Tony and Jabari. Battle of the Boston Pimps. Maybe it could be a new reality series. I tried to empty my brain of thoughts about Richie and Richard and save them for Susan Silverman. Why I paid her the big bucks.

When I arrived Susan was wearing a navy suit jacket

and skirt, white shirt underneath. I noticed, and not for the first time, that in addition to a beauty that seemed almost effortless, she had a sensational figure.

I began by telling her of my conversation with Richie the night before, and Kathryn's impending departure for Los Angeles.

"I should fix her up with an old boyfriend of mine out there," I said.

"The agent," she said.

"Good memory," I said.

She smiled.

"Tony Gault is his name," I said.

"It did not end well between the two of you, as I recall," she said.

"Multiple times," I said. "But you know me. I'm a game girl."

"You're not here to talk about old boyfriends, I'm guessing," she said.

I sighed. It sounded as if it had come from a whole church choir of sighers.

"Richie keeps telling me we can handle this," I said.

"Having a child," she said. "Or at least sharing one."

"Maybe he can," I said. "I don't think I can."

"Up to now," Susan Silverman said, "this is something both of you have only imagined in the abstract."

"Only this is no longer symbolic thinking," I said. "Maybe I know myself better than I ever have, more than somewhat because of you. And I know that I'm not ready for this. And might not ever be ready, not that I've yet mentioned that to Richie."

"But you've said you're quite fond of the boy," she said.

"And could likely learn to love the boy," I said. I sighed again. "Just not in my own space."

I surprised myself by how hard I stepped on the last word. Susan Silverman waited now. She was good at it. I'd always thought she could win medals for waiting.

"I've been able to create enough space for Richie and I . . ." I reached up with my right hand, as if trying to somehow catch the right word. "For us to *function* successfully as a couple."

She nodded.

"But you fear that three will not fit in the space you describe," she said.

"Things have been so much better for us than I ever thought they could be after Kathryn gave him a child," I said.

"A child she is now giving right back."

"I was thinking about this last night," I said. "It's not as if I had a vote when she got pregnant. And I certainly don't have a vote about the child now."

"A person for whom you have no use still exerts this kind of control over your life."

"Even when her skinny ass is about to be on its way to the airport," I said.

"Are you at least able to put yourself in her shoes?" Susan Silverman said. "Whether it was her choice or not, she has been a single mother for the past six years. It was Richie's decision to end the marriage. The decision she makes now might be selfish. But not malicious."

I felt myself smiling.

"Do I sound selfish right now, or malicious?"

"Maybe if Kathryn were here," she said, "she'd be able to put herself in your shoes."

"I don't think I can do this," I said.

"But just because you think you can't, because of the way your life is constructed, doesn't mean you can't," Susan Silverman said. She smiled. "You're a game girl, after all."

"Viewing the boy as a complication instead of as a wonderful child always makes me feel like a bad person," I said.

"Not one of the rules of engagement in here," she said.

"I feel like I'm projecting," I said.

"Said the patient to the therapist."

"There's one other thing," I said. "I feel as if Richie is being a little controlling here when he keeps telling me we can do this."

"How so?"

"Because every time he says that, what I'm hearing is that we *should* be able to do this," I said.

"Maybe it's something the two of you need to discuss."

"Maybe it is," I said. I ran a hand through my hair. "What a mess."

"Which is how you describe your professional life at the moment," she said.

"I know both Tony and Jabari are lying to me," I said. "It's part of the pimp handbook. I just can't decide which of them is lying more. And who would have profited more from Lisa Morneau's death."

"Or maybe," she said, "the question ought to be: Who has most to lose?"

We both stood now, with a familiar and practiced synchronicity.

I smiled.

"That," I said, "is a very good question."

"Try not to sound quite so surprised," Susan Silverman said.

45

TONY MARCUS HAD gone to ground, according to both Vinny Morris's contacts and Spike's. Apparently Gabriel Jabari had done the same. Perhaps each was regrouping, and plotting his next move. As always when dealing with any level of thug, I reminded myself I was not dealing with master criminals here. Both of them were smart. Just not nearly as smart as they thought they were.

They still operated off the codes of the streets that had produced both of them. What was happening between them in real time, whoever turned out to be responsible for the murders of the two women, was a variation of a basic street-corner stare-down. You dis me, I dis you. You don't take a step back? Neither do I. Never show weakness, until only one was left standing.

Or neither. But if both of them did go down, two more would step up to take their places. It was the order of things in what my father had always called the world of fuckery.

All of this I contemplated on the long walk back to River Street Place. Had I ever walked eight miles in the same day, at least not when on a sightseeing tour in a city like London? I could not think of a time when I had. Maybe I was in training for the Olympics of fuckery.

When I finally returned home, I walked Rosie and fed her earlier than usual. I still had not heard from Darcy about Jabari's fingerprints. I had not heard back from Jake Rosen. For this one afternoon, I was about as close with cops I knew as I was with pimps I knew. I wondered what Dr. Silverman would make of symbolic thinking like that.

I walked up to the fourth floor and put on my smock and tried to paint, but could not. So I showered and made myself a cup of strong English tea. I thought about lacing it with some Irish, as a way of bringing the two countries closer, but did not.

I needed to take some sort of action that was not simply *re*action. I considered two of my favorite rules of top-flight detecting:

When in doubt follow someone.

Or annoy someone.

I decided to combine them with Natalie. We were, after all, neighbors. So by six o'clock I was about fifty yards from her building on Revere Street, having found a parking spot on the street that gave me a perfect view of the front door. Maybe it was a sign. Maybe my luck was changing. The lights of her apartment were fully lit.

I had no real plan. I was just hopeful, because of the hour, that she might come out the front door at some point and head off to dinner. If she had called a car service, or had a car of her own parked on the street, I would follow in mine. Or follow her on foot if she was walking to a restaurant nearby.

The temperature outside had dropped again. I thought back to the night Spike and I had staked out Suite. Jabari had, at least indirectly, led us to Natalie that night. Maybe she could lead me somewhere tonight.

I was sitting behind the wheel, listening to *Eric in the Evening* play jazz on WGBH, when a car pulled up in front of Natalie's building. A woman got out of the backseat, fumbling around in her purse, probably for her keys.

When she had them in hand, she turned just enough in my direction that I got a clear look at her face, and saw that it was Olivia Hewitt.

46

OLIVIA HEWITT HAD said something to me about having a good woman in her life. Now she was letting herself into Natalie's building with her own key.

"Oh, ho," I said.

I WAITED A few minutes and then locked my car and walked to the front door of the building and pressed the speaker button and waited.

"Who is it?" Natalie said.

"Sunny Randall," I said.

"Go away," she said.

"I think not."

"We have nothing further to say to each other," she said.

"But I have much I want to say to you," I said. "And Olivia. And if you don't invite me in, I will stay right where I am and call your ex-husband and ask him why he thinks one of his top managers is hanging around with you."

Five seconds later the door clicked open. In I went. I really was everything a good neighbor should be, including being well-armed.

"I SHOULD HAVE shot you a long time ago when I had the chance," Natalie said.

"This might sound as if I'm splitting hairs," I said. "But I don't recall you ever really having the chance."

Natalie and Olivia sat next to each other on the couch. Olivia was wearing a black sleeveless dress that I was not entirely certain fit the season. I couldn't help but notice that her upper arms were extremely well toned, for a woman of a certain age.

Natalie wore tight gray jeans and a white pullover. Everything about the air around them, and the energy, told me they were a couple. There was a bottle of white wine in an ice bucket on the table, and two full glasses in front of them.

I sat in the same chair in which I'd sat on my previous visit.

I nodded at Olivia and said, "You've apparently switched sides."

She smiled, almost imperceptibly. I knew I was being catty, being fixed on the work she'd obviously had done. Normally I wouldn't stoop to that level, but it had been a rough couple weeks.

"Are you referring to my sexual preference?" she said. "Because this one has always been mine."

"I meant professionally," I said.

"Did you follow me here?" Olivia said.

"I was watching Natalie's building, actually," I said.

"Why?" Natalie said.

"I was hoping I might stumble upon something resembling a clue," I said. "And, apparently, I have."

Natalie and I stared at each other. Olivia stared at Natalie. Neither offered me any wine.

"Are you going to tell Tony?" Olivia said. "If you do, he'll kill me, too."

"'Too'?" I said.

"Like Lisa and Callie," she said.

"I'm still trying to determine who killed Lisa and Callie," I said.

"It had to be Tony who had it done," Natalie said. "Lisa knew too much. And Callie must have known at least some of it."

"Then why hire me?" I said.

"Ask him," Natalie said. "He's your client."

"I'm actually my own client these days," I said.

"Only one would have you," Natalie said.

She placed her glass on the table and took Olivia's hand.

"What I'd like to know," I said, "is how the two of you being together fits with what's going on between Tony and Gabriel Jabari."

I looked at Olivia. "Did you tell Gabriel Jabari which establishments like your own the cops could hit?"

"I don't have to answer that," she said.

"No," I said, "you don't. But somebody certainly had an insider's knowledge about clients, and teenage girls."

Olivia simply shook her head and drank some wine.

I was aware of music playing in the background. It sounded like some kind of violin sonata. If I wasn't talking about a couple of pimps with a madame and ex-hooker, and didn't have a gun in my purse, the scene couldn't have been more civilized.

"Clearly you have us at a disadvantage," Natalie said.

"Boy," I said, "you can say that again."

"If you tell Tony," Olivia said, "he might kill us both."

"Natalie won't believe this," I said. "But I mean neither of you any harm."

Olivia Hewitt drank more wine. Her hand shook slightly, but she managed not to spill what was left in her glass.

"Tony is slipping, that's just my view," Olivia Hewitt said. "If it's not Gabriel, it will be someone else."

"The devil you know," I said.

Olivia looked at Natalie again. Natalie nodded, as if encouraging her to keep going.

"I told Natalie a few weeks ago," Olivia said, "that I wonder sometimes if Tony is even totally in charge of his own operation any longer. This was even before Lisa left. It's as if, I don't know how to put it, he's being run somehow."

So Lisa wasn't the only one who thought that.

"Was this something you just intuited?"

Natalie smiled. "'Intuited,'" she said. "You always did have the words."

Olivia said, "I'd ask him about making some changes with our online advertising. In the old days, he'd say yes or no, thumbs-up or down, right away. Now he'd tell me he had to get back to me. I told him that in light of what was happening around the country, even hiring young girls for some of the brothels was far too risky. He told me I was right, that he was going to close them down. But then a couple of days later he changed his mind. Then he changed the subject and told me that everybody in the whole business was getting younger except him, and that he needed to adapt."

"Just not for long," Natalie said.

"Gabriel is going to take over eventually?" I said.

"Gabriel, me, Olivia," Natalie said.

"Can I ask you something?" I said to her. "Why doesn't Jabari just kill him and be done with it?"

"Too easy," Natalie said. "He wants to torture him first."

"Sounds like he's waited a long time to get even," I said.

"Long as me," Natalie said.

Without being asked, Natalie told me that she and Olivia had come up together on the streets. By the time Tony and Natalie had been married and divorced, Olivia was in New York City working for Patricia Utley at a brothel near the Museum of Natural History, with an eye on working in management herself someday.

"So you were willing to return to Boston and go back to work for Tony?" I said.

"Only in the short term," Olivia said. "Patricia joked that it was like giving me an out-of-town tryout before I came back to New York." She shrugged. "But then one day I ran into Natalie at Max Mara. On Newbury Street? We've been together ever since. And I've stayed with Tony longer than I ever intended."

"Then Gabriel came back to town," Natalie said. "That just accelerated things."

"So you all really are in this together," I said.

Olivia said, "What Tony didn't know was that I was using him. As a way of getting us where, and what, we want."

"Which we're close to getting," Natalie said.

"Unless Ms. Randall here gets in the way," Olivia said.

"I don't think she will," Natalie said.

"Why would you possibly trust her?" Olivia said.

The two of them were suddenly talking about me as if I weren't there. I smiled at them, just to give myself something to do.

"She usually does what she says she's going to do," Natalie said to Olivia. "On top of that, she has to know that if she does anything to jam us up, I'll tell Gabriel to kill her."

"He says he's not a killer," I said.

Natalie smiled. "First time for everything," she said.

She stood then and walked across the room and opened the door. I walked through it and down the steps and out onto Revere Street. Before I walked to my car I looked back up at the apartment. The two of them were standing in the front window, staring down at me. I resisted the urge to wave. Instead I got into my car and drove home, wondering just how much sisterhood a sister could handle these days.

47

I HAD CALLED SPIKE on the short ride home and given him the bumper-sticker version of what had just happened. He said he was on his way.

"Slow night?" I said.

"There are no slow nights at Spike's," he said. "There are just some nights not as fast as the others."

"What about the meteorologist?" I said.

"A cold front has moved in," he said. Then he said, "But as we like to say in television, the bigger breaking news here is that Tony might not be the lead dog everybody still thinks he is."

Within the hour Spike and I and Rosie were on the couch in my living room, Rosie between us, a bottle of Jameson Black Barrel in front of us. Spike was drinking his with ice. I was having mine neat, with water on the side.

"So if Tony isn't calling the shots for Tony anymore, who the hell is?" Spike said.

He was wearing one of those untucked shirts, distressed jeans, battered and bruised and beloved Doc Martens.

"Maybe that's the secret about which is he most afraid," I said.

"You can't be the biggest and baddest if somebody else is running the show," Spike said.

"But all I keep hearing is that Tony has been consolidating power while a lot of the old bosses have faded away," I said. "Or started to, the way Desmond has."

"Maybe Tony has formed an alliance with some of the younger guys who have stepped up with the old guard like Gino Fish and Joe Broz and even Antonioni gone," Spike said. "I don't know all the new players and neither do you. I don't even know who's running Antonioni's outfit now. Do you?"

"I don't," I said. "But even if there's been some kind of merger or acquisition, why would Tony give a rip if people knew that?"

Spike sipped some of his drink and smacked his lips and smiled.

"Maybe he just doesn't want everybody to know he might not be the cock of the walk," Spike said.

He held his drink up closer to the lamp next to the couch, as if to see it in a better light. "Did you know

George Bernard Shaw once called whiskey 'liquid sunshine'?"

"I do," I said.

"So why isn't this whiskey shedding any light for us?" he said.

He put his head back. I did the same.

"You're gonna laugh," I said. "But I think Tony did love her."

"Too much of a romantic to laugh," Spike said. "Even if we are talking about Tony Marcus."

"So who's got enough juice to boss a boss like Tony?" I said.

"You're going to find out, aren't you?"

"I am," I said.

Spike turned and presented his glass to me. I touched it lightly with my own.

"I'll drink to that," he said.

We both did.

48

RICHIE AND KATHRYN had enrolled Richard in the Kingsley Montessori School on Exeter Street, between Newbury and Commonwealth. Richie called the next morning and asked if after school he could drop Richard off with me before he drove Kathryn to the airport.

"Pretty sporting of you to be her ride to Logan," I said.

"A form of closure," he said.

"For now," I said.

I told him I would be happy to spend time with Richard, and might even take him out for an early dinner.

"He likes being with you," Richie said.

"Before he needed a father figure in his life," I said. "Now he needs a mother."

A few minutes later I called Richie's father.

I MET DESMOND Burke at the Warren Tavern on Pleasant Street in Charlestown, a couple blocks away from the Bunker Hill Monument. I knew enough of my local history to know that the place was named after Dr. Joseph Warren, who had been a charter member of the Sons of Liberty and who, before he died at the Battle of Bunker Hill, had sent Paul Revere off on what became a fairly famous ride.

Desmond and I sat at a table near the window. Two bodyguards, neither of whom I recognized, sat at the bar. Desmond and I both ordered clam chowder. He ordered Shipyard ale to go with his. I went with iced tea. I was babysitting his grandson later.

It was as if he'd aged ten years, or more, since Felix had died saving his life, taking the bullet intended for Desmond. He'd never had much color, but today his face looked as white as the Irish knit sweater he was wearing, set off only by eyes the color of coal. He was still running what was left of the family business, even without Felix to run it with him. But Richie said the old man's heart was no longer in it.

"I need a favor," I said when the waiter had brought our drinks.

"I owe you one, don't I, though?" he said. "You saved my life."

"You don't owe me anything," I said. "And have already paid me handsomely when I expected no payment at all."

"Not the way it works in my world," he said. "An eye for an eye cuts a lot of ways."

"I've been working on a case involving Tony Marcus," I said.

"When I heard," Desmond continued, "I thought you'd turned into a right *moran*."

The Irish in him coming out. *Moran* meant fool. Or worse.

I could see his grandson in his eyes. But the boy's eyes were constantly full of wonder. The old man's had seen too much, the wonder in them drained out long ago, replaced now by ashes.

"So ask what you're here to ask," he said.

"Is it possible," I said, "that Tony Marcus has taken on a partner?"

"I never trafficked in women, by the way," Desmond said. "Or children."

"I know that."

"What kind of a man puts children on the street?" he said.

He shifted slightly in his chair to stare out the window.

"Have you heard anything?" I said.

"You hear things," he said, turning back to me, looking as if even that small movement had exhausted him. "There's even been a rumor about that Antonioni might have had another son no one knew about."

"A name?"

He shook his head. "My interest in Albert Antonioni died when he died."

I thought: *After you had him killed and dumped off the coast of Rhode Island.*

"But could this person already have enough strength to throw in with Tony?" I said.

"It's possible," he said. He waved a hand that looked as thin as paper in front of him. "You get tired," he said.

"What would Tony have to gain, or lose, from such a business relationship?" I said.

"Loss of face, certainly," Desmond said. "It is the only thing that matters to some of these *morans.* Before Whitey Bulger lost power, perhaps you know, he lost face."

"Could you ask around?" I said. "Two women have died because of this case. I want to find out why."

"Women from the whorehouses," he said.

He pronounced it *hoor*houses.

"Yes," I said.

He said he would try. He repeated that he owed me. I repeated that he did not. He called for the check. As soon as he did, I saw the two men at the bar get off their stools, almost as if they had snapped to attention.

"My grandson is a gift," he said.

"He is," I said.

"You'll help Richie with him now that she's leaving?" Desmond said.

"I'm going to try," I said.

He took money out of a clip thick with it, and threw some bills on the table. Then he stood.

"I'd like you to do more than try," he said.

He made his way across the front room. But as he got to the door, he stopped, turned around, and came back to our table. Something in him seemed to have changed. Somehow he did not look old, or frail, or tired now. He was Desmond Burke.

"Be careful with this, Sunny," he said.

He almost never called me Sunny.

"Always," I said.

"Men like us," he said, "will do anything to hold on to what we have."

Now he left.

49

RICHIE DROPPED HIS son off at about 4:30. He said he was heading back to pick up Kathryn at the Four Seasons. I did not tell him about my lunch with his father. Perhaps he already knew. If he did, he didn't mention it. But he already had enough on his plate today.

Richard hadn't even taken off his coat yet, but Rosie was already sitting on his chest and lapping his face. I saw Richie smiling at the sight of them. I put my arms around him, and kissed him harder than I'd planned.

"It's all going to work out," he said when we both pulled back.

"Pretty to think so," I said.

When he was gone, I asked Richard how he was doing, having to say goodbye to his mom.

"I'm okay," he said. "My dad says I have to keep being brave."

I smiled at him.

"Guess what?" I said. "He's always telling me the same thing."

"But it's hard sometimes," the little boy said.

"Is it ever," I said, then asked if he wanted to change the subject.

"Yes, please," he said.

"You like pizza?" I said.

"We didn't have pizza in London that much," he said. "Mom said it wasn't good for me."

Another reason to hate her.

"Well," I said, "how would you like to go have the best pizza?"

"Can Rosie come with us?"

"No," I said. "But we'll bring some pizza back for her."

"Is pizza good for dogs?" he said.

"Absolutely," I said.

Then the two of us got into my car and drove to Santarpio's.

THE WARREN TAVERN was an older Boston landmark. Santarpio's had better pizza.

It was on Chelsea Street in East Boston, close enough to the airport that you could shuttle there from Logan. It had become even more of a local legend in my lifetime because the father of Mike Eruzione, the captain of the "Miracle on Ice" Olympic hockey team, had bartended there for years. I wasn't much for hockey. That was Richie's favorite sport, even more than baseball. But everybody in Boston knew the name Eruzione, because he'd been the one to score the winning goal against the Soviets in what even I knew was the greatest game ever played.

My own father had been taking me to Santarpio's since I was Richard's age. The place had been around since 1903, and the owner, Frank Santarpio, used to joke that they had to finally build an airport nearby so that people could fly to Boston if they wanted one of his pies.

I parked on Bremen Street. When we were inside we went to our left and into the back room, and scored a table under a picture of Mike Eruzione.

"Who's that?" Richard said.

"A famous hockey player whose dad used to work here," I said.

"My dad likes hockey," he said. "He told me he's going to take me to a Bruins game."

"The two of you are going to do a lot of things together," I said.

"With you, too?" he said.

"You bet," I said.

We ordered an Italian cheese, large. When Richard asked why I had ordered such a big pizza I told him I wasn't just bringing some home for Rosie, but maybe even for my friend Spike.

"Is Spike a dog?" he asked.

I told him no, but that Spike was even more loyal than one.

The little boy didn't talk more about his mother

leaving, nor did I. We just ate pizza. I happily watched him eat. I asked him if he was excited about his new school. He said he was excited and scared at the same time.

"New things," I told him, "can be both."

"That's what my dad says," Richard said. "You sound like him sometimes."

"You're very smart," I said.

"Thank you, Sunny *ma'am*," he said, and smiled at me as he did. It was, I had decided, a pretty spectacular smile.

When we finished eating and the leftovers had been packed into a small pizza box, I told Richard we should get going, so as to be back at my house when his father got back from the airport. So we came down the ramp out front, went straight to the corner, and walked the fifty yards to Bremen. Then I unlocked the car, secured Richard into the booster seat that Richie had remembered to leave on my doorstep. The pizza box was next to Richard in the backseat. He said he would guard it for Spike and Rosie.

I was about to get behind the wheel when I felt the gun pressed into the small of my back, knowing exactly what it was even with my peacoat on. I had no chance to clear my own gun out of my purse, not that I would even have considered it with a little boy in the backseat.

"Remember me?" he said. "The Harvard man?"

He leaned in close to my ear now.

"Who snuck up on who this time, little girl?" he said.

50

YOU'RE SCARING A little boy," I said, trying to keep my voice both low and calm.

"Sunny?" Richard said from the backseat.

"It's all right," I said. "I'm just going to shut the door so my friend and I can talk."

I did that.

"The boy isn't a part of this," I said.

"Sure he is."

"What do you want?"

"What," the voice behind me said. "Got no smart shit to say to me now about who got the gun and who doesn't and who's the badass and who's not?"

I kept hoping that someone would come walking down Bremen Street. No one did.

I waited.

"What I am here to tell you," he said, "is that if you don't stop nosying around where you shouldn't be nosying around, no telling who might get hurt."

"Who sent you?" I said.

"Somebody wants you to stop nosying around," he said. "Somebody wants me to tell you to just go live your life while you still got one. A life, I'm talking about. You and yours."

He jammed the gun harder into the small of my back.

"Nod if you understand what I'm telling you," he said.

I did.

"Can't get nowhere by threatening you?" he said. "So now the message is we dialing things up."

"Message delivered," I said. "Now let the boy and me leave."

"Not before you reach into your purse and take out the gun I know you got in there, and hand it to me," he said.

I took the .38 out by the handle and put it in his free hand without turning around.

"Now you get in your hooptie car and put your hands on the wheel and count to twenty," he said. "And if I see you turn around before I'm gone, I just might start shooting and let the bullet figure out where the fuck it wants to go."

He pressed himself into me again.

"We clear?" he said.

"Crystal," I said.

I got inside the car. Put my hands on the wheel, ten o'clock and two o'clock, just like they taught you in driver's ed. Then I counted and waited.

"Sunny," Richard said. "I'm scared."

"It's fine now," I said. "Sunny ma'am would never let anything happen to you."

"Was he really your friend?" he said.

"No," I said. "Just someone trying to play a dumb game."

As I put the car into gear and pulled down Bremen, Richard wanted to know why, if it was just a game, I had a gun.

"It's part of my job, carrying one," I said.

"Will that man give it back to you?" the boy said.

"Eventually," I said.

51

I KNEW LITTLE AT this point about being a parent, but I was already getting a crash course about how resilient children could be.

By the time we got back to River Street Place, Richard informed me that he was already hungry, and asked if he could have some of Spike and Rosie's pizza. I asked if he wanted it heated up. He said he would be fine eating it the way it was. I set him up at the table in the kitchen. He asked if it was all right to feed Rosie some.

I smiled at him and said, "That's between you and Rosie."

Then I said: "Are you okay?"

He nodded, looking at me with big, dark eyes.

"That was just something I call dumb-guy stuff," I said.

He tilted his head slightly, suddenly curious.

"Do girls do dumb-guy stuff, too?" he said.

"You have no idea," I said.

He was still at the table when Richie got to the house. I didn't even wait for him to take his own peacoat off before telling him what had happened at Santarpio's, keeping my voice as quiet as I could, leaving out nothing.

"He had a gun out," Richie said when I finished. "Near my child."

"Yes," I said. "He was on me before I could do anything about it."

"Do what?" he said. "Start shooting with my son in the car?"

"Richie," I said. "I know you're upset. I'm upset."

He took in a couple big gulps of air, let them out.

"I know," he said.

"No more pizza!" we heard from the kitchen, and then the sound of the boy's laughter.

"He threatened my son," Richie said. "I can't let that stand."

"I don't know who he is, or who sent him to follow me in the first place," I said.

"I'm going to find out," Richie said. "Or my father is."

"Please don't," I said, and then told him about my lunch with his father, and what we had discussed, and once again asked Richie to please let me handle this.

"How did handling things yourself work out for you tonight?" he said.

I had no answer for that.

"Who would do something like that in front of a child?" Richie said.

"People like this," I said.

"Like my father, you mean."

"That's not what I meant," I said.

"You've accepted my help before," Richie said. "And Desmond's."

"And I promise you," I said, "I will ask for it again if I need it."

"You don't want me to tell him," he said.

"For now," I said.

"Secrets," Richie said, shaking his head.

"Your family is good at them," I said.

"I will protect my family," Richie said.

"I've protected it, too," I said.

We stood there, as we heard another shout of laughter from the kitchen. Richie took my face in his hands and gently kissed me.

"I love you," he said.

"I know," I said.

"But I can't let him be around you right now," he said.

"I know," I said.

Richard came running into the front hall, chased by Rosie. When he was close, I leaned down and took his face into my hands. He looked up at me and said, "When can I come back, Sunny ma'am?"

"Soon," I said.

They left. I watched them go. Sometimes being brave wasn't all it was cracked up to be.

* * *

AN HOUR LATER Darcy Gaines called and told me that the prints had come back and that Gabriel Jabari wasn't his real name, but that he had done time at Dannemora in upstate New York, a felony for pimping and pandering in what Darcy called the big, bad city.

"What's his real name?" I said.

"Gabriel Lister," she said.

We go way back, Natalie had said.

"Gabriel Jabari's real name is Gabriel Lister," I said.

"Yup," Darcy said.

It was as if the air around me in the kitchen had suddenly rearranged itself, and then distilled somehow. I took in some of it, then slowly let it out.

"Is there a next of kin listed as an emergency contact on his sheet, by any chance?" I said.

"As a matter of fact, there is," Darcy said. "A sister in Boston, lived on Revere Street. Natalie Goddard. Must be her married name."

"Not exactly," I said.

"You know her?"

"As a matter of fact, I do," I said.

"Is this helpful?"

"Extremely," I said. "Thank you."

"You're welcome."

I stared through the liquid sunshine in my glass.

"You know how you hold a grudge?" I said to Darcy.

"How?"

"You wait," I said.

52

YOU'RE JUST BRINGING me into this now?" Phil Randall said. "Something like that could affect a senior citizen's self-esteem."

"Daddy," I said, "your self-esteem could survive a carpet bomb."

We sat across the kitchen table from each other. I'd thought about calling Lee Farrell, with whom I'd had no contact lately, except that I wasn't ready, or willing, to tell Lee who Gabriel Jabari really was. I wasn't ready to share that information with him, or with Jake Rosen. Maybe I would when I figured out where Gabriel being a brother to Jermaine and Natalie fit into the whole cockeyed scheme of things.

So I'd called my dad. He said he was free for the evening because my mother was out to dinner with her bridge group. Knowing of my mother's fondness for bourbon, I told him I hoped one of the other club members was the designated driver. He said Millie was.

"Against all odds," he said, "Millie took the cure."

I had made coffee for us. My father looked as dapper as always: Harris tweed jacket, zippered sweater underneath it. His cologne gave off a scent that I'd always thought should be marketed as "Dad."

"I knew you would have disapproved of my original understanding with Tony," I said.

"You think I hadn't heard?" he said. "I was just waiting for my pumpkin pie to tell me herself."

"I kept thinking I could get ahead of this," I said. "But I've been a couple of moves behind from the start."

He grinned. "Sounds like your mother's bridge group," he said.

Then: "Catch me up."

I did. When I finished he said, "If this was all about revenge from the start, the other brother has been extremely patient, and gone to some trouble to keep his true identity a secret. But why kill the women?"

"Natalie said something about Gabriel wanting to torture Tony first. If Tony really loved Lisa, killing her would certainly fit into that category."

"Why kill the other woman, though?" Phil Randall said.

I shrugged. "To get to Lisa?"

"Unless Tony really did it," my father said.

"Or neither of them did," I said. I sighed. "See what I'm up against?"

I'd tried to discourage him from driving into town, because I knew he liked driving at night less and less as he got older. It was why something stronger than caffeine had been out of the question.

He leaned forward.

"Who has the most to lose?" he said.

"My therapist asked the exact same question," I said.

"Think of the money you could save by talking out your problems with me," he said.

"What about sex?" I said, grinning at him.

"Don't make me wash your mouth out," he said.

"I keep telling myself I'd like to figure this all out before anybody else dies," I said.

"Where are Tony and the other fellow now?"

"I can't seem to locate either one of them," I said.

"You're usually good at finding people," he said.

"Sunny Randall," I said. "If you've lost a pimp or whore, I'm your girl. Maybe I should have it printed on my business cards."

"Maybe it's best to go back to the beginning," he said.

"Tony," I said.

He smiled and nodded.

"Who wanted my help until he didn't," I said.

"Maybe he still needs it and just doesn't know it," Phil Randall said.

"But if he knew that his ex-wife had another brother, there was no reason for him not to mention that by now," I said.

"You know what I always say about your criminal

element," he said. "If they had real brains, there'd be way more streets named after them."

He put his arms around me at the door, kissed me on the cheek, and briefly made me feel safe before he left. I walked Rosie after that and carried her upstairs and put her on the bed while I got ready for sleep. There was something bothering me, on the periphery of memory, the edges of what I knew and didn't know. Something I felt I had missed. Something someone had said. Or something I already knew without knowing that I did. I kept reaching for it, but it was like trying to pin mercury, before I finally fell asleep.

53

AT NOON THE next day I was standing at the bar at Buddy's Fox, the place starting to fill up with another surprisingly good lunch crowd. As usual I looked as out of place in this place as Tony Marcus would have looked singing lead for the Mormon Tabernacle Choir.

I asked the bartender if Tony was around. He shook his head.

"Ain't here," he said.

"Might he be later?"

"Ain't been here for a couple of days," the bartender said.

"What about Junior or Ty Bop?" I said.

"Where Tony is, they is," the bartender said.

I handed him my card and asked him to have Tony call me if he did happen to show up in the next few hours, and went outside and got into my car and drove to Suite.

I wasn't sure when places like Suite opened for business. It turned out to be two in the afternoon. I didn't think Gabriel would be around in the afternoon, but decided to go in anyway. There wasn't the same kind of crowd here as at Buddy's Fox. Maybe Gabriel should think about offering some tasty appetizers in addition to the strippers.

I ordered a club soda and asked the bartender here when Gabriel generally showed up.

"When he feels like showing up," he said, placing my drink in front of me.

"Does he ever show up in the afternoon?" I said.

"He's kind of a late riser," the bartender said.

"If he shows up, please tell him Sunny Randall was looking for him," I said. "We're old friends."

He was tall and black, with a shaved head and biceps I thought qualified as a new wonder of the world. When I handed him my card he looked at it, tore it in two, and let the pieces fall to the floor behind the bar.

"Or not," I said.

I could go tell Natalie that I knew Gabriel was her brother. But for now I didn't see how that got me any closer to where I wanted to go. Maybe I really should just kick the can to Lee Farrell, or Jake Rosen. Or both. Lee wanted to catch a killer and put him in jail. Jake wanted to put Tony in jail.

For all the new intel I had acquired over the past couple days, all I'd really accomplished was getting a gun pulled on me when I had a six-year-old boy in my car. Me. The big talker. *You can't threaten me.*

So they hadn't.

They'd basically threatened Richie's son instead.

I drove to Revere Street and double-parked in front of Natalie's building and rang the bell. No one answered. I got back into my car and drove to Olivia Hewitt's brothel. I didn't know what I wanted to ask her. Maybe about Gabriel. Maybe I just longed for human contact at this point. But no one answered the door. They either weren't open yet or were closing permanently after the busts in Cambridge and Charlestown. Darcy said that sometimes places like this, no matter how well or long established, were there and gone.

It was starting to get dark when I returned to River Street Place. I parked my car in the back, came around to the front door, unlocked it, and saw Gled standing in the front hall.

I started to reach inside my purse. He shook his head. His left arm was still in a sling. His right hand, at his side, had a gun in it.

To Gled's right, I saw Gabriel sitting on my couch, Rosie next to him, on her back as he scratched her belly.

"Dogs love me," he said.

Then he said we needed to talk.

Again.

54

IS THERE ANY point in me asking how you got in?" I said.

I honestly couldn't remember if I'd set the alarm or not. Even when I told myself to set it every time I went out, sometimes I forgot.

"It was Gled," he said. "He's good at shit like this. Met him in Little Odessa a while back." He paused. "In Brooklyn."

I told him I knew where Little Odessa was.

"No shit," Gabriel said, "before that the boy was with the damn KGB. His specialty was making people disappear."

"Good to know," I said.

I took the chair across the coffee table from Gabriel.

"Why are you here?" I said.

"I want to ask you if you're trying to get me killed," he said. "Why the fuck did you tell Tony my real name?"

"I didn't," I said.

"Well, somebody did," Gabriel said.

"The cop who told me, she wouldn't talk if you waterboarded her," I said. "And the only other person I told was my father."

"Who I hear is a cop," he said.

"Retired."

"Well," he said, "somebody told Tony. Who got word to me couple of nights ago that I better back the fuck off, because next time he wasn't missing. Me and Gled, we been on the move a little bit ever since."

"I haven't talked to him since either he killed Lisa or you did," I said.

"How many times do I got to tell you it wasn't me?" he said.

"Till I convince myself it wasn't you?"

He was in a black suit, a black shirt, and a black tie. Shiny black cap-toed shoes. Sapphire cuff links that looked real to me. He'd become some dude since Dannemora.

"Let's back up," I said. "How'd you go from Gabriel Lister to Gabriel Jabari?"

"Never saw myself as a Lister," he said.

"So how'd you come up with Jabari?"

"There was a basketball player at Duke had that name," he said. "I just tried it on for size one day and thought it fit me like this suit I got on right now. Put me in touch with my African roots."

Rosie got off her back but stayed where she was, letting him rub her neck, the little tart.

"How long have you been planning to come after Tony?" I said.

"Since Jermaine," he said. "But I was only fifteen at the time. Wasn't ready. Living with an aunt. Natalie was doing everything back then to keep me out of her world. And Tony's. I don't think she ever told him about me. Turned out to be a good thing."

"And Natalie was willing to wait while you were reinventing yourself?" I said.

"We both buy into all that shit about revenge best being served cold," he said. "Natalie just knew that when I finally did make it back to Boston, it would be time. Only now everything has gotten fucked up, including me losing the damn element of surprise."

"Did you tip the cops about Tony's houses?" I said.

He showed me all those white teeth. "Probably was just a concerned citizen doing that," he said.

"Where do you think Tony is right now?" I said.

"I find him, you'll be the first to know," he said. "Time to stop fucking around and end this thing, so I can get on with my business." He smiled again. "And his."

"I didn't tell him about you and Jermaine and Natalie," I said.

"You sure you didn't tell anybody else besides your father?"

"Just him and Rosie the dog," I said.

"Ask you something?" he said. "Where were you when you talked to him?"

"In my kitchen," I said.

He nodded, then put a finger to his lips and got up and walked out the front door, motioning for me to follow him. Gled did the same. The three of us walked all the way out to where the Navigator was parked.

"Maybe you being surveilled," he said. "You ever think of that?"

I had not.

"By Tony?" I said.

"Uh-huh," he said. "Didn't you ask me one time if I broke in here? Maybe it was just another time when you had it wrong on me."

It had never occurred to me, not once, that the break-in could have been not to find something but to *plant* something. But maybe it should have.

Jabari said, "Gled, you go back in the kitchen now and do that spyware shit you do for me sometimes, see if you can find a little something something."

"He can do that?" I said.

"One more thing he learned in the mother country," Gabriel said.

To Gled he said, "Me and her will go back and sit back down in the living room and keep talking some shit to each other. You find anything, you come get us."

Gled reached into his pocket, came out with what looked to me like the newest version of the iPhone. He placed it in the palm of his left hand, the one in the sling, tapped on some keys.

"His phone is a bug detector?" I said.

"Uh-huh," Gled said. "So is yours if you are knowing how to work it and be finding EMF."

"EMF," I said.

"Electromagnetic field," he said.

"Think of him as a high-tech meter reader," Gabriel said. "We go somewhere for a meeting with people I ain't vetted to my satisfaction, Gled here does a quick sweep, so I know it's not the same as them wearing a wire."

We all went back inside. Gabriel Jabari told stories about prison, and more about how he'd made his way back to Boston. It didn't take Gled long. Ten minutes later he motioned to me from the entrance to my kitchen. When we were both in there, he got down on his hands and knees. So did I. Underneath the butcher-block table, stuck in a corner, was what looked to all the world like a small black lug nut.

Gled checked the rest of the house after that. When he finally came back downstairs he looked at Gabriel and shook his head. When the three of us were back outside, Gabriel said, "You ought to start trying to figure out what else whoever planted that thing knows you don't want them to know. You said you was being followed, right?"

"I was."

"Maybe they just hedging their bets."

"All I want to know is who killed those women," I said. "I just need a little more time."

"Well, you out of time," Gabriel said. "Because if I find Tony Marcus before you do . . ."

Gled opened the back door of the Navigator for him. Gabriel got in.

"Funny how this shit can work out, you think about it," Gabriel said. "Might be the people you can trust the most on this thing right now are my sister and me."

I told him he might be right. Gled closed the door. But before he walked around and got into the driver's side, he whispered something in my ear.

As I was headed back up the walk, I heard Gabriel call out to me.

"Cute damn dog," he said.

55

I CALLED SPIKE A little after seven and told him I was on my way over to Spike's. He asked if there was any reason in particular, other than me missing him.

"I want an adult beverage and I want to talk," I said.

"Two of my three specialties!" he said.

Right before I left the house, Jake Rosen called.

"Gotta say," he said, "my life has gotten a lot more interesting with you in it."

"Did you call to tell me that?" I said.

"No," he said. "I called to see if you wanted to have a drink and help me figure out where Tony Marcus might be."

"I don't know."

"Me neither. Lost track of him a couple of nights ago."

"Thought you knew everything."

"Not always," he said. "So what about the drink?"

I told him he could meet me at Spike's. A half-hour later we sat at a round corner table in the back room. Jake was in his basic uniform, and had ordered one of Spike's IPA's with a funny name. Spike and I were drinking a red wine blend that he promised me I'd love, and did, as it turned out.

"Is she a pain in the ass with you?" Jake said to Spike.

"On the contrary," Spike said. "I find her a sweet trip downriver to a gentle shore."

"Isn't that a way people describe dying?" I said.

"Is it?" Spike said. "I just thought I was being lyrical."

"Jabari and his man Gled came to my house tonight," I said to Jake Rosen.

"They looking for Tony, too?" he said.

He drank some beer. The label said *Funky Buddha*.

"He wanted to tell me again that he didn't kill Lisa Morneau," I said.

Rosen grinned, and raised his voice slightly. "Jesus, Sunny, as opposed to what," he said. "Making a full confession? Telling you he just couldn't deal with his guilt any longer and had to come clean to you?"

He drank more beer. He seemed just slightly lit to me, if not drunk, as if he'd had a few before meeting us. And was still cute in a good-guy, bad-boy way, no getting around that, even if he was as full of himself as ever. Maybe when this was all over, we could go out and get lit together some night, just to celebrate.

But there was nothing to celebrate yet.

"I keep wondering why Jabari would risk going down on a murder rap when it's Tony he's after," I said.

"All that matters in the end is that I'm after Tony," Rosen said. "And I'm gonna get him before Jabari does, and even before Darcy does, unless you keep pissing people off and getting in the way."

"I've clearly pissed somebody off," I said, and told him about having a gun pulled on me outside Santarpio's, with Richard in the backseat.

Spike had gone to check on something in the kitchen.

"Bringing a kid into it is some serious shit," Rosen said. "But these are bad men. And bad men will do anything to hold on to what they have."

"That's what Desmond Burke told me," I said.

"He ought to know," Jake said.

"Somebody thinks I know more about Lisa Morneau than I actually do," I said.

"Other than the guy who killed her," Rosen said, "you were the last one to see her alive. Maybe that's what they still want to know about."

He finished his beer. "She didn't tell you something at the house that could hurt Tony?" he said. He grinned. "And help me?"

"I told you before," I said. "I'd tell you if I did."

"Would you?" he said.

Spike sat down as Rosen stood up, reaching for his wallet. Spike shook his head. "On the house," he said.

Rosen gave me a long look.

"I keep wondering whose side you're on," he said.

"Mine," I said.

Just like Tony Marcus, I thought.

"And mine," Spike said.

Rosen walked through the back room and past the bar and was gone. We both watched him go.

"I think he might have a thing for you," Spike said.

"I have enough men in my life. Good and bad."

"You never told me what you wanted to talk about," Spike said.

"I think I may be figuring things out on my own," I said.

"Was it at least something I said?" Spike said.

"Not exactly," I said.

He drove me home. Even though Gled had found no further listening devices, I still decided to make the calls I needed to make while I walked Rosie. As always, I wasn't being paranoid, just extremely alert. First I called Lee Farrell and asked him a question I should have asked him before.

Then made another call and left this message on voicemail:

"Got a proposition for you."

Then I went upstairs and slept like a baby.

Starting to feel like a babe again.

56

I SPENT A LOT of the next day on the phone. I did not tell Spike what I was planning. I knew I could not tell Richie. I briefly thought about running it all by Jesse Stone, but suspected he would try to talk me out of it, too.

Even if I was right, I still needed help.

Just not theirs.

This had to be my show now. I was the one who had put a target on two women, whether I'd meant to or not. I was the one who had to make things right. In the world of bad men and fuckery, I was the one who had to be in charge tonight.

A little after six, I finally called Jake Rosen and told him to meet me at the brownstone Tony and Lisa had shared.

"I got him," I said.

"Tony?" he said.

"Yeah," I said.

"You're telling me you beat me to him?" he said.

"Pretty sure," I said.

"On my way," he said.

I LEFT THE front door open for him. I was in the living room, where I'd met Tony the night after he'd hired me. It really hadn't been that long ago, but it already felt like last year, just because so much had happened since. Callie and Lisa and Paradise. Harvard Stadium and Santarpio's. Natalie and Olivia and Gabriel Jabari né Lister. A listening device under my own kitchen table.

And having spent five minutes, tops, with Lisa Morneau.

I heard the door open and close and then Jake was with me in the living room, looking around approvingly.

"Nice crib," he said.

"You bet," I said.

"This was their love nest?" he said.

"Apparently so," I said.

I motioned for him to sit down. He took the couch, then grinned and patted the area next to him. "Plenty of room next to me," he said.

"You don't give up," I said.

"Like Churchill said," Rosen said. "Nev-ah surrend-ah."

I took the chair across from him.

"You really got Tony?" he said.

"What I've got," I said, "is a bunch of pearls I think I can make into a necklace, with your help."

"I occasionally forget you were a fine arts major," he said.

"The finest," I said. "Now here I am with one of Boston's finest."

"Just not the way he wants you to be with him," Rosen said.

"Nev-ah surrend-ah," I said.

"But that's not why we're here," he said.

"Nah," I said.

"You're telling me Tony killed her even though he loved her?" he said.

"Tony did love her," I said. "He just didn't trust her enough. But then he doesn't trust anybody." I shrugged. "Part of being Tony."

"Not following," Rosen said. "What does that have to do with him killing her?"

"He didn't kill her," I said. "But I'm pretty sure you did."

57

ROSEN DIDN'T ACT shocked. Or angry. He went for amused.

"I'm waiting for the punch line," he said.

"None forthcoming," I said.

"So, wait," he said. "You dragged my ass over here to tell me I did it? It's like the tennis guy said that time. You cannot be serious."

"Call it more of a working theory," I said.

"While I call bullshit," he said.

"Not sure I can prove it," I said. "But I think I'm right."

"Why for fuck's sake would I kill Tony's girlfriend?" he said.

"Don't forget her friend Callie."

"Got it," Jake said. "I take time off from trying to take down Tony to take out two hookers."

"See, that's a key element to my working theory," I said. "I don't think you're actually trying to take Tony down. I think you two are partners."

"Okay, now we've crossed over the bridge into Crazy Town," he said.

"That's not an actual place," I said.

"Tonight it is," Rosen said.

"Don't think so."

"People talk a lot of shit to me all the time," Rosen said. "Part of the job description. But you win. Like, going away."

He ran both hands through the thick hair, in exasperation.

"Thing is, I actually do like you," he said.

"Is that why you're still here?" I said.

"I'm fascinated about this working theory of yours," he said. "Why don't you run the whole thing by me, while I *am* still here."

So I did. Told him again that I just couldn't make Jabari for the killings, no matter how hard I tried. Told him I could never reconcile Tony hiring me and then breaking into my house. Or killing Callie after I'd already told him Callie had told me nothing useful about Lisa. Or following Lisa to Paradise.

Told him there was a lot I didn't know yet, but figured I could find out later, maybe even from Tony himself.

"Good luck with that," Rosen said.

"Because he won't talk?" I said. "He's always loved talking to me."

"Then he'll tell you what I'm telling you," Rosen said. "That this is all bullshit."

I smiled.

"You said I was the last person to see Lisa alive," I said.

"So?" he said.

But I saw something happen with those blue eyes. No fun in them now.

"I never told you about meeting Lisa," I said.

"Sure you did."

"No, I didn't. Didn't tell Tony at the time. I only told Lee Farrell. But when I called Lee last night, he told me he'd never told anybody. So the only way somebody could have known that is if they were the one who broke into my house, locked my dog in a closet, and planted a bug in my kitchen."

I reached into my pocket and came out with the device that had been under the kitchen table and placed it on the table in front of him.

"You know what the guy who found it told me after he did?" I said.

"Can't wait to hear," Rosen said.

"Police issue," he said.

He leaned back, folded his arms across the bomber jacket. "You're embarrassing yourself, Sunny. No shit."

"I think you planted the bug," I said. "I think it was your guy who followed me to Harvard Stadium, thinking I might be leading him to Lisa. And your guy who followed me to Santarpio's the other night. Just to keep tabs."

"My guy."

"Gangs, guns, girls," I said. "Probably a gang guy, acting like one of your whores. And then outside Santarpio's, the guy told me you couldn't ever get anywhere by threatening me."

"So what."

"I only said that to you," I said.

"You must have said that to somebody else in your life," he said.

"Not anybody he would know," I said. "Except for you. When Lisa did come to my house that night, she was babbling about Tony getting with the man to stay the man. You know what I finally decided? *You're* the man she was talking about. Later on, somebody told me they thought someone might be running Tony. I think the someone is you, Jake. I think you're the one who decided to become an entrepreneur. I don't know what you've got on him. But it must be something good."

He shook his head.

"The balls on you," he said.

"That's what Tony always says," I said.

"Sunny, listen to yourself," Rosen said. "You're the one who's babbling here. Either Tony or Jabari is playing you, and you're just slow to catch on. It's the old poker line. If you can't identify the sucker at the table after a few minutes, the sucker is generally you."

"I don't think so."

"I didn't do it," he said. "Any of it."

I shook my head. "As bad as it would have been for his image to have it out there that he was in business with a dirty cop," I said, "you were the one with everything to lose if it got out about you. Lisa never came right out and said what she knew and what she didn't. But when she ran, even a cool guy like you panicked."

"Forget about painting," he said. "You should have been a writer."

"You probably lost your shit when Tony hired me without telling you," I said. "But you couldn't turn finding her into a full-time job. You already had one of those. So you figured I might help you, as long as you knew what I had every step of the way. You beat it out of Callie that Lisa was up in Paradise before you killed her and dumped her. The bug in my kitchen picked up her telling me she was going to The Fens. I didn't know where the house was. But you did. Then you got there first, and eliminated the threat once and for all."

He looked at his watch.

"I can hear how you've talked yourself into this," he said. "And I guess I can't talk you out of it. But it's not me. I told you before. I'm one of the good guys."

"Maybe once."

"Say you're right about all of this, just for the sake of this conversation," Rosen said. "Could you ever prove any of it in a million years?"

"She can't," Tony Marcus said, walking through the kitchen door and looking like a million damn dollars. "But I can."

He was smiling.

"Bitches," he said. "They sure can talk."

58

IF I HADN'T gotten Jake Rosen fully engaged with the story I'd just told him, Tony Marcus's presence certainly did.

I was briefly concerned that Rosen's response would be to go for his gun. But he did not. He just stared at Tony, shaking his head, almost in wonder.

"You're with her?" he said. "You've got to be fucking shitting me."

Rosen nodded at Tony.

"Where's your boys?" he said.

"Didn't need them tonight," Tony said. "Got this girl right here."

Tony stood a few steps inside the room. He had left his topcoat behind in the kitchen. He wore a navy suit with rather wide pinstripes, a spread collar, a thick-knotted bloodred tie, and a pocket handkerchief in the same color.

"You and me both know that a lot of what she's saying is true," Tony said. "What I didn't know until tonight, and Sunny laid it all out for me as nice as she did, was who killed Lisa over there in The Fens, at a place you used yourself from time to time when you wanted to get your ashes hauled."

Rosen stood. "How about I just get out of here now?" he said.

"How about you sit the fuck down?" Tony Marcus said.

If Rosen *had* been running Tony, he wasn't now. But as I was well aware by now, Tony's relationships were always transactional, at best.

"You kill her, Jake?" Tony said. "Like you killed that young girl the other week?"

"She OD'd!" Rosen yelled.

"This is me you're talking to," Tony said. "That girl was the one freaked out Lisa once and for all."

"I'm a cop, for chrissakes," Rosen said.

"Did you kill Lisa?" Tony said.

"No, for fuck's sake!"

"*Did* you kill her and want me to think Jabari did it?"

"His number was on her phone!" Rosen said.

The balloon had finally gone up.

"What phone?" I said.

Rosen looked at me, then back at Tony. Opened and closed his mouth again.

"The phone I took off her body and have stashed in

my house?" I said. "The one only I knew about until I told Tony about it tonight?"

"You told me about it," Rosen said to Tony.

"Hell I did," he said.

"Then why'd you try to shoot Jabari after that?" Rosen said.

"Because at the time I didn't think it could be nobody except him," Tony said. "Now I got all this new information at my disposal."

Rosen's gun was out in a blink, and he was up and off the couch, so he had both Tony and me in front of him.

"Pick a lane, Tony," he said. "Me or her."

Tony smiled again.

"Picked one already," he said.

Then it was Ty Bop coming through the kitchen door, his gun pointed at Jake Rosen.

"How many times I got to tell people that pimps lie?" Tony Marcus said.

59

MY GUN WAS in my purse in the kitchen, but was of absolutely no use to me now. From the start, just about everybody involved in this case had been telling me not to get caught in a crossfire. But now here I was.

"You gonna shoot a cop?" Rosen said. "Seriously?"

Ty Bop wore a gray hoodie with a green Celtics shamrock on the front, what looked to be brand-new Timberlands, and jeans that made his legs look as skinny as swizzle sticks.

The .45 in his right hand had a suppressor on the end of it.

"Shoot a cop in front of a witness whose old man is a cop, too?" Rosen said.

"You're the one who drew down," Tony said.

"Why do you believe her and not me?" Rosen said.

"Same reason I hired her in the first place," Tony said. "She good at finding shit out."

Rosen took the blue eyes off Tony and put them on me.

"You were a cop yourself," Rosen said. "You know that the phone means nothing. Which means you've got nothing."

"Probably so," I said.

He looked back at Tony. "You and me need to talk later," he said. "Just the two of us. Settle things."

"What Lisa said she was going to do with Tony that night," I said. "She just never got the chance."

"Walking out of here now," Rosen said.

"Suit yourself," Tony said.

"You're letting me walk away, just like that?" Rosen said.

"Uh-huh," Tony said.

Rosen backed around the couch and toward the door, reached behind him and opened the door, his eyes never leaving Ty Bop.

When he was outside, Tony and I walked to the window and saw Rosen backing down the front walk. It was why he didn't notice the black Navigator parked on the street as he was putting his gun back in the holster underneath his bomber jacket.

By the time Gled was behind him, it was too late for Rosen to do much about that. Gled's gun was already out and in Rosen's back. Then there were two other guys out of the Navigator and throwing Rosen into the backseat and the door was closing behind him.

"You worried about security cameras on this street?" I said to Tony.

"Seems like couple of them down all of a sudden," he said. "And one more pointing the wrong way."

"Imagine that," I said.

"You feel bad about this?" Tony said to me.

"He killed two women," I said. "Three if you're right about the girl you say didn't OD."

"He liked 'em young," Tony said. "Kid in a candy store."

"But was right about one thing tonight," I said. "I had no way in hell of proving it."

"No way he could have known she came to your house," Tony said. "Not without help."

"Nope," I said.

"Boys will be boys," Tony said.

"Won't they, though," I said.

"No way he could have known about the phone unless he took it off her and put Jabari's number in it and put it back," he said.

"Nope."

"He didn't beat up on Lisa 'fore he shot her, the way he did the others," Tony said.

"Maybe he knew he didn't have time," I said. "Like a john on the clock."

I faced him fully now. "What did he have on you?" I said.

"Got sloppy and had a pimp done the way I had Jermaine done that time," he said. "Rosen had proof. Once he did, he had me by the balls. Finally ran myself into a cop who could have put me down for good. Once he started running all those young girls, was nothing I could do about it. And some of the shit he did to them, that was on me. I coulda stopped it and didn't. Maybe could've saved that one girl. If I had, maybe Lisa wouldn't've run."

"What goes around," I said.

"So I decided the best thing to do was give him a piece, keep him happy," Tony said. "Only then he wanted more to keep quiet. Give a mouse a fucking cookie. I didn't know Lisa knew that I was the one getting pimped out, and by a cop this time. But like I told you: Girl was smart." He closed his eyes and opened them and said, "Too smart for her own good in the end."

We both turned to stare back out the window at the snow. The black Navigator was long gone.

"Tell me again what the big Russian's specialty was?" Tony said.

"Making people disappear," I said.

"I needed somebody like him before I went into business with a cop," he said.

"Live and learn," I said.

"Not the cop," he said.

Ty Bop was no longer in the room. Tony took out a cigar, snipped off the end, and slowly lit it with a lighter I thought might have cost as much as my car. I thought of a story my father had told me once when we were passing the statue of Red Auerbach in Faneuil Hall, that in the old days when Auerbach was coaching the Celtics, he'd light up a victory cigar at the end of games.

"You and Gabriel come to an understanding after I talked to both of you?" I said.

"Took some persuading, not gonna lie," he said. "But at the end, the boy made a practical decision that I was worth a lot more to him alive than dead. Same with Natalie. And her new girlfriend."

"You're going to let that go, Olivia being in with them while she's been working for you?" I said.

"We all on the hustle," Tony said, "one way or another."

"You have to give Gabriel a lot?"

"More than I wanted to, and more than I gave Rosen," Tony said. "But remember how I told you you didn't want to be looking over your shoulder the rest of your life? Ain't no different for me."

"You going to be able to trust them?"

He smiled. "Fuck no," he said.

Then he shook his head, still smiling. "But it's like a damn family business, you think about it. Me and the Listers. They just A-Listers now."

He blew a perfect smoke ring in the direction of the ceiling.

"We all whores," he said.

Then he winked at me.

"'Cepting you, of course," he said.

I told him, not so fast, I was about to call in the favor he'd promised me.

60

COUPLE OF THINGS," Darcy Gaines said.

We were back at the Dunkin' in Brighton a couple days later.

"First of all," she said, "Jake Rosen seems to have dropped out of sight."

"Has he done something like that before?" I said, before casually asking her to pass the sugar.

"Apparently so," she said. "But then he's always seemed to be operating off his own set of rules."

I told her I'd gotten that same vibe off him myself, but hadn't talked to him since earlier that week.

"He say anything about some undercover thing he might have had going on?" Darcy said. "A reason he would have gone dark, even temporarily?"

"No," I said. "But he was always talking about having to go see some guy."

She bit off the end of a cruller, then washed it down with coffee. I sipped my own coffee. I still liked it better than Starbucks.

"The other thing that's happened," she said, "kind of amazing, is that a string of those pop-up brothels, the ones being worked by a lot of kids, suddenly closed down, all the way from the Rhode Island border to Lowell."

Almost like Lisa Morneau's dying wish, I thought.

I shrugged. "Maybe you scared them right out of business, Lieutenant Gaines," I said.

"Doubt it," she said. "Don't know that I ever could have proved that Tony was behind them, at least not enough to stand up in court."

"Gotta admit, though," I said, reaching over and picking up her cruller and taking a bite out of it. "Sounds like a happy ending. Right?"

"For us," she said. "Not the kind the idiots are used to in places like that."

WHEN I GOT back to River Street Place, Richie and Richard were already inside. The first thing I saw, and heard, was Richard happily chasing Rosie up the steps.

I hadn't seen the little boy since Santarpio's.

Richie and I sat at the kitchen table. Maybe someday I would tell him everything that had happened, and how it had happened. But for now, I just told him that as far as I was concerned, the case was closed.

"You know who did it?" he said.

"Think so," I said. "Just can't prove it."

"Was it Tony?"

"It was not."

"Can you tell me who?"

I told him.

"That cowboy cop you told me about?" Richie said.

"Yes."

"Where is he now?" Richie said.

"Gone," I said.

"Tony have something to do with that?" he said.

"Only in a peripheral way," I said.

"There's more to the story, isn't there?"

"Always."

"But you're safe from him?"

"Yes," I said.

Then I said, "I'm so sorry that he put your boy in the line of fire."

"I know you are," he said. "So am I."

He looked at me with eyes he shared with the boy. Then he smiled. In that moment I knew I loved both of them, just perhaps not in the way Richie wanted. Or I wanted.

"I'm going to need some time to figure things out," he said.

"Back at you, big boy."

Richie said, "Before there can be a three of us, I have to get to know him better. And maybe myself."

"I know," I said.

"I have to learn how to be a father before I can be anything else," he said. "I know I keep saying that you and I can make this work. But before that, I have to."

"You're a fast learner," I said.

I placed my hand, open-palmed, in the middle of the table. He placed his hand on top of it. Then he picked up my hand and kissed it and went and called out for his son.

A few minutes later, they left.

A few minutes after that, I put on my running clothes and jogged over the Fiedler Footbridge and then down along the river, running toward the Mass Ave Bridge in the morning sun, the day feeling like early spring. I was still trying to feel guilt about Jake Rosen, but could not. Maybe Tony Marcus was right. Maybe sometimes street justice was the best you could do.

I ran faster once I made the turn, the wind at my back now. Just not as fast as Lisa Morneau had run that night. When I was back home, I showered and dressed and felt like I was the one who looked like a million damn dollars.

Then I put Rosie in the backseat of my car and the two of us drove to Paradise.

ACKNOWLEDGMENTS

Lieutenant Commander Donna Gavin, Boston Police Department.

And, as always, the home team:

Daniel and David Parker, Ivan Held, Sara Minnich, Esther Newberg.

TURN THE PAGE FOR AN EXCERPT

PI Sunny Randall has relied on the help of her friend Spike in times of need, and when Spike's restaurant is taken over under a predatory loan agreement, Sunny finally has a chance to return the favor. As she begins digging into the life of the hedge fund manager who screwed Spike over, she finds this new enemy may have the backing of even worse criminals. When a college student separately reports being the victim of a crime and the two cases become entangled, one thing is clear: Sunny has been poking a hornet's nest from two sides, and all hell is about to break loose.

1

I WAS IN MY brand-new office over the P. F. Chang's at Park Plaza, around the corner from the Four Seasons and a block from the Public Garden, feeling almost as cool as Tina Fey.

I'd just walked through the door that had SUNNY RANDALL INVESTIGATIONS written on the outside, put on some coffee, sat down behind my rustic wood Pottery Barn desk. All in all, I was everything a professional woman should be, if you didn't count the Glock in the top right-hand drawer of my desk.

There were two chairs on the client side of the desk, a small couch against one wall, and a table on the other side of the room that I used for painting when I needed to take a break from world-class detecting. It housed my pads and boards and a palette and all the other tools of a world-class watercolorist's trade.

"Forget about the gun," Jesse Stone said. "If somebody shows up and threatens you, just pull a paintbrush on them."

"What about the boxing classes you made me take?" I said. "You should see how good my right hand has gotten."

I had signed up for a half-dozen at the gym an old boxer named Henry Cimoli owned over near the harbor.

"Here's hoping you never need to throw it," he said.

Jesse. Chief of police, Paradise, Massachusetts. On-again, off-again boyfriend. Mostly on over the past year. I had given in and started calling him that, my boyfriend, just because I hadn't found a better way to describe his role in my life. We were still together, anyway, even though we were mostly apart, our relationship having survived the virus. We were official, as the kids liked to say, even if we hadn't announced it on Instagram, or wherever kids announced such things these days, in a world where they found everything that happened to them completely fascinating. Jesse and I had been as close as we'd ever been before the virus caused the world to collapse on itself. Now we'd once again grown more used to our own social distancing, and for longer and longer periods of time, him up in Paradise, me in Boston.

But still official, at least in our own unofficial way.

"I feel like Jesse and I are happy," I said to Spike the night before, over drinks at Spike's.

"Low bar," he said. "For both of you."

"Come on," I said. "I've got a stress-free relationship going, money in the bank, my own office, I've still got Rosie the dog, I've even lost five pounds, not that you seem to have noticed."

"Just like a big girl," Spike said.

"Not as big as I was five pounds ago," I said.

"You also still have ex-husband issues," he said, referring to Richie Burke, still in Boston, still in my life as he raised his son from his second marriage.

"Do not," I said.

"Do so," Spike said.

"You sound childish," I said.

"Do not," he said. "Do not, do not, do not."

Spike and I had been celebrating the fact that I'd finally gotten paid by Robert Magowan, who owned the second-biggest insurance company in Boston. Magowan had hired me to prove that his wife had been cheating on him. This I did, well over two months ago. Then he refused to pay, and kept refusing, until Spike and I had finally shown up at his office and Spike threatened to shut a drawer with Magowan's head inside it. That was right before I handed Mr. Magowan my phone and showed him the images of him in bed in a suite at the Four Seasons, park view, with Lurleen from accounting, and wondered out loud who'd win the race to the divorce lawyers, him or the missus, once the missus got a load of what I thought were some very artsy photographs.

"You were only supposed to follow *her*," he said.

"Well," I said, "to put it in language you can understand, I thought I might need additional coverage."

He'd proceeded to transfer the money over speakerphone from an L.A. branch of Wells Fargo while Spike and I watched and listened.

On our way out of the office Magowan had said to me, "They told me you were a ballbreaker."

"Not like Lurleen," Spike had said.

I knew I could have handled Magowan myself. I'd brought Spike along just for fun. His, mostly. He'd gone through a bad time during the pandemic, nearly having lost Spike's at the worst of it. But he'd come up with the money he needed at the last minute, thanks to a loan from one of his best customers, a young hedge-fund guy named Alex Drysdale, who spent almost as much time in the place as I did.

Spike still wasn't back to being his old self, but threatening to kick the shit out of Robert Magowan, even if it hadn't come to that, had made him seem happier than he'd been in a year. And more like his old self.

He was about to pay off his loan this morning, having invited Drysdale to the restaurant so he could hand him the check in person. The thought of that made me smile, just not quite as much as the memory of the ashen look on Magowan's face when I showed him the pictures of him and Lurleen in one particular position that should have had its own name, like a new yoga move:

Downward dogs in heat.

The sound of my cell phone jolted me out of my reverie.

The screen said *Spike.*

"Sunny Randall Investigations," I said brightly. "Sunny Randall speaking. How may I help you?"

"I need to see you right away," he said.

His voice sounded like a guitar string about to snap. I realized I was standing.

"What's the matter?" I said. "Something's the matter. I can always tell."

"I just knocked Alex Drysdale on his ass, is what's the matter," he said.

"The guy who loaned you the money?" I said. "*That* Alex Drysdale?"

"I wanted to kill him," Spike said. "But I stopped after breaking his fucking nose."

"Spike," I said. "What the hell happened?"

"He stole my restaurant."

There was a pause.

"Wait, let me amend that," Spike said. "I mean *his* restaurant."

I told him I was on my way, ended the call, grabbed my leather shoulder bag, remembered to turn off the coffee machine, locked the door behind me, ran down the stairs.

I had started to believe that maybe God, at long last, had stopped being pissed off at everybody.

Obviously She hadn't.

2

PAYBACK REALLY IS a bitch," Spike said. "Only it turns out Drysdale's the bitch."

We were seated at the bar. Spike had a Bloody Mary in front of him so big it looked like a fire hydrant. He also had a glass filled with ice next to it, and would occasionally pluck out a cube and press it to his cheek. Spike said that after he hit Drysdale, the two guys with him—neither of whom, he said, looked like fund managers—hit him back. I knew how hard it was to get the better of Spike in a fight, even when it was two against one. But they'd managed.

"At least you got your shot in," I said.

"I even managed to get some good ones in on the extras from *The Sopranos*," he said, "before one of them kicked my legs out from underneath me and the other just kicked the shit out of me."

"Literally kicking you while you were down," I said.

"My upper body is already starting to look more colorful than Pride month," he said.

Drysdale, he said, finally told them to stop; he didn't want Spike scaring the customers.

"Called them *our* customers," Spike said, and drank.

I asked then how Drysdale had done it, if he could explain it to me without trying to sound like Warren Buffett.

"I'm too stupid to sound like Warren Buffett," he said. "I'm the one who let him pick my fucking pocket in broad daylight."

Drysdale had been a regular at Spike's from the time he turned it from a sawdust-on-the-floor to an upscale restaurant on Marshall Street that had become one of the hottest places in town, not just because of the food, but because of the bar crowd, which could include professional athletes and local TV personalities and politicians and the lead singer from Dropkick Murphys and young women from the modeling agency that had opened around the corner. Drysdale was good-looking, a big tipper, often came in with a beautiful woman or left with one. And was rich as shit. He finally became aware that Spike, even with the government loans and takeout business and furloughing of a lot of the staff, was about to shutter the place. So he offered Spike the loan that he needed at a two percent rate, on one condition:

He didn't tell anybody about the terms.

"I'm a one-percenter," he joked to Spike, "but let's keep that two percent between us."

Spike had been a business major at UMass. When Drysdale presented him with the document, he told Spike to ignore all the bullshit language about floating rates and warrants and even what would happen if Spike somehow still had to declare bankruptcy down the road, that it was all boilerplate stuff and would never come into play until maybe the next pandemic in another hundred years or so.

"We're friends," Drysdale said. "We could have done this on a handshake. But my lawyers are making me."

Spike was one of the smartest people I knew, on every subject except maybe the periodic table. But desperation made him careless, and so did trust in what he considered a real friendship. The wolf was at the door and he needed his money, as he said, right fucking now.

"Stay with me," he said, knowing I was often challenged doing the math on a dinner check with girlfriends.

I stayed with him, but barely, as he began to speak of floating rates and cash positions that Spike said he never could have met, the ones Drysdale had assured him he didn't need to worry about. And interest coverage. And revenue targets for a business that had no chance to meet those until the pandemic was over. Spike never knew it, but by the time Spike's started making money again, by the time he could finally see some daylight, it was too late.

"But the only one who knew that, from the start, was my pal Alex Drysdale," he said.

Then Drysdale came through the door a couple hours ago with his bruisers and handed Spike his check back as soon as Spike handed it to him, saying he could keep it, he'd basically been in default on the loan from the beginning.

I said, "Are we getting anywhere near the bottom line?"

"He now owns Spike's is the bottom line," he said. "He even showed me the part of the agreement where he was entitled to a special dividend for what he called his 'consulting' services."

Spike put air quotes around *consulting.*

"Consulting on what?" I said.

"Fucking me over," Spike said. "It was at that point that I dropped him. Cost me a bunch of my new Doppio napkins because of all the blood. I was actually hoping he might bleed out and my problems would be solved."

Spike drank more of his Bloody Mary. I idly wondered if it was his first of the day. He rarely drank this early. But these were special circumstances. I was starting to think about asking him to build a Bloody for me.

"You know what he said when I asked him why?" Spike said. "He said it was for the same reason dogs lick their balls. Because they can."

At that point, Spike said, Drysdale turned and walked out.

"What am I going to do?" he said.

"I believe you mean what are *we* going to do?"

There was a flicker of light then in his eyes, for the first time since I'd arrived. Not much. A little. I was telling him what we both knew in that moment, that I was here for him the way he had always been for me. I was his wingman now. Just far cuter.

"Have it your way," he said. "What are *we* going to do?"

I smiled at him. It was as big as I had. Trying to tell him that things were going to be all right, even if I had no idea how.

"What the horny insurance guy said I did to him," I said. "We're going to *break* this dog's balls."

3

BEFORE I LEFT I told Spike not to do anything stupid.

"Don't you mean more stupid than I already did?" he said. "It would make me as dumb as a hamster."

I told him I would call him later. He said if I couldn't reach him that would mean he was passed-out drunk. I kissed him and told him we'd figure a way out of this. He said I was full of it, but that he still loved me. I told him I loved him more.

I was supposed to have lunch with Lee Farrell at the Legal Sea Foods across from my office. I hadn't seen him for a few weeks, not since he'd caught the disappearance of a local social media sensation named Carly Meme that the cops were treating as a possible homicide. Carly had made a huge name for herself as an influencer, pushing products and places to people her age and getting paid handsomely to do it. It was just one more thing that made me feel old. I used to think influencers were guys like my friend Wayne Cosgrove at *The Boston Globe.*

To make things far racier in all media, it turned out that Carly Meme—real name Carlotta Espinoza—had been the girl-on-the-side for Jack Norman, the most powerful political consultant in the state and right-hand man and fixer for Carlton Miller, who owned half of downtown Boston and was in line to be the next treasury secretary, if you could believe what you read. Of course, Norman had been extremely married for the past hundred years or so. He hadn't graduated to suspect yet, remaining the ever-popular person of interest, swearing that he had nothing to do with Carly's disappearance, that he'd been nothing more than a mentor to her. I told Lee one day that I'd never heard not being able to keep it in your pants described as "mentoring."

But when I called to make sure Lee and I were still on, I went straight to his voicemail. Got no immediate reply to my text. He had either forgotten or was too jammed up with the case.

With lunch taken out of play, and not feeling particularly hungry, I decided to do what I often did in moments of great uncertainty.

Go annoy someone.

The someone was Alex Drysdale, whom I suspected was enough of an arrogant asshat to meet with me, even knowing how close I was to Spike.

Drysdale had asked Spike, when he first became a regular, if it was worth taking a shot at me.

"You can go ahead and fire," Spike told him. "But you'd miss."

Alex Drysdale, at least for a few months, remained undeterred. He'd never pushed too hard, never made me feel uncomfortable or too close to being Me Tooey. Maybe it was because Spike was always close by. Or me having told him, when asked, that I did indeed have a gun in my purse and so knew how to use it. He'd finally given up, still acting shocked that someone he found attractive didn't return the feeling.

One night, when it was just Spike and me and him at last call, Drysdale had said, "Well, at least you let me down easy."

"Dude," Spike said, "how can you be down if you were never up?"

I still had Drysdale's office number in my phone to go with his cell number, because he'd given me both. I called the office number, told his assistant who I was. She put me right through. I asked if I could come by his office. He said to come ahead. There was no point in him asking why I wanted to see him or me telling him.

"You're not going to finally shoot me, are you?" he said.

"To be determined," I said, and he reminded me that his office was at One Financial Center.

"Where else?" I said.

The Dean of American Crime Fiction

Robert B. Parker